Savage Storms 3

Meesha

Lock Down Publications and Ca$h
Presents
Savage Storms 3
A Novel by *Meesha*

Meesha

Lock Down Publications
Po Box 944
Stockbridge, Ga 30281

Visit our website @
www.lockdownpublications.com

Copyright 2022 by Meesha
Savage Storms 3

All rights reserved. No part of this book may be reproduced in any form or by electronic or mechanical means, including information storage and retrieval systems without permission in writing from the publisher, except by a reviewer who may quote brief passages in review.
First Edition February 2022
Printed in the United States of America

This is a work of fiction. Names, characters, places, and incidents either are products of the author's imagination or are used fictitiously. Any similarity to actual events or locales or persons, living or dead, is entirely coincidental.

Lock Down Publications
Like our page on Facebook: **Lock Down Publications @**
www.facebook.com/lockdownpublications.ldp
Book interior design by: **Shawn Walker**
Edited by: **Kiera Northington**

Stay Connected with Us!

Text **LOCKDOWN** to 22828 to stay up-to-date with new releases, sneak peaks, contests and more…
Thank you.

Submission Guideline.

Submit the first three chapters of your completed manuscript to ldpsubmissions@gmail.com, subject line: Your book's title. The manuscript must be in a .doc file and sent as an attachment. Document should be in Times New Roman, double spaced and in size 12 font. Also, provide your synopsis and full contact information. If sending multiple submissions, they must each be in a separate email.

Have a story but no way to send it electronically? You can still submit to LDP/Ca$h Presents. Send in the first three chapters, written or typed, of your completed manuscript to:

LDP: Submissions Dept
Po Box 944
Stockbridge, Ga 30281

DO NOT send original manuscript. Must be a duplicate.

Provide your synopsis and a cover letter containing your full contact information.

Thanks for considering LDP and Ca$h Presents.

Acknowledgements

2021 was a very trying time in my life, I fell off tremendously with my writing. I want to thank my readers for sticking with me through these trying times, without asking any questions. It makes my heart swell to see many of you are rockin' with me beyond books and I greatly appreciate that. I have so much in store for you guys and hopefully, I can mentally get them out in a timely matter.

This book is dedicated to all of you, and I love every one of you with everything in me. I promise to continue to bring the heat and will never disappoint you guys. Y'all will get the best of me at every turn. XOXO

#Iamtheghostwriter

Meesha

Previously on Savage Storms...

Phantom

It's been a month since Scony put the buzz in my ear about the connections involving Heat. We searched high and low for that nigga and he still hadn't emerged from the rock he was hiding under. None of the people who worked for Heat knew where he was, at least that was the lie they told. I didn't believe a word of that shit.

We got down on a couple of the members of the Black Kings crew before Brando's lieutenant called for a truce. Dreux told his ass Heat was on his own with the bullshit, but we didn't have a problem clearing the roads of their asses. The way we were laying their men down, I guess the rest of them wanted to keep breathing. For the time being they were straight, unless they decided to renege on what they said.

Layla and I had been having so much fun since she was released from the hospital. It took three days for my baby to open her eyes and smile at me. I never left her side and had the best alibi when the police came to me with a bullshit lie about me killing Butch. Tiffany sent them my way when she found his bitch ass sprawled out in her front yard with his brains splattered everywhere.

Stone and Scony wasn't playing. They took care of that shit with Butch and kept my hands clean. Both of them wanted to get his ass for what he did to Layla, but mainly because he couldn't keep his hands off a woman. I really didn't give a fuck about him putting his hands on Tiff, it's when he involved my daughter in that shit.

Chanel was trying her best to stay on a professional level with me, it wasn't working for her though. She was able to provide enough evidence for me to get full custody of Layla. Her services were no longer needed, but it didn't stop her from calling my phone multiple times a day. Tiff wasn't feeling that at all, because she was granted supervised visitation every other weekend. I had a phone filled with vile text messages from her and I looked at them and laughed without responding.

"Daddy, somebody's at the door!" Layla's voice snapped me out of my thoughts, and I jumped out of my bed and raced downstairs. "Whoever it is been ringing the bell for a long time."

"I'm sorry, baby. Think about what you want to eat while I answer this door."

I opened the door and was surprised to see Kenzie standing on my porch. She had been calling every day to check on Layla, but still hadn't said too much to me. So, to see her standing before me; yeah, I was dumbfounded.

"Hey, can I come in? I have something I wanted to give Layla in person."

Stepping to the side, I waited on her to collect the packages she had sitting on the side of the porch. Kenzie had gifts as if it was Christmas in the summertime. All I could do was shake my head when she handed the bags to me and turned to go back to her truck. She came out with a pink and blue electric scooter. Kenzie bought knee pads, elbow pads, and a helmet to match. Layla didn't need that shit, but who was I to tell her how to spend her money.

"Layla! Where you at, baby girl?" Kenzie hollered as she entered my crib. She pushed the scooter to the middle of the floor and took the other items from my hands and placed them on the couch.

"Kenzie!" Layla said, running from the kitchen right into Kenzie's back. She wrapped her little arms around her waist tightly. "You bought all this for me?"

Her eyes lit up like a Christmas tree and it made my heart pump wildly in my chest. Layla didn't get that excited seeing her own mother, but it was a different story when Kenzie was around. Anyone that didn't know them would think they were mother and daughter when they were together.

"Yes. I thought about my favorite girl when I was out and about today. You are better now, and I want you to have fun. I'm going to take you to the park, if it's alright with your father, so you can ride that," Kenzie said, turning Layla around to see the scooter.

"Oh yeah! I like that, Kenzie! Thank you so much!"

"I charged it up and it's ready to go." Kenzie handed Layla one of the bags with a smile on her face. Layla sat on the couch and reached in the bag. She pulled out an iPad and squealed like a pig going to the slaughterhouse. "That's for when you want to talk to me. Now, you don't have to call from your daddy's phone. My number is already stored. I don't want to hear about you crying about your mama not giving you your phone anymore, you don't need it."

Layla thanked Kenzie again, going back into the bag. My daughter pulled out clothes, shoes, hair bows, barrettes, and a couple of little purses. Kenzie went all out for my daughter, and I appreciated it. Layla danced around swinging her gifts. Kenzie's phone rang and she dug in her purse before she missed the call.

"Baby girl, take all of that up to your room," I said, helping her put everything back in the bags.

"Can I go to the park with Kenzie?" Layla was pouting hard to get me to say yes. There was no way I could tell her no after that. "Please, Daddy!"

"Yes, Layla. We can go out to eat after the park. How about that?"

"Yay! Thank you, thank you, thank you. I'm going upstairs to change. I have to be cute to hang out with Kenzie," she said, snatching the bags before running upstairs. "Oh, Kenzie. Would you put my hair in four ponytails?" She paused on the stairs.

Kenzie shook her head yes as she continued her phone call. That was good enough for Layla, because she sang all the way to her room.

I do my hair toss
Check my nails
Baby, how you feeling?

I had to laugh because her little ass was something else. Long as she was happy, that's all that mattered. I checked out the scooter and I wanted to take it for a spin myself. Glancing up at

Kenzie, my joint started getting happy as I looked at the way her ass fitted in her Fabletic leggings. She matched from head to toe in turquoise and black. I zoned out and didn't realize I was caught red-handed, lusting over her thick ass.

"You like what you see, Xavier?" Kenzie smirked.

"I'm not going there with you Kenzie. I won't let you catch me in your web of bullshit today. How are you?"

"I'm good, now that my lil baby is beyond happy. I'm going upstairs to get Layla's hair right. Phantom, when you need her hair done, call me. I don't mind seeing your number, long as it's about Layla."

"You sound like a baby mama, and you don't even have kids," I laughed. "Stop the madness. You can act as if you don't fuck with me, Kenzie. I know better, shawty."

"Whatever. I have to hurry because Kayla is going to meet me and Layla at the park down the street from my house."

"Oh, it's just you and Layla riding out, huh?"

"You can come along. Khaos is coming after he finishes whatever he's out doing. That way, you will have someone to keep you out of my face."

Kenzie left the conversation hanging and ran up the stairs two at a time, until she was out of my sight. The way the muscles in her legs flexed made me think about the last time them muthafuckas were wrapped around my neck. She knew exactly what she was doing, and I had a trick for that ass real soon.

***

We were having a good time in the park talking, smoking, and watching Layla ride the fuck out of her new scooter. Kenzie hooked her hair up in the four ponytails Layla requested, and added a few braids and pink and baby blue ribbons and balls. My baby was cute in her pink capris, baby blue and pink tank, and a pair of pink and baby blue high-top Chucks. She looked like a miniature Kenzie riding up and down the bike path.

Khaos had called to see where I was and when I told him I was at the park with the ladies, he said he was on his way. Kenzie kept looking around with a worried expression on her face, which made me glance around myself. I positioned my Glock on my hip just in case.

"What's the matter, Ken?" I asked, walking over where she was standing with Kayla.

"It feels like someone is watching us. Every time I look around, I don't see shit though. Maybe it's just all the shit going on that's bothering me. I'm good, don't worry about it. I'm sure it's nothing." She tried to smile, but it never reached her eyes.

I looked over Kenzie's head to keep an eye on Layla and I saw her making her way back to us. Khaos was walking across the parking lot with something in his hands. I knew damn well he didn't bring nothing for Layla's ass. I didn't think my ears would be able to handle another round of squealing from her. As he got closer, I saw what he had in his arms, and I shook my head.

Kenzie saw him approaching, but Kayla's back was turned. Khaos put his finger to his lips, indicating to Kenzie not to say anything. In his arms was a white baby pit with a blue collar around his neck. Seeing the dog brought a smile to my face because that lil muthafucka was pretty as fuck.

"Hey, baby," Khaos said, kissing Kayla on the neck when he got close to her. She turned around and her hand went straight to her mouth when she saw the puppy.

"Oh my God! He is so cute!"

Layla heard the excitement and rode her scooter over full throttle. "Uncle K, you bought me a puppy! Thank you, it's so cute," she said, jumping up and down.

I looked at Khaos and the smile he wore a minute ago faded away as he looked down at his lil homie. "Layla, this one isn't for you. It's for Kayla. I'll take you to the pet store to pick you out a puppy tomorrow."

"No, the hell you won't! You keeping that muthafucka at yo' crib because it's not coming to my shit."

"But, Daddy!" Layla whined. I gave her the look and even though she shut right the hell up, it didn't stop the tear from sliding down her pretty little face.

"Layla, you can't get everything you see. You ain't never thought about having a dog until now. The answer is no, so clean your face and ride your scooter or we can leave."

"I'm not ready to leave!" She stomped her feet and crossed her arms. I lunged at her and Kenzie scooped her up and walked her away. Her little ass was beyond spoiled and I played a major role in that shit, but I would whoop her ass without thought when she got like that. When I said no, I meant it.

"My bad, Cuz. I shouldn't have told her that," Khaos said, handing the puppy to Kayla.

"You don't have to apologize. Layla needs to learn that she can't have every damn thing," I said, rubbing the top of the dog's head. "Is that a blue nose?"

"Hell yeah. When I saw that muthafucka, I had to have it. It reminded me of this feisty, sexy, aggressive female I know." Khaos licked his lips as he gazed at Kayla from the bottom of her feet to the top of her head. She missed the seductive way he bit his bottom lip, because she was checking out the collar around the dog's neck.

"Khaos, why does this damn dog have a diamond tag? That's too much." Kayla held up the puppy and sure enough, the word *Snow* was shining bright in diamonds. When Snow opened his eyes, they were the color of the bluest ocean. That shit called for me to take my phone out to take a pic.

"Nothing but the best for you, queen. I wanted to name him Kane, but that shit was already taken. I don't need him thinking I'm calling his punk ass when I'm actually talking to you."

"He is so beautiful. Thank you, Khaos."

"Get ready, Kayla. Look at his paws, he gon' be a beast. His structure is already forming. How old is this puppy, fam?" I asked as my eyes traveled across the grass where Kenzie and Layla were standing.

Savage Storms 3

Tiffany was stomping on the grass in their direction and I headed that way before anything could transpire. Khaos and Kayla was right behind me, because this bitch wasn't even supposed to be anywhere near my daughter. Tiffany's voice could be heard from the minute she addressed Kenzie as, "Bitch."

"Watch yo' tongue, Tiffany. I would hate to fuck you up in front of your daughter. I'm trying to teach her the right way of life, please don't take it there," Kenzie said, a little too nicely.

"You're not supposed to be teaching her shit! She has a whole mother to do that!"

"I haven't seen you do anything motherly since I've been around. Save that shit for somebody that don't know you in real life. Get out of my face with all that gibberish."

Kenzie grabbed Layla's hand and turned to walk away from Tiff. I started running and scooped her ass up before she could hit Kenzie in the back of her head. Tiff started hitting me in my chest, but that shit was nothing to me.

"Why the fuck are you even here, Tiff?" I asked, putting her down once I reached the pavement in the parking lot.

"I want to see my daughter! Seeing y'all shower her with gifts, then seeing y'all in the park like one happy couple is fucked up, Phantom! That's our child and you are letting that bitch play mama to her! I won't stand around and watch that shit happen!"

"Stay yo' ass away from my shit and you wouldn't see anything." I know what I said wasn't making matters any better, but Tiff needed to hear it. "Watching my every move is only going to fuck with yo' head. Stop doing that shit. We will never be a family, Tiff. I have my daughter because you didn't know how to take care of her. Without me providing for her while in your care, she wouldn't have shit. Layla is where she belongs, with me."

"You never cared about me, Xavier. Layla is the only thing you wanted out of our relationship. I've always come second to her spoiled ass!"

Tiffany was showing her true feelings toward my daughter, and I didn't like the way it sounded. How the fuck could a mother be jealous of her own child? She was acting like a bitter ex, fighting for a spot another woman was able to secure after she fucked up. But she was spitting venom towards her own child.

"Get the fuck away from me, Tiff. It's fucked up how you're talking about my daughter. And you call yourself a mother." I turned and walked away from her and she started calling out to Layla.

"Lay-Lay, come here, baby." Layla stared at Tiffany and walked in the opposite direction to get her scooter. "Fuck all of y'all, including that little bitch you're always protecting. You're gonna wish you never crossed me, Phantom."

Kenzie rushed past me to get to Tiff, but I grabbed her around her waist as Tiff got in her car and drove away. I couldn't let Kenzie beat her ass while my daughter was present. I wasn't going to stop her the next time though. Tiffany was foul for saying fuck my daughter. Saying that shit about me was cool, but my daughter? Nah. She violated in the worse way.

"She needs her muthafuckin' ass beat for the shit she said! Don't ever stop me from reaching out to touch her bum ass ever again. That was the perfect time to beat the fuck out of her." Kenzie was mad and I didn't blame her. I had my reason as for why I didn't let her put hands on Tiff and that was Layla.

We walked back to where Layla was and headed back to the truck. Tiff had messed up our outing and I just wanted to get my daughter away from the park. I was putting Layla's scooter in the back of Kenzie's ride, and she was standing blowing off steam with Kayla and Khaos.

"Layla, get over here, that's still considered a street," I heard Kenzie say to my daughter. I laughed lowly because Tiff was right, Kenzie did fill the role of being Layla's mom.

Lifting my arms to close the back of the truck. The revving of a car caught my attention and I turned abruptly. Layla was taking her time getting out of the middle of the parking lot and my eyes grew wide as I saw the car gunning toward my daughter. I pushed off the truck and made a dash toward Layla. Before I could get to her, Layla tried to run and fell. The back tires caught both of her legs and kept going. My heart plummeted to my feet as I saw my daughter lying on the ground.

"Layla!" I yelled out as I fell to my knees by her side. My baby's legs were positioned in an odd way, and I knew they were both broken. The tears flowed down my face as I listened to Khaos on the phone with 911.

"I'm killing that bitch soon as I make sure Layla is okay," I heard Kenzie yell as I hugged my baby.

Meesha

Chapter 1

Phantom

The ambulance was there in a flash. Once Layla was situated in the back I jumped in right behind the stretcher. The paramedic was shooting questions at me, and I responded without taking my eyes off my daughter. The tears and her sobs had me crying silently as I held her hand. Her legs were stabilized so she couldn't move them. I knew both were broken, but I hoped it wasn't bad as it looked. Once we got to the hospital in record time, Layla was rushed straight to the operating room because the paramedics had called the incident in ahead of time.

"Daddy!" Layla cried out as they pushed her through the double doors.

"I'm right here with you, baby," I reassured her as the doors slowly closed. One of the nurses stopped me from going further and there was nothing I could do to get back there with my baby. "I love you, Lay!" I yelled before the doors closed completely. Layla's cries could still be heard as I turned away.

Sitting in one of the chairs in the lobby, my head fell in the palm of my hands for a few seconds. I lifted my head as the automatic doors opened, Khaos and Kayla raced across the room. The worried look on my cousin's face was one I hadn't seen in a very long time.

"How is she, fam?" he asked, pacing in front of me nervously.

"I don't know. They rushed her to the back. Her legs looked pretty bad. It was nobody but God that spared my baby, man. I'm glad only her legs were hit. She thought quick on her feet when she attempted to run. If she hadn't fallen, she would've been in complete path of that car. But she's still breathing and that's all that matters to me." I glanced at the door and then back at my cousin. "Where's Kenzie?"

"She was driving behind us, but she didn't pull in the lot. I've been calling her phone and she's not answering," Kayla responded as she tapped away on her phone. "I just texted her."

"Kenzie is in full Storm mode. I knew she wasn't following us. I noticed the minute she turned off. Tiff deserves what's coming to her stupid ass. The bitch is that malicious to run over her own daughter! She could've killed her! Soon as I get an update on baby girl, I'm hittin' the pavement to find her funky ass myself."

Khaos was fuming and I didn't blame him. I was wondering what the fuck Tiff was thinking as she drove the car into her own child. The thought of killing her ass was the furthest thing from my mind. I just wanted to see my baby and make sure she was good. All the shit we had encountered in a short period of time, and everything we had to tackle head-on as a team, my baby's wellbeing trumped it all. Everybody would have to carry on without me.

"Do what you have to do, Cuz. I'm not leaving this hospital long as my daughter is lying in this muthafucka. Tiff can only run so far. There's nowhere she can go that I won't find her. The mother of my child or not, she gon' get what's comin' to her. Any muthafucka that comes for my family, especially Layla, don't have a leg to stand on with me."

Biting my bottom lip, I fought the tears that threatened to fall from my eyes. I was hurt about what happened to my daughter. She didn't deserve to be laid up in the hospital by the hands of her trifling ass mama. Scared was an understatement. I was terrified because I didn't know the extent of her injuries. I was hotter than volcanic lava because Tiff could've directed her anger towards me. She should've shot my black ass instead of going after my heart.

"Xavier!" my mother's voice filled the room as she hurriedly entered the waiting room. Standing from the chair, I met her halfway and fell into her outstretched arms. I used the top of her head to rest my chin as the tears I tried so hard to hold in ran down my face.

"What happened, baby? Kannon called, saying I needed to get here because something happened to Layla."

I heard my mother speaking but I couldn't respond. The words were caught in my throat, and all I could do was sob while squeezing her tightly. She rubbed my back while I cried. After a few minutes, I finally released the hold I had on her. Guiding me by the hand to the row of chairs, my mama sat and tugged my arm to do the same.

"Sit down, baby, and talk to me. What's wrong with my grandbaby?" she asked once I was seated beside her.

I sat with my head held low, trying to figure out how to tell my mama what happened. After a brief pause, I finally just let the words flow from my lips. "We were at the park because Kenzie bought Layla a scooter and wanted to see her ride it. She was having fun, when Khaos arrived with a puppy for Kayla. Lay got upset because she realized the puppy wasn't for her. Mama, I chastised her."

I broke down as I recalled the words I'd said to my daughter. It was my fault Layla felt she was entitled to any and everything she wanted. I gave her damn near anything she asked for because she was a very good child. My baby. Wiping my face with my shirt, I continued talking.

"Kenzie walked off to have a talk with Layla, and Tiff came out of nowhere, talking shit. She and Kenzie had words and almost came to blows, so I stepped in. I told Tiff to go about her business. She got pissed and stormed off. I thought she was gone, but she doubled back as I was loading the scooter into the truck and hit Layla with her car. The bitch didn't even stop."

My mama gasped as she covered her mouth with her hand. She was in a state of shock from my details of what happened. At that moment, we were crying together. Her body quaked as she tried her hardest to control her cries. Khaos came over and wrapped his arms around both me and my mother, letting us know he was there without saying a word. We were a close-knit family and always there for one another.

As we pulled apart, two officers exited the double doors Layla was rushed through when she was brought in. I watched as they slowly made their way in our direction. The officers crept forward,

I guess for us to get through the moment we were sharing. Me on the other hand, I used that opportunity to prep my mama to stay quiet.

"The police are about to come over here. I got this, Ma. Don't say anything please," I said, staring down at her.

"Tell them the truth, Xavier. Allow the police to do their job," she whispered.

"Nah, that's too much like right. Tiff isn't getting away that easily. Sit right here and let me handle this my way."

I could tell she wanted to protest but I wasn't trying to hear any of that shit. If I had to spend the rest of my life behind bars, it would be worth it. That bitch was going to pay for hurting my baby.

"Phan, I'm about to take Kayla home. We left Snow in the car, but I'll be back within the hour," Khaos said, giving me a brotherly hug.

"You don't have to rush back. I'll be alright." Khaos' lip curled up as he side-eyed me with a grimaced expression.

"That's my lil homie back there. I'll be back."

Kayla came over and hugged me and my mother before leading the way to the exit, with Khaos behind her. The officers walked over and stood before me. "Parents of Layla Bennett?"

"Yeah, I'm her father, how is she?" I asked.

"According to the doctor, she's still in surgery. Layla is a very lucky little girl. She will need extensive physical therapy after all of this, but her youthfulness will play a major role in her recovery."

The news relieved a lot from my mental and I relaxed just a little bit. There was more to come from the officers, I knew. Their job wasn't to deliver messages from medical personnel. Just as I predicted, the stream of questions started.

"Mr.—"

"Bennett," was all I said, folding my arms over my chest.

"Do you know who could've done this to your daughter?"

"No," I replied.

"What color was the vehicle? Do you recall?"

"The car was red. I don't know the make nor the model, because the only thing I saw was the back end before going to my daughter's aid." I purposely gave the wrong information because as I said to my mother, I was taking this case on myself. Tiffany's car was a smoky gray color, far from the red I'd described.

"Why was Layla in the way of the car, Mr. Bennett?"

The officer was lowkey trying to imply I was negligent with my child, and I didn't like that shit at all. I calmed down briefly, knowing my daughter would be alright, but I was heating up once again as the question danced around in my head. "She wasn't in the way of the fuckin' car! I was putting her scooter in the truck, and she was standing behind me. Don't you dare try to—"

"Relax, sir, I'm only doing my job by asking the necessary questions. We want to catch the scumbag who hit your daughter and drove off. We have no more questions at this time. Is there a way for us to contact you if anything else arises?"

Giving them my number was the last thing I wanted to do, but I had to play my part. As I recited my business number to the officer, I felt my mother's arm wrap around my waist. I was ready to rip dude's head clean off his shoulders. If I'd seen that shit about to happen, it would be me in surgery instead of Layla. The officers thanked me for my time and left the building. I sat down and pulled my phone from my pocket. Dialing Kenzie's number, her phone rang until the voicemail picked up.

"Kenzie, whatever you're doing, leave it alone. Come to Emory now!"

Meesha

Chapter 2

Tiffany

"Fuck! What did I do?" I asked myself as I hit the steering wheel repeatedly.

Tears streamed down my face as I relived my actions back at the park. Seeing my daughter disappear under the car and the jolt of the tires as they hit her small frame, I wanted to stop and make sure she was alright, but I knew I couldn't. Phantom was going to kill me. Now, I had to get out of Georgia. There was no way I'd be able to walk freely after what I did.

Speeding in the direction of my townhome, I thought about it and detoured. My house would've been the first place Phantom would look for me. I truly didn't intend on hurting Layla. I wanted to hurt Phantom, but I knew Layla was the key to doing just that. Satan had taken over my thoughts, because I couldn't believe what ran through my mind, and flowed out of my mouth as I yelled out loud.

"He wanted her ass, now he can have her in his heart forever, after he buries her six feet under," I yelled angrily as I drove without a destination in mind. "How dare he have that bitch playing mama to my child! Phantom allowed her ass to buy Layla shit, comb her hair, and let her know it was okay to call the bitch on the phone—Fuck Kenzie! She's the reason my daughter wanted nothing to do with me."

I had an angel and the devil on each shoulder, taking turns with my mental. I was confused as fuck riding through the streets of Atlanta. Truthfully speaking, my emotions were in disarray. I didn't know if I felt sorrowful or evil. Fuck it, I felt it all. Layla didn't deserve what I did to her, but she was the ultimate sacrifice for the bullshit her father put me through. Now, let that shit ride his conscience.

Phantom knew I loved him with everything in me, and he still chose another woman over our family. The reason I was with Butch in the first place was because Phantom didn't want me anymore. All he had to do was come back and none of this shit would've happened.

I found myself on the other side of town, going down the street where Mya lived. My heart broke in pieces as I remembered my friend was no longer around for me to vent to about my baby daddy. At that point, I knew there was nowhere I could run. I relied on Phantom for my finances, and I didn't have a job. The little bit Butch did wasn't nearly enough, but he was no longer around to help either. I had a few hundred dollars in my bank account, but it wouldn't be enough for me to relocate. Seeing the yellow tape lying on the front yard of Mya's house made me step on the gas without stopping.

"I have to get out of here. I'm on the top of Phantom's retaliation list and I don't have the means to disappear. What am I going to do?" I asked in a panic.

Getting to Junction, Kansas, was my only hope. My parents moved there late last year, and Phantom had no idea. The only problem with that, neither of them wanted anything to do with me because of my relationship with Butch. My parents always thought I put Butch before Layla. My mother always suggested I give my daughter to her father because she said I wasn't fit to care for her.

It was my fault for constantly calling my mother when Butch would whoop my ass. I should've kept the shit to myself and dealt with it on my own. It was too late to try to recant all of that mess. What happened couldn't be fixed. If word got out to them about what I'd done to Layla, the police in Kansas would be waiting for my arrival to haul me off to jail. It was on me to make sure they never found out.

Driving around aimlessly, I grabbed my phone to make a call I hoped would work in my favor. Summer was Mya's friend, and I was an acquaintance off the strength of my friend alone. With her not being around, I didn't know how Summer would react to me calling her on some desperation-type shit. Summer was my only hope to getting out of the state. If she didn't agree to help, I was fucked. I knew she had the means to get me away from the trouble

I'd gotten myself into, would she be willing to help was the question.

"Hey, Tiff. Long time no see, what's up?" Summer asked soon as she answered. I drove silently without responding. The words I was thinking couldn't make its way out of my mouth. I didn't know exactly how to state the reason of my impromptu call. "Are you still there?" Summer asked with worry in her voice.

"Yes, I'm still here. Can I come over? I need someone to talk to," I stated nervously.

"Yeah, come through. I know you miss Mya. Hell, that was my bitch and I feel the same way. We may not have hung out together without her, but the times we did, we had a good time. I'll be here for you any way I can in her absence. I'll be waiting for you to pull up."

"Thank you. I'll be there in about twenty minutes. Wait, is Heat there?"

Summer breathed hard into the phone and smacked her lips before answering. "That's a story we can touch bases on when you arrive. To answer your question, no, he's not here. It will be just you and me for as long as you need to vent."

"Okay. I'm heading your way now."

I took the next right and hopped on the highway. Glancing down at the gas hand, I started praying because I was damn near out of gas. There was no way I was about to stop at a gas station so close to my house to fill up. I would have to push it until I was sure I wouldn't run into anyone associated with Phantom, before I felt comfortable stopping.

About five minutes away from Summer's house, I stopped and got gas and a Black & Mild. I didn't even smoke those damn things, but I didn't have any weed to settle my nerves. Once I finished filling up my tank, I got comfortable in the driver's seat and pulled my seatbelt over my body. My phone chimed in the cupholder, and I looked down seeing a text message notification. As I reached for my phone, my hand shook like a dope fiend in need of a hit. The message was from Phantom.

Meesha

Baby daddy: The shit you did was fucked up. You better run while you have the chance. When I see you, bitch, you gon' wish you would've taken yo' ass home like I told you to. If my baby has to suffer, you already know you gon' get it ten times worse. It's one thing to fuck with me, I can handle that shit. You fucked up when you brought my daughter into your malicious muthafuckin' ways. You fucked up, Tiff, and I will have no mercy on you, bitch!

Scared was an understatement, my ass was petrified. Phantom never threw out idle threats, he made nothing but promises, and I knew he was going to come for me with a vengeance. Turning the key in the ignition of my Camry, I struggled to put the car in drive because all the strength left my body after reading the message. My phone chimed again, and I didn't even bother to read the message. Instead, I peeled away from the pump and raced to Summer's house.

When I pulled into her driveway, I disabled the ignition, grabbed my purse and phone. The device was chiming a mile a minute and piqued my curiosity. I opened the message tab and Phantom was talking about burying me alive, soon as he caught up with me. My stomach started churning and it felt as if I had to throw up. I checked my surroundings before I jumped out of the car and ran up the steps leading to Summer's front door. The door opened and she stood in the doorway with a strange look on her face.

"Tiff, what's wrong with you? I was watching from the window, and you took off soon as you got out of the car. Not to mention, you look like you've seen a ghost."

"I'm okay. Can I come in please?" I asked, glancing behind me. Summer strained her neck to see what I was looking at. She motioned for me to enter but checked to see if anyone was outside her house once more.

I walked slowly to her dining room table and sat in the nearest chair and buried my head on top of my arms. The tears flowed from my eyes because I didn't know if Phantom was going to find me or not. The only place I could go to lay my head was my house and I couldn't even return to pack a bag if I wanted to live another day. The sound of the chair to the left of me scraped against the floor and Summer placed her hand on my shoulder.

"Tiffany, what's going on?" she asked.

I looked up and wiped the snot from my nose with the back of my hand. Summer scrunched up her face and got up. When she returned, she had tissue and sanitizer in hand and placed it in front of me on the table.

"Clean your face and tell me what brought you all the way to my house. You're running from something or somebody, Tiff. Is Butch whooping yo' ass again?"

I was surprised she knew what was going on between me and Butch. Mya must've been telling her all my muthafuckin' business. There wasn't a need for me to get mad about it because there was no way for me to snap on Mya about revealing the shit she had told. After getting myself together, I placed my head in my hand and closed my eyes.

"Butch was killed a while back." Summer gasped but didn't say a word for a few minutes, then she sighed heavily.

"Tiff, I'm sorry he's dead, but that shit was wrong on his part. I never said anything about what he was doing to you because it wasn't my place. Every time Mya told me about him putting his hands on you, I prayed you would leave him alone before you ended up in a pine box. No matter what the hell is going on, you don't allow no man to beat on you. I know you loved him, but that didn't warrant you to stay and get pounded on."

Summer should've said something long before because I needed to hear that shit back in time. It was too late to give me a prep talk about the abuse I endured. Butch paid for what he did to me and other things throughout his life. He was the least of my worries, I had bigger fish to fry.

"It's easier said than done. Leaving an abuse relationship takes time. A woman can't just get up one day and say, 'I'm leaving.' It's an immediate death sentence, Summer. So many people say leave and don't look back, that's not the way it works. I don't have to deal with the abuse from Butch any longer—"

"You bet not deal with that shit from anybody else either! Live and learn, Tiff. Since you were forced into the single life, you can go take your baby daddy back from that beauty thug." Summer laughed but I didn't crack a smile. "Damn, you just gon' hand your family over to that hoe without a fight?"

"Summer, I will never be in an intimate relationship with Phantom again. I fucked up." I was so ashamed about what I'd done to my daughter, I couldn't even look Summer in the face. Reality sunk in and I was hurt to the core.

"What did you do? Fuck that, use Layla to make his ass come back. You know she is the key to keeping him close. Make her the pawn, bitch!"

"I already sacrificed her," I wailed. "Summer, I need your help. I got mad at Phantom for having that bitch around my daughter and let my anger take over. I hit Layla with my car and kept going. I'm so sorry for what I've done."

The room became so quiet, you could hear a cat piss on the carpet. Summer's mouth was wide open, and her eyes bulged. The shock was evident on her face and tears threatened to fall from her eyes.

"Tiff, noooooo!" Summer shrieked. "That's not the way to get that man's attention. Yes, you fucked up and Phantom is going to kill you! Please tell me Layla is okay."

"I don't know! I drove away fast as I could. I had to get away from there. Phantom has been texting me with threats. Please help me get away from here. Please!"

I pled with everything in me and hoped like hell Summer would be willing to help me out. By the way her posture stilled, I knew she wasn't going to do shit for me. She was disgusted by what I'd done, and I couldn't blame her. Whatever Summer threw at me, I deserved it. If she beat the hell out of me, she had every right to do so.

"That's your muthafuckin' daughter, Tiffany! She was brought into your life so you could protect her from all evil and you're the bitch she needed to be protected against! I can't believe you used a dangerous method and put your own child in the mist of the madness. When I said use her as a pawn, I was thinking more along the lines of prohibiting Phantom from seeing her, not hitting her with a fuckin' vehicle!"

"I don't get you baby mamas! Stop thinking with your pussy and glow the fuck up on these niggas!" Summer was angry and she was speaking truthfully, and every word hit me like a bag of rocks. I felt every last one of them. "Tiffany, hearing what you did got me wanting to call Phantom myself and tell him where the fuck you are. But seeing I just lost a friend, I won't lead you to your final resting place."

Summer got up from the table and left the room. I bit down on the nail on my index finger as I waited for her to return. After about ten minutes, I grabbed my purse and chucked my phone inside to make a dash for the door.

"Where the fuck you running off to?" Summer's voice startled me, and I turned slowly in her direction. "I thought you wanted my help." She had three bundles of bills in her right hand and a small brown bag with a handle in the other.

"I do. I thought you were setting me up by calling Phantom."

"Bitch, if I wanted to call that nigga, I would've done it in your face. Take this money and go wherever you going. Don't contact me ever again. I can't stand the bitch Phantom is fucking with, but you should've run her ass over instead of Layla. If this money runs out, that's all you getting out of me. There's no more where that came from. Take care of yourself and stay prayed up. After the shit you pulled, you gon' need it."

I took that as my cue to leave Summer's home. I thanked her for the money as I stood by the door. "I'm so sorry—"

"Tiff, I'm not the one you need to be apologizing to. Save that for your daughter. Get the fuck out my house."

Summer walked around me with a disgusted look on her face and opened the door as she waited for me to leave. In the back of my mind, I thought she was going to kick me square up the ass, but she didn't. Instead, she slammed the door soon as I crossed the threshold, causing me to stumble a little bit.

Meesha

When I made it to my car, I peeked in the bag and pulled out one of the bundles. Summer was generous enough to give me fifteen thousand dollars and sent my ass on my way. "Thank you, Jesus! Now, I can get away from Atlanta without looking back. Layla, Mommy's sorry, baby. I love you," I said out loud as I backed out of the driveway.

As I merged into traffic, I decided I would just pop up on my parents and surprise them. I had damn near fourteen hours to think of a lie to tell once I got to Kansas.

Chapter 3

Summer

Watching Tiffany leave her bum ass out of my driveway, it took everything in me to give her that money. There was no way in hell I would do such a thing to a child. When I went into the guest bedroom, I contemplated calling the police to come lock her ass up, but that wasn't my business. No matter where she went, Phantom was going to find her. I was going to be waiting for the breaking news segment when her body was found, and I was going to keep my mouth closed because I didn't know shit.

She pissed me off and I didn't get a chance to tell her about Heat's muthafuckin' ass. I hadn't seen him in damn near three weeks and didn't know what the hell was going on with him. Heat's claim to leave town for business wasn't sitting well with me because he had never left for weeks at a time. When I called his phone the last couple times, he let the voicemail pick up and that was unusual too.

I'd heard in passing he was responsible for a nigga named Brando being dead and skipped town. The Heat I knew, the man I fell in love with, would never run from a muthafuckin' thing. I was going to give him time to get his shit together and let him do what he had to do. But whenever I was in close proximity of his ass, I was going all in.

As I headed up the stairs to my bedroom, the doorbell chimed, halting my steps. No one ever came to my home unannounced, and it couldn't have been Tiff because I saw her drive away. Since learning of the shit Heat could be involved in, I was very leery about many things that went on around me. The doorbell sounded a second time as I slowly made my way to the door. There was a silhouette of a gentleman on the other side, and I had no clue who he could've been.

"I'm sorry if I startled you," the unknown man spoke to me through the door. He could see me standing in view through the square piece of thick glass in the door. "I'm lost and would love if you allow me to use your phone."

I'd seen this very scene played too many times on the *Investigation Discovery Channel*. The female was always found deceased or missing. Nope, I wasn't falling for that shit.

"We live in the times where everybody has some type of cellphone. I'm not comfortable allowing a complete stranger in my home. I won't be able to help you, sir." My voice quaked a little bit and I hoped like hell he didn't pick up on it.

"Baby girl, my cellphone died. Yes, I am in a vehicle, but I forgot my charger back home. I'm not a serial killer, rapist, or none of that other shit. My name is Savon Cole. I live 2351 Campus Way North in Lanham, Maryland. I'm here in Atlanta on business. I am a lawyer and I'm scheduled to meet up with a client's family. I just need to use a phone, ma'am."

Maybe he was truly lost. Nobody would give their whole name and address if they were on bullshit, right? I peeked out the side window and damn near saturated my pants with my juices. Mr. Savon was fine. He was dressed in a gray business suit with a rose gold tie that accentuated the pale pink shirt that hugged the muscles of his chest. The waves in his head were making me nauseous as he glanced down at his watch. I envisioned running my hand over them while pushing his head deep into my love box. Those thoughts alone had me twisting the locks to let him use my phone.

"Don't make me regret my decision. I'm going to let you come in, but please don't try anything, because I will light your ass up."

Knowing I was lying my ass off, I had to chuckle a little when he smiled, showing the whitest teeth I'd ever seen, outside of a toothpaste commercial. I stepped to the side so he could enter. The way his junk was on display in the front of his slacks almost had my tongue wagging like a thirsty puppy.

Savon cleared his throat, snapping me out of the trance I'd slipped into. "Um, your phone, please," he said, adjusting his dick without shame.

"Oh, yeah. You can have a seat in here." Leading the way to the living room, I motioned for him to sit on the couch. "I have to go into the other room to grab my phone. Don't touch anything and everything will be cool."

"I don't need to take anything from you or anyone else. As a matter of fact," he sighed, standing to his feet. "Here's a little something for your trouble."

Savon pulled money from his pocket, peeled off a few bills, and held them out to me. I looked down at the money and shook my head no, before walking away from him. I didn't need his money in order for him to use a phone I had unlimited everything on. After checking the kitchen, I remembered I left my phone upstairs in my bedroom when I finished talking to Tiffany.

My hormones were telling me to change into something comfortable, but my mind was screaming, *bitch, don't you dare*! He may still be a murderer. I had to go with my mind because I wasn't into that hoe shit anymore. At least I wasn't, but my yoni was thinking of a master plan with her freaky ass. Instead, I hurriedly grabbed my phone and headed back downstairs to the stranger in my house.

A man of his word, Savon was seated in the same spot I left him. He glanced up at the sound of me descending the steps. *Damn, he's fine*! I said to myself. The woman in his life is one lucky bitch.

"Here you go." Holding out the phone for him to take, our fingers slightly touched, and an electrical current traveled up my arm.

"Thank you. I know I may be asking for a little too much, but would it be possible for me to use your restroom? I've been driving for quite some time today."

"Sure. There's one down that hall." I pointed. "And it will be on the right."

Savon nodded as he followed my directions, and I watched every step he took. He'd taken my phone with him and I rushed behind him but he had already closed the door to take care of his business. "Hopefully, he wasn't the messy type. I have all types of pussy shots in that damn phone," I mumbled to myself.

Walking into the kitchen, I started prepping the chicken I had took out earlier for the fajitas I craved for dinner. Periodically, I would check the time on the microwave because Mr. Sexy hadn't come out of the bathroom. Just as I was about to go knock on the door to make sure he didn't fall in, he rounded the corner.

"Sorry I took so long. Do you by chance have a notepad and a pen, so I can copy the directions to my client's mother's house?"

"Sure." Reaching into what I called my junk drawer, I handed him the paper and pen he requested. "Are you finished with my phone?"

"I kind of put the information in your notes. Soon as I copy the information, I'll be good as finished." Savon scribbled away as I looked on. "Do you have any idea if there's an Apple Store close by?" he asked, handing over my phone. "There's no way I'll be able to function without my phone for three days. By the way, sorry for interrupting your time."

"Stop apologizing. It's alright. I'm glad I was able to help you out. I won't lie, I was scared as hell to even allow you inside. So much is happening in the world, you know? Can't trust everybody. It's good to know you're not a killer." Savon licked his lips while scanning my body from the top of my head to my camel toe. The leggings I wore left nothing to the imagination.

"Nah, I don't have a violent bone in my body. Hurting women is not my forte. Now, I'll slay pussy without thought."

That last sentence had me blushing like a schoolgirl with a crush. I walked out of the kitchen to get away from the advance he was hoping I caught. Returning a few seconds later, I handed him an extra charger and adapter I had. Placing it in his hand, I went back to cutting up the chicken I'd left on the counter.

"You can take that with you. No need for you to wander around blindly trying to find a store without GPS."

"Are you sure? I can pay for this."

"No. I'll be alright without it. I appreciate the gesture, though." I smiled as I put the chicken in the skillet.

"Well, I've taken up enough of your time, Miss—"

"Summer. My name is Summer." There I was, blushing again.

"I was wondering," he paused as he licked those pink succulent lips of his. "Can I have the pleasure of taking you out for dinner tomorrow night? Maybe you can show me around your city."

I didn't know anything about this man, and he was ready to take me out. Too bad I couldn't accept his offer. As bad as I wanted to say yes, there was no way I could lead him on in that way. Heat was still a factor in my life, even though he had been missing in action and was nowhere to be found.

Savon waited patiently for my response. Heat said many things to let me know he wasn't ready for a relationship, but my loyalty was solid even if I didn't get it in return. That's the type of woman I was. When I was with someone, I was all in regardless of the circumstances.

"Thanks, but I'll have to decline. I have a man—"

"Fuck yo' man, ma. That nigga don't have shit to do with me. I've been in your crib damn near an hour and *yo' man* hasn't called, text, nor walked through that door."

Dressed in a suit and tie, with his Gucci Vanilla cologne saturating my nostrils, Savon went straight hood on my ass. It let me know he used to be in the streets at some point of his life and it turned me on. The seat of my leggings was drenched. My hand went to my neck as I clutched my imaginary pearls.

"I'm not trying to be your man, yet. All I want to do is get to know the beautiful woman that saved the day for a straggler like myself. Plus, I've never been to Atlanta before today. I won't ask again though. In fact, be ready at seven o'clock sharp. Get sexy for me, okay?" He winked and saw himself out.

A bitch was stuck in the same spot long after his fine ass left my house. He didn't say anything else after he laid down law about dinner the next night. I'd never had a nigga command me to do anything, not even Heat. Savon had me mentally going through my closet for something to wear. Even though I kept telling myself I wasn't going with him.

Meesha

As I locked the door, I turned to head back into the kitchen when I spotted the money on the coffee table. At first, I just stared at it, but then I picked it up and thumbed through the bills. There were ten, crisp one-hundred-dollar bills in my hand. Yeah, Savon will see me for dinner at seven o'clock on the dot for sure.

Chapter 4

MaKenzie

So much was going through my mind as I followed Khaos to the hospital. My intentions were to check on Layla, but Storm had a different game plan. We got caught at a red light and I strummed my fingers on the steering wheel as I urged the light to change. When it finally did, Khaos went through the intersection, and I hit the corner and headed for the highway. Soon as I merged into traffic, I pressed the gas pedal and high tailed my whip in the direction of Tiffany's house. My phone was going off every few minutes but answering the muthafucka wasn't on my list of things to do.

    Trying to calm myself down before I made it to my destination was an epic fail. The scene at the park kept playing in my mind. The bitch hit that baby with no fuckin' remorse. The guilt was eating me up, and in a flash, revenge wiped that shit right out of my system. Tiffany was going to die by my hands soon as I found her.

    I pulled into Tiffany's driveway and slammed the gear in park. My fingers caressed the gun I had sitting between my legs, and I jumped out. Her raggedy ass car wasn't in the driveway, but that didn't mean she wasn't home. Storming up the steps, I gave the door three swift kicks until it gave way. The door bounced off the wall with a thud and I grabbed it and closed it best I could.

    With my pistol aimed, I crept slowly through Tiffany's house, ready to pull the trigger. It was quiet as hell and there wasn't one light on in the place. Still, I didn't let my guard down as I checked every square inch of the place. Once I determined no one was there other than myself, I started searching for any clues I could find. After what she'd done, it looked like Tiffany got out of Dodge. At least if she was smart, that's what she would've done.

    I ransacked her bedroom and came up empty. I went into the closet, and nothing seemed to be missing. There was luggage still on the floor and clothes still hung neatly on hangers. I overturned shoeboxes and threw them behind me when nothing of importance was found inside. I checked shelves and every crevice, until I found a wooden storage box hidden in the back. Carrying the box into the bedroom, I decided to take it with me and go through it thoroughly back at my place.

Not giving a damn about Tiffany's broken front door, I dumped the box in the trunk. Soon as I sat in the driver's seat of my ride, my phone started ringing again. I still wasn't ready to talk to anyone. I was pissed because I didn't get the chance to reach out and touch that bitch. Whoever was blowing my shit up would have to wait until I got to the hospital. I knew it wasn't anybody other than Kayla or Phantom. I would listen to the bickering and bitching when I saw them in the flesh. Until then, nah, I was good.

About twenty minutes later, I was pulling into a parking spot right outside the hospital. Phantom stepped out the doors and looked around until he spotted my car. He came marching towards me with his face balled up in anger, fists clenched at his sides, and his jaw locked like an enraged pit bull. I had to brace myself for whatever he threw my way. Opening the door, I stepped from the car and before I knew it, Phantom was hovering over my small frame.

"Where were you? Don't lie either. I'm asking because I already know the truth."

There was no reason to lie to anyone. I always stood on my shit, and it wouldn't waver that day. How Phantom knew my whereabouts was a mystery I wasn't going to dwell on because it was nothing to me.

"I went looking for your pitiful ass baby mama. She's not getting away with this bullshit," I calmly said as I looked up at him. "When I catch her, it's lights out."

Phantom sighed without taking his eyes from mine. His expression was serious. I knew he was about to dig deep, and I wasn't going to like what came out of his mouth. I propped my hip on the side of my car, folded my arms, and waited.

"Do not go after Tiffany—"

"Fuck that—"

Phantom stepped closer. "Kenzie, don't ever cut me off when I'm speaking," he said, clenching his teeth. "Shut up and stop being so damn combative! Listen sometime, you may learn something. Stay the fuck away from Tiff! I'm gon' handle her my way. You won't spend a day in jail behind her shit."

"I've killed niggas before they could see it coming without getting caught. I don't need you to protect me from nothing! Who are you to tell me what I can and cannot do? Like I said, your bitch of a baby mama is dead on sight. What she did to Layla was wrong. She won't walk around thinking shit sweet without a care in the world."

The tears that stung my eyes caused me to turn away from Phantom. He had seen me cry one too many times and I refused to let him see that shit again. Composing myself, my hard demeanor was back in place, and I was ready to go toe-to-toe with him over the situation.

"I take it you didn't find her."

"Nope. Regardless of what you say, I will search high and low until I sniff her stupid ass out. Layla is someone that's important to me and nobody, and I mean nobody, fucks with the people closest to me!" I scoffed. "We have enough shit going on and this bitch want to add running her own daughter over to the mix. Do you know how I feel, knowing I could've saved Layla from that travesty? My whole body shut down and I watched that shit happen right before me. There was nothing I could do after the fact other than run to her side."

A tear escaped my eye and Phantom wrapped his arms around me and held me tightly. I sobbed as the event replayed in my mind. The way Layla cried out in pain, tugged at my heart. Thinking about her brought me back to the reason I was at the hospital.

"How is she?" I asked, wiping my face as I stepped away from Phantom.

"They just moved her to a room about thirty minutes ago. The surgery was a success, and the hardest part is going to be the physical therapy. Lay will have to work hard to walk again. I will do any and everything to make sure she pushes forward with all her might to get back to her normal self." Phantom looked away from me blinking repeatedly. "I know you love my daughter, Kenzie. What about her daddy? I need you by my side."

"My feelings for Layla have no reflection on you and me, Phantom. I will be there to help care for my girl long as she needs me. As far as my feelings for her father, we are friends. Please take me to see Layla so I can see she's alright for myself."

I all but dismissed Phantom and I didn't feel bad about telling him the truth. I didn't want his love, but that didn't mean I hadn't dreamt about the sex. That's about the only thing Phantom could get out of me, because I wasn't built to be held down by anyone. As I neared the automatic doors of the hospital, I waited until he caught up because I left him standing alone by the car.

"You're on the list. You can come see Lay anytime of the day and stay overnight if you want."

Phantom walked past me and I followed him inside. Obtaining my pass, he led the way to the elevators and the moment was like déjà vu from the last time Layla was admitted in this very hospital. My little princess couldn't catch a break. This was going to be the final time she ever got hurt if I had anything to do with it.

It was ironic Layla was on the same floor from the last time, and two rooms down. Meaning she had the same doctors and nurses that helped her before. Phantom stepped into the room first but stopped abruptly. He closed the door and turned to me.

"Kenzie, I want you to be on your best behavior. Everyone is here for Layla, okay?"

I was puzzled because I didn't know why he felt the need to give me a prep talk before I could go in to see Layla. The first thing that came to mind, Tiffany was in the room. I tried to push my way around him to open the door, but Phantom wouldn't budge.

"Tiffany better not be the muthafucka you're protecting on the other side of that door, Phantom," I sneered. "If she's in there, I'm going to jail today, I promise. Move out of my way." Trying my best to keep my cool, I was getting frustrated because he wasn't attempting to move as I had asked.

"Tiffany isn't in there, but Chanel is. No, I didn't invite her," he paused. "The last time Layla was hurt, it was arranged beforehand, if she was brought to the hospital, Chanel was to be called. You have to understand, she's my lawyer and I'm going through a custody battle to get my daughter. I don't want you to get into any altercation with her."

Confusion was what I felt as Phantom spoke. I didn't give a damn about his *lawyer*. I said all I needed to say to her the last time I laid eyes on her.

"That's *your* lawyer. You said all that to say what, Phantom? I'm not your woman and there's nothing for me to understand. Whoever you want in your life is on you. What you should be doing is having this talk with her because if she disrespects me, I'm gonna react. It won't have anything to do with the relationship you have with her. I could careless, honesty. Can I go in and see Layla now?" My patience was almost nonexistent because I'd been through too much in a day's time. Phantom grabbed the doorknob and entered the room.

"It took you long enough," his mother said soon as he stepped into the room. When I appeared behind him, she started shifting in her seat. "Hello, Kenzie."

"Hey, Karla. How is she?" I asked as I stepped closer to the bed Layla was lying in.

"The nurse came in and gave her pain medicine. She just drifted off to sleep about five minutes ago."

Holding onto Layla's hand, Phantom pulled a chair behind me and pushed my shoulder gently to sit down. The sound of lips popping could be heard, and I chuckled. Chanel was big mad, but I hoped she knew to keep that shit to herself. Adjusting myself in the seat, I spoke into Layla's ear so only she could hear.

"Everything will be alright, baby. I'm here to help you through all of this. You are strong, you are brave, you are powerful, you are going to be okay—and nothing can stop you. I will be here to motivate you to keep moving, Layla. We have a long road ahead of us, but I'll be here every step of the way. I love you, Pumpkin." Kissing Layla on her cheek, I continued to hold her hand as I watched her little chest rise and fall.

"Bitches will say anything to a kid to get closer to the father," Chanel huffed under her breath.

My head swiveled in her direction, but Phantom was already on that shit. He grabbed Chanel by the arm and led her out of the room. I followed their movements and saw Chanel snatch out of Phantom's grasp. I turned towards Karla's voice soon as she started to speak.

"Thanks for ignoring Chanel's foolishness. I don't know what's going on with her. She's been really cranky when my son is mentioned as of late."

"Layla doesn't need any negative energy right now. Chanel is in her feelings and I'm going to leave it at that. I'm only here for Layla."

"Kenzie, my son has deep feelings for you."

I shook my head as Phantom's mother tried to talk on his behalf. I really didn't want to hear any of what she had to say about his feelings. He knew how I felt and even if I did want to pursue something with him, it wouldn't be the right time, because he was banging his lawyer. There was enough static between me and Summer. Adding another bitch wouldn't be good for anybody on the opposing team. I was good on all that female jealousy shit.

"You do know he and Chanel is a thing of the past, right?" Karla paused to see if I was going to respond. Obviously, she had no idea they had rekindled their sexual flame. I wasn't going to be the one to deliver the news to her though.

"I don't know anything, Karla. It's not my business, to be honest. Phantom and I are friends, nothing more. Again, the only thing tying me to your son is that little girl lying in that bed. I'm the next thing to a mother for Layla besides you, and I'm going to play my role to the best of my ability. Her mother did the unthinkable and now it's time to show her what a real mother's love feels like. Phantom does not have to be my man in order for me to achieve that."

Sitting close to the bed, I held onto Layla's hand as I looked over her little body. The sight before me tugged at my heartstrings, but I didn't allow my emotions to show. Karla didn't say anything more about Phantom and I was glad about that. The last thing I wanted to do was disrespect her in any way. After a while, I was ready to go.

Standing to my feet, I looked at Layla and moved a strand of hair from her face. I kissed her cheek and made my way to the door. "I'm going to get out of here. Call me if I'm needed to stay with her overnight, because someone needs to be here around the clock. I'll see you later, Karla."

"Okay. Drive safely and get some rest. Thank you for loving Layla the way you do. She thinks so highly of you, and I appreciate you for treating her like she's yours."

"You don't have to thank me. I promise to always be in Layla's life, no matter what." With that, I left the hospital room and couldn't wait to get home and continue my hunt for Tiffany.

Meesha

Chapter 5

Chanel

"Get your hands off me, Xavier. I have the right to speak my mind." Snatching my arm from the hold he had on me, I stopped in my tracks, daring him to try that shit again.

"Chanel, don't push me. You can speak your peace with anybody, that *is* your right. But I've warned you once about Kenzie. I won't be responsible for what happens if she attacks. You're pushing your luck calling her out of her name."

"I can call her whatever the fuck I choose. She's sitting in that room as if she's Layla's mother and here I am, basically begging her father to give me some type of attention. The shit is foul, and I won't stand back being quiet, as if we have nothing between us."

My feelings were exposed for everyone in the hall to see, I didn't care. Xavier was going to hear me out whether he wanted to or not. If he thought he dragged me out of that room for show, he had another think coming. Kenzie or whatever her name was, had his ass rattled. Not I though. I knew my voice had risen a little bit too much when a nurse rushed in our direction and a couple of patient's doors crept open. When she got a few feet away from us, I could see the frown upon her lips.

"This is a place of business. There are children in the rooms on this unit and your altercation is one none of them should be subjected to hearing about. Many of those children are fighting hard to overcome illnesses out of their control, and need all the positive energy their little hearts can muster right now. Frankly, I have to ask you to take this one outside. Mr. Bennett, your daughter isn't too far away, and you know her condition. Be mindful of that, please."

"I apologize, ma'am," Phantom said, once again snatching me by my arm and damn near dragging me to the elevator.

Repeatedly pushing the button on the panel, I tried my best to get away, but his hold was solid that time around. When the doors opened, he shoved me inside and was in my face with the quickness. Soon as the doors closed, Phantom went in on me.

"I'm trying my best not to choke the fuck outta yo' ass," he said through his teeth. "I want you to hear me and hear me good. Don't feel as if you have to beg me for shit! There's no need. We've been done, Chanel."

"You weren't saying that when—"

"That was pleasure for the both of us," he sneered. "There were no feelings involved, at least not on my part. We knew what the fuck we wanted at the time. Grow the fuck up! When you parted yo' legs like the red sea, I walked on your juices like Jesus walked on water. Live with that shit, I have."

The doors opened and Phantom stalked off the elevator, with me on his heels. I should've just left and got in my car, but no, I had to address what he'd said to me. There was no way he didn't feel the same spark of our lovemaking I felt. Phantom's pace quickened as he crossed the parking lot. I gripped the back of his shirt and he twisted out of my grasp. Stumbling slightly, my ankle rolled, causing me to yelp out in pain. He glanced back but didn't stop moving forward.

"This conversation is far from over, Xavier!" I cried out as I limped behind him. Knowing he wasn't going far, he hit the button to unlock his truck and opened the driver's door. I paused to remove my heels and watched as he leaned his upper body into the truck and came out with a blunt in his hand.

"Go home, Chanel. I don't want to discuss nothing outside of my custody case. I can do without all the dramatics. You know I can't stand that shit, but here you are, showing your ass. Tiffany brought enough drama into my life, and you saw firsthand how that turned out for her. I never thought you would be on the same childish shit you ridiculed her about every chance you got."

Phantom shook his head and lit the blunt he held between his fingers. After taking a puff, he blew the smoke out through his nose. "Females are a trip. If y'all would learn how to do shit without getting in your feelings, the world would be a better place.

Savage Storms 3

That's too much like right because y'all would find something to bitch about either way," he said, hunching his shoulder.

"No, if niggas stop fucking women, making them feel special in the moment then act as if y'all don't give a fuck, you muthafuckas wouldn't have nothing to worry about. Keep that shit funky!"

"You must be referring to Devin, because there was never an indication I gave two fucks about you. If your idea of feeling special is the way my dick forever curved to your pussy, so be it. That's all on you, Chanel. Whenever I want to slide through yo' crib, you gon' open the door with ease. We'll do the sexual tango and I'm gon' dip afterwards. Ain't shit gon' change, baby girl. That shit dead though, we ain't never going that route again in life."

Phantom smoked half of his blunt, while I stood stupidly as his words resonated in my mind. The blood boiled through my body as I restrained myself from knocking his muthafuckin' head into the side of his truck. Professional Chanel wasn't present. I had transformed into the hood bitch I kept hidden once I graduated law school.

The man standing before me had a lot to do with the reason I went back to school and got my degree in law. I loved him enough to obtain the shit that would save him from doing twenty-to-life in anybody's prison system. And the muthafucka stood before me, without a care, talking out the side of his neck.

"All these so-called feelings didn't emerge until you saw someone else getting close to a nigga. Where were your feelings when I was all about yo' ass, Chanel? Your feelings didn't exist when you were giving the pussy you claimed was all for me to another nigga, in my shit! It don't even matter, man," he said, waving his hand at me.

"Xavier, that was a mistake! How many times do I have to say I'm sorry?" My eyes burned as the tears welled in my eyes. "Devin never meant anything—"

"Yet, you continued to fuck him after I caught you trickin' off! Get the fuck outta here with that bullshit. Call that nigga and whine to his ass, because I don't want to hear it."

The fire left his eyes and his face lit up instantly. His demeanor changed prompting me to follow his gaze. The bitch that obviously had his heart stepped off the curb and they spoke to one another without words, from a distance. The way he lusted over her had me heated. When Phantom pushed off the truck, I politely placed my hand on his chest to halt his movement.

"Where do you think you're going?" I asked, stepping in front of him.

"Move yo' ass out the way. It's none of your business, but I'm going to make sure my woman is good. Is that alright with you?" He smirked before heading in the direction of Kenzie's car.

Instead of walking the short distance to my car and going home, I followed behind his ass like a lost puppy. While he thought what he'd just said was amusing, Phantom had caused problems with me he wasn't equipped to handle. I watched while he attempted to hug the hoe, only for her to keep taking steps away from him.

"This nigga begging, getting no play. Dumb ass," I muttered to myself. "Hey, Xavier, I'm about to head out."

"Aight, be easy," he said, without looking my way. "I'll call you later when Lay wakes up."

My mouth turned upward into a smile. "Okay, that's—"

"Chanel, go home. I wasn't talking to you."

Kenzie laughed as she walked around Phantom to get into her car. "Handle that, then we can discuss us. I want no parts of the added drama that's sure to come your way."

"Bitch, he's not going to handle shit! I've been here before you and I'm not going anywhere. But I'm going to let him cap in peace, because I know what it is in private." Phantom stared daggers into my soul but I didn't care. He needed to stop playing with me.

"I'm going to be the bigger person and act like I didn't hear you disrespect me for the second time today. With all the pent-up frustrations I have in me right now, I would be wearing orange before the sun sets. I guess lawyers aren't as professional as they appear when big dick is involved. I'll let you have that though. Phantom, get a muzzle for this bitch. You already know how I roll." Kenzie got in her car and peeled away without thought.

I smiled devilishly and didn't think shit of it. The nerve I hit in that bitch's nervous system was golden. Her mind was going to be wondering if Xavier was with me, every time he was out of her damn sight.

"What the fuck is wrong with you, Chanel? We just had a whole spat about this shit! Man, move the fuck around before I lay hands on you, for real."

Phantom was pissed. I wasn't about to allow him to play in my face as if I didn't mean shit to him. His dick told a different story than the words that spewed from his mouth.

"Stop fronting! That little girl doesn't even want your ass! Stevie Wonder can see that shit plain as day. I'm going to need you to stop playing with me, Xavier."

"Nah, you need to stop playing ya'self. You're fired, bitch! I'll find somebody else to handle the affairs with my daughter."

Phantom left me standing there looking dumb as he made his way back into the hospital. A lot of evil things ran through my mind. Everything he said went in one ear and out the other. Xavier may have fired me as his lawyer, but he would forever be in my life.

Meesha

Chapter 6

Heat

Nicassy's been on my dick since the day I allowed her to swallow me whole. She had a sex drive that I couldn't seem to keep up with. To be honest, I wasn't feeling any of the sexual interactions between us. The sex was great, but I felt as if I was cheating on both Summer and Kenzie with her. Summer had been blowing my phone up and I felt bad because I had her under the assumption I was out of town on business. In reality, I was only about forty minutes away.

Taking a chance of being tracked down by Brando's gang was something I didn't want to do. Rocko had been keeping me up to date about what was going on in the city. Even he had to disappear from the limelight. Rocko had some of the young cats looking out and that's how he received his information.

We lost a few of our soldiers in the process, but there was nothing I could do about that with the position I was in. I'd been getting many calls from my team, but they got the voicemail, just like Summer's ass. When Rocko informed me about the Black Kings making a truce with Phantom after they tried to take out Storm and Kane, I knew that shit wasn't going to hold too long. Spike wasn't going to lay low when his brother was killed and the person that killed him was nowhere to be found. He was out for my blood, and he was going to knock off as many of my people, until I felt the pain he did when he lost his brother.

I didn't give a fuck about that because I made sure my ducks were in a row before I left. My grandmother was safe in my home down in Miami and I had moved my parents away years prior. My baby mama hadn't been seen since the night she attempted to set me up to be robbed and killed by her stupid ass brother. She knew to stay out of sight, because she would be joining his ass soon as she popped up.

"What has you deep in thought over there?" Nicassy asked as she stood in the doorway of my office. She wore a shirt that barely covered her lower region and I had to squeeze my shit to calm his ass down.

"Business. I have to go out for a little bit later. Are you gon' be aight staying here alone?"

"Why can't I go with you?" she asked.

Sitting back in my chair, I thought about the watered-down version of what happened to her and decided to take it up a notch. It was time for me to drop names and hopefully it wouldn't jar her memory too much.

"Come in and take a seat, Nicassy," I said, motioning her to sit on the couch. Joining her, I turned and took a deep breath. "As I told you when we first arrived here, someone tried to kill you. It's not safe for you to go out. The best way for me to protect you is to keep you hidden."

"You have explained that and I'm hearing you, but *who* tried to kill me? The only thing you told me was someone was sent to kill the man I was hired to take out and blew his house up with me inside." She waited patiently as I struggled with the words I wanted to say. "You don't have to soften anything up. Give it to me raw and uncut. I can handle it, I promise."

"I'll start from the beginning, and you can stop me if anything comes back to memory." She nodded her head, and the movement gave me the okay to go forward. "I met Kenzie and Kayla when they saved my life one night at the club I own. The way they handled themselves was impressive and I wanted them on my team."

"I remember Kenzie and Kayla! They are my sisters from back home in Chicago. I haven't seen them since their grandmother passed away, and I have been wondering where they were. Do you have a number for them so we can reunite?"

There was no way I would give her access to Kenzie and Kayla. She didn't know they were no longer the same people she would remember. Storm and Kane was the side of them that would come for her. It was up to me to prepare Nicassy for the evil twins they had become.

"Let me finish bringing you up to date and I will allow you to determine if you still want to contact them or not. As I was saying, I brought them on as part of my team and they told me they had another member to their circle. That's how you came on and moved to Atlanta. I trained and enhanced all of your abilities to protect yourselves. The line of work I was in required you ladies to be strong, able to hold your own while in the streets."

"You trained us to be the assassins you told me about before?" she asked curiously.

"Yes. I trained y'all to kill people for a living, Tornado."

"Tornado? Who the fuck is that and how long have I been doing this shit?" I laughed because she was shocked to hear what she'd been doing for money. "I remember helping Kenzie and her family with a situation before, but I didn't think it went to that extreme. Wow."

She somewhat remembered little details about Kenzie and Kayla, and it was good things. I was about to shut her down and fill her in on the not so good things about her so-called sisters. There was no other way to get her to side solely with me and not them.

"Tornado is the name you wanted to go by on the job. Kenzie is Storm and Kayla is Kane. Short for Hurricane. The three of you were my Savage Storms and worked very well together until things between you and Kenzie took a turn for the worse."

"Storm is the one that tipped the guy off I was hired to kill?" I nodded my head yes. "Why would someone I loved turn her back on me like that? This isn't making sense." The excitement she expressed a moment prior was replaced with one of sadness.

"Kenzie found out the two of us were messing around behind her back."

"Wait a minute! You were dealing with both me and Kenzie at the same time?" Nicassy jumped to her feet and stood over me.

"I'll explain if you give me the chance to do so. Please don't jump to conclusions. Our affair was a mistake we both made, and I've apologized time and time again to both you and Kenzie. It was never supposed to happen, Nicassy. But it did."

Meesha

I pulled her onto my lap, and she slid onto the couch just as fast. With her head held down, Nicassy fumbled with the bracelet on her wrist. The way she was breathing let me know she was trying her best to control the anger she chose to hold inside.

"Kenzie and I were connected from the moment I laid eyes on her. The love we shared was something I wouldn't trade for anything in the world. We grew apart after she and Kayla moved back to Chicago after the passing of her grandmother. The twins weren't taking on any jobs during that time, but you came back to Atlanta and did a few jobs on your own. One night we were partying at Club Heat, and we were both pretty faded. One thing led to another, and we slept together."

The fabricated story rolled out of my mouth with ease and there was no doubt, Nicassy believed every word. It was never my intention to hurt her feelings, but I had to make the shit believable in order for my plan to work. She was soaking up everything I said, but she had yet to interrupt me.

"Kenzie chose the next morning to come back to Atlanta and found you in my bed. The two of you fought and your relationship hasn't been the same since. Me and Kenzie are no longer together, but she still held resentment towards you for what happened between us. You chose to go on an undercover job in Houston and Kenzie found out where you were. She tipped off Stone and told him the real reason you were there. That's when the explosion happened. Since you are here listening to me tell you all of this, that means she didn't succeed."

Nicassy stood and started pacing back and forth. There was going to be a lot of wear and tear in the carpet when she was done. My phone started vibrating in my pocket, but it wasn't the time for me to take any calls. I would deal with whomever it was after I got everything under control with Nicassy.

"Speak your mind," I said, attempting to break the silence that had taken over the room.

"I don't know what to say. Me and Kenzie is feuding over a man and to top it off, I get hurt and the only person I could remember to call was the man that once belonged to someone I called my sister. Do you know what type of code I broke fucking with you? There's no coming back from that, Heat! Now I'm hiding out because Kenzie wants me dead."

"We got over the initial affair thing. Kenzie was the one that took it too far when she tried to have you eliminated permanently. I'm not going to let her get away with what she has done. It's very important for you not to contact her. You are safe long as everyone thinks you are dead."

"What the fuck! I'm deep into some shit I know nothing about and now I have to live my life as if I'm in a fucking witness protection program! This is not the way I wanted to ever live life. Who is this Stone person, Heat?"

"Stone is the owner of Club Onyx—" I clamped my mouth closed because I'd given too much truth. Nicassy started crying and stormed out of my office. Following behind her, I didn't get the chance to console her because by the time I climbed the stairs, the door to the guest bedroom slammed hard. When I turned the knob, it was locked.

"I'm sorry, Nicassy. I didn't want you to be in the dark about what is going on. I'll see you when I return in a couple hours." She didn't respond so I walked away without trying to get her to talk to me. Hopefully, she missed when I mentioned Club Onyx.

***

Before I left the house, I went back to Nicassy's room and made another attempt to talk to her. She didn't open the door so again, I let her be. In the car, I thought about the things I had planted in her head, and I felt kind of bad about what I'd done, but it was necessary. Grabbing my phone, I called Summer, but she didn't answer.

Pulling into her driveway about an hour later, I got out the car and fumbled with my keys. I let myself inside and Summer was dancing around to Mary J. Blige's "Real Love," singing at the top of her lungs. She had on a pair of short shorts, a tank top, and footies. The curve of her hips swayed, and my eyes roamed over her body lustfully, causing my joint to swell.

"Real love. I'm searching for a real love. Someone to set my heart free, real love. IIIIII'mmmmm searching for a real love."

Summer was singing that shit with her chest. The way she was performing, there had to be a nigga in her ear. Her hair was rodded flowing down her back, nails done, and a big smile on her face. She had no clue I was coming through, so she didn't do all that shit for me.

"Having fun?" I asked over the music as I leaned against the wall with my arms folded over my chest.

"Heat! Oh my God, what are you doing here?" Summer ran across the room and jumped into my arms. "I've missed you, baby. Wait, is it safe for you to be here?"

Cupping her cheeks in my hands, I kissed her lips as I gazed in her eyes. "What do you mean, is it safe? I've been taking care of business. I figured I'd come through to see how you been doing."

"You don't have to keep lying to me, Romero. I've heard about what you did to Brando. People are looking for you, babe. I don't want anything to happen to you."

"I'm straight. Stop listening to the shit you hear in the streets. Whatever happened to Brando had nothing to do with me. I'm not worried about nobody coming for me, but I am worried about you watching out for yourself. And don't be out here trying to replace me. I know I haven't been around, but you still belong to me."

She sucked her teeth in aggravation, and I smacked her ass in return. The heat between her legs resonated through my shirt and I knew her kitty was ready. Leading the way to her bedroom, Summer knew what time it was.

Laying her gently on the bed, I grabbed her shorts and pulled them swiftly from her body. Her inner folds glistened with her juices and my mouth watered with anticipation. I ran my thumb over her nub as I watched her eyes slowly close. Summer's pussy was the best I could get, since I fucked up with Kenzie.

I got in position by lying on my stomach like a sniper. Her legs opened wide as an invitation for me to feast on her goodies. I ran my tongue along her slit and Summer purred seductively and pushed her lower region into my mouth.

"Oh, shit! Just like that!"

Hearing her moans turned me on more than I already was. I separated her folds and wrapped my lips around her pearl, sucking softly. The tremors of her legs let me know she was on the verge of erupting in my mouth.

"Fuck!" she screamed passionately as she grasped the back of my head. "I'm about to cum! Yes, yes, aaaahhhhh!"

Summer's sweet secretions glided down my throat, and I caught every drop. The taste of pussy almost always quenched my thirst. After what I'd done to her, I was still thirsty. As she came down from the euphoric high I'd put her in, she pulled my arms until I was towering over her frame.

"I've waited weeks for this. I need you inside of me."

Summer looked so sexy lying with her eyes half closed. She placed her hand into the front of my pants, but my dick laid flaccid in my boxers. My pipe was dead to the touch, and he had never been inactive in a moment of desire. Summer didn't try to hide her disappointment.

"What's really going on, Heat?" she asked with an attitude.

"I have a lot on my mind, I guess. Pleasing you orally is all I'm able to give, Summer. I'm sorry." Closing my eyes, the image of Nicassy riding my dick displayed behind my lids.

"It's been weeks since you've had sex with me. Your sex drive is always on go, and you have never turned down the opportunity to do so with me. Who is she?" Summer scoffed as she threw her leg over my head and stood from the bed.

"You're always thinking another woman has something to do with everything. Stop that shit, Summer. You know what's going on in my life right now. I came here to check on you. To make sure you were good. That other shit, was an added bonus."

Summer walked toward the door and snatched the shorts I'd thrown behind me from the floor. I sat up on the bed and watched as she dressed and felt bad that I couldn't give her what she wanted. In a flash, the hurt turned into anger, and I let out a long sigh because I knew she was getting herself geared up for a major tirade.

"Whatever. I'm good. You saw me, now you can leave. Your dick ain't working for me, so that means it has a new owner. I don't give a fuck what you say, somebody is getting the goods and it's probably that bitch, Kenzie."

"I didn't come to argue, Summer. Think whatever you want because that's something I'm not about to dwell on today. You're obsessed with Kenzie and she's not even a factor in my life. Believe it or not, we would be further than we are, if you worried about yo' damn self. The insecurities you have is fuckin' shit up between us because you know I hate to be questioned about bullshit. I'm gon' leave, but before you go out and do something stupid, remember there's niggas gunnin' for me. You would be the perfect way for them to get to me. Keep that shit in mind."

I stood from the bed and took a few steps toward the door. Instead of Summer letting the bullshit go, she decided to push the knife deeper into her own heart. "You don't even claim me as your woman! Ain't nobody worried about me on account of your ass. See your way out and don't worry about me contacting you after this shit."

It didn't make sense to go back and forth with her. I was better off walking away so she could drive her damn self crazy, alone. I looked at Summer one last time and left out of her bedroom. Stopping in the bathroom downstairs to wash my face, I noticed a pair of cufflinks on the countertop. Everything started coming together for me. The hair, happy mood, and the way she told me to leave without much of a fight. Summer's hoe ass had a nigga whispering sweet nothings in her ear. *"She better keep that shit out of sight or that's her ass,"* I said to myself as I washed the remnants of her snatch from my face.

Savage Storms 3

Chapter 7

Stone

The moment I left Summer's house, I hit up Scony. She was definitely an easy target to get at. All it took was a good-looking nigga like me to come dressed to impress and show up at her crib, looking like a million bucks. It didn't take long for me to download the tracking app on her phone. Whenever Heat decided to call, I'd be able to track his shit, as well as every move both he and Summer made.

I won't lie, baby girl was bad. My thoughts were to smash her ass for the fun of it. She was going to go for a good roll in the hay, no doubt. The lust in her eyes told me all I needed to know. My mind went back to the conversation I had with Scony.

"What you got for me, Stone?" Scony asked soon as he answered.

"My plan is in motion. I just left Summer's crib and I'm taking her out tomorrow night. I came up with a story about being lost and gained entry into her space. Then when she allowed me to use her phone, I excused myself to the bathroom and planted a tracking app on her phone. Now, we wait for that nigga to contact her. After that, we'll be burying his ass."

"Damn, nigga, you didn't waste no muthafuckin' time," Scony laughed. "How long you plan on staying in the A?"

"Nah, this nigga needs to be found pronto. He fucked up putting a hit out on me not once, but twice and failed both times. Heat will pay for that shit in blood. As far as my stay in Atlanta, it depends on how long it takes Heat to get in touch with his bitch. In the meantime, I'm about to finesse her ass for the hell of it."

"Go for it, homie. Just make sure you strap up. There's no telling how many dicks she had since her so-called man bailed on her. Don't fall in love, this shit is business."

"Scony, you're talking to me like I'm a young sap out here, man. I know how to fuck the bitch senseless and slit her mutha-

fuckin' throat in the process. Too bad we need her ass to get at the big fish."

I smiled as I finished getting dressed for my fictitious date, shaking the conversation with Scony from my mind. Sliding my feet into my Giuseppe dress shoes, I looked in the mirror and liked what I saw. A nigga cleaned up well when needed.

It was almost time for me to put my game face on and pretend to get to know Summer. I'd already bought a dozen roses and made reservations for dinner. Grabbing my wallet and stuffing it in the back pocket of my slacks, I snatched my keys and cellphone from the dresser and made my way to the door. Making sure to pick up the bouquet and the keycard from the table, I whistled as I pulled the door open.

I turned a few heads as I strolled through the lobby and made my way to the Mercedes Coupe I'd rented for my stay in Atlanta. My phone vibrated in my pocket as I crossed the parking lot. Hitting the button to unlock the doors, I pulled my phone out as I climbed inside, placing the flowers on the passenger seat. There was a message from the encrypted app I'd installed on Summer's device.

Bae: Wyd

Summer: None of your business, Heat! You showed me everything I needed to know when you were here. What do you want?

Bae: Get out your feelings, Summer. You got a whole attitude about the make-believe shit you conjured up in yo' head. The nerve of you when you had a nigga in yo' shit, but you worried about what the fuck I'm doing.

Summer: Ain't nobody been in my house! Don't try to turn this around on me.

Heat: Whose muthafuckin' cufflinks on the counter in the downstairs bathroom?

A smiled spread wide across my face because his ass saw my shit in her crib. He caught the bait and it let me know he'd been to see her at some point since I'd left. Stealing a glance at the clock, I had a little time to spare before we had to be at the restaurant. I was eager to see how this shit show was about to play out. It took Summer a few minutes to respond but eventually she did.

Summer: Cufflinks? Ain't no cufflinks in that bathroom. Gone with your bullshit, Heat. Feel free to fuck whomever because I don't care no more.

Bae: That's because I got the muthafuckas with me!

I put the gear in reverse, laughing heartily as I backed out of the parking lot. Placing my phone in the holder, I drove in the direction of the highway. As I stopped at a red light, a message came through. Heat responded with an image of my cufflinks and the monogram letters were in plain sight. If he was in his right frame of mind, that alone should've told him I was on his ass like flies on shit. But his concern was focused on who was getting that pussy while he was in hiding.

Summer: I've never seen those a day in my life. Miss me with that nonsense. Bye, Heat!

Heat continued to text, but Summer refused to respond. She was probably walking around nervous as hell, hoping that nigga didn't come back to fuck her up. I turned on the radio because I was tired of hearing myself laugh. I smooth sailed soon as I hit the highway to Summer's crib.

Now that Heat had hit her line, I had tabs on his ass. Hitting a few buttons, I was able to track his movements. When the red dot appeared with his name on display, it showed he was right on her street. This nigga was texting instead of walking in the house to confront her like a real man. That alone caused me to go into another fit of laughter. I was still about ten minutes from Summer's house, so I pushed the gas pedal and sped to my destination.

A few minutes later, a beeping sound brought my attention back to my phone. His ass was on the move, and I tried my best to keep my eyes on the road while trying to see where the fuck he was headed at the same time. Making sure I didn't run into somebody's shit, I quickly glanced back at my phone and the nigga was gone.

"Fuck!" I said as I hit the steering wheel. "I'll have to figure out what happened once I get back to my laptop at the hotel," I said frustratedly to myself. "This muthafucka just pulled a Houdini on my ass."

***

I walked up to Summer's door and it opened soon as I reached out to ring the bell. Damn, she was sitting in the window like a kid waiting on their deadbeat to show up. Fighting hard not to laugh at the shit going on in my head, I gave her a once-over from the top of her head to the bottom of her pretty feet.

Summer stood before me in a cream-colored pantsuit that hugged her in all the right places. The cropped top showed off her toned stomach and navel piercing. A pair of peach, open-toed stilettos adorned her feet, showcasing her pretty pink toes. My eyes traveled back up, and she had a sheepish smile on her face.

"Hello to you too, handsome," she said, putting her hand on her hip.

"You are beautiful. These are for you," I said, handing her the flowers.

"Thank you. Let me put these in some water and grab my purse. Come in, I won't be long."

I stepped inside and watched every swivel of her hips as she walked away from me. Knowing her bitch ass man was still in the vicinity, I had to keep watch at the door and off her ass, in case I had to beat Heat's muthafuckin' body if he decided to double back.

"Okay, I'm ready. You look real spiffy, Mr. Cole."

Opening the door, I held it open so she could walk out ahead of me, but thought twice about it, and pulled her back slightly. Discreetly, I checked the perimeter to make sure everything was cool before I allowed her to step outside. Summer looked at me strangely and became fidgety as she peeked her head out of the door.

"Is everything okay?" she asked nervously.

"Yeah, when I drove up, there was a nigga out here that looked out of place. Don't mind me, I'm always cautious in neighborhoods I know nothing about. I'm quite sure everything is good." The lie seemed to work, but I could tell she was feeling a sense of uneasiness.

Summer fumbled with her keys, and they fell from her hand as she tried to lock the door. Bending down to retrieve them, I handed them to her. Summer's hands were steadier that time around, allowing her to lock her door successfully. She took a deep breath and walked down the steps with me on her heels.

When we got to my car, I opened the passenger door for her and she eased in with a smile. Closing the door, I walked around the front as I scanned the block. There was nothing out of place, so I hopped in beside her and started the engine.

"I hope you're hungry. I made reservations and we need to be there in the next fifteen minutes."

"I'm starving. I've been waiting for this date all day. You kind of piqued my curiosity, Mr. Cole."

"My father is Mr. Cole. It's alright to call me Savon. You don't have to be so formal, sweetheart. Tell me all about your curiosity. I would love to hear all about it."

Summer and I talked the entire time I drove to the restaurant. When I pulled into the parking lot, she gasped. I gave her a side glance and her eyes were gleaming. I knew I made the right choice choosing the upscale restaurant. Driving into the valet lane, I got out as the attendant approached the car. Handing over my keys and taking the ticket, I walked around, opening the door for Summer. I led the way into the establishment with my hand on the small of her back.

We were seated promptly. The candlelit environment made the moment very intimate. Summer was acting a little shy and I knew she wasn't used to being courted the way I'd done. That nigga Heat needed to step his game up. It was going to be hard for him to top the shit I had planned for her gullible ass. Taking her back to the suite I reserved for our after-dinner activities, was going to put the icing on the cake. There was no way she would know which hotel, I was staying in. She was going to be thinking about

Savon for the long haul and might try to stalk a nigga before I could make my getaway.

"I've always wanted to come to this place. Thanks for bringing me."

"Oh, this shit is small to a giant, baby." I smiled, showing off my dimples, making Summer squirm in the seat across from me. "Talk to me. Tell me something good about Summer."

"There's not much to tell really. I was born and raised here in Atlanta. My parents decided to move away when my father retired. They live in Las Vegas now and are enjoying life. I have two sisters, both are married and have their own lives. They moved away to see what life was like outside of Georgia. I'm the only one that couldn't let the peach go. It's all I know," she said, hunching her shoulder,

"I guess that's where a nigga like me comes into play. If we get to know each other on every level, maybe I can introduce you to many more first." I took a sip from the water the waitress placed on the table after we were seated.

"Savon, that sounds good, but I told you yesterday, I'm in a relationship."

I laughed as I sat back and draped my arm on the back of the chair next to me. "Your man is not a factor tonight, or any other night, when you're in my presence. You wouldn't be sitting across from me now if he was. This is our night, and we won't discuss *yo' man.*"

"Okay, before we put that subject to rest, can I ask you a question?"

"Sure. Talk to me."

"Did you leave a pair of cufflinks in my bathroom yesterday?" Summer stared intensely across the table at me. I knew I had to come correct when I answered.

"Yeah, I did. I couldn't remember where the hell I left them. Did you bring them with you?" I asked.

"Um, no," she said, glancing everywhere but at me. "My man came over earlier today and he found them. He took your cufflinks from my house and texted me with a picture after talking shit about someone being in my house."

"It's cool. I can get another pair. I'm sorry for that hiccup, Summer. When I washed my hands, I took them off to roll up my sleeves. I guess I forgot to pick 'em back up. If I messed things up for you, I apologize."

At that moment, the waitress came over, interrupting our conversation. We looked over the menu and placed our orders. Summer ordered lobster, crab, and a sirloin steak with potatoes and asparagus. Money wasn't an issue, but she was definitely paying for all that shit with her ass tooted up in the air. Fuck she thought? I ordered a steak, baked potato, and broccoli. For extra measures, I requested a bottle of their finest wine. May as well get the party started early. The waitress collected the menus and Summer wasted no time getting back to the conversation we were having before we were interrupted.

"Back to what we were talking about. There's no way you could mess up something that's been messy for quite some time. To be honest, I should've walked away from the relationship a long time ago. I've been through too much bullshit with this man, but that's the choice I made."

"You can't help who you love, baby girl. There's always going to be trying times in any relationship. I can tell you not going anywhere when it comes to yo' nigga. You're only feeling the way you are because you're with me. I'm just something for you to do right now. I want you to put all thoughts of your relationship to the side and enjoy the time we have together."

I needed her ass to stay with that nigga so I was going to let her think I would play second fiddle to his ass. The way she smiled let me know she was game. I laid the shit on thick, letting her know what I was willing to sacrifice.

"Summer, I don't give a fuck about your man. Whatever you got going with him, is between y'all. It doesn't have anything to do with me. Like I said before, when you with me, nothing else matters. You can be my woman whenever you want to be." She looked taken back by what I said, but I kept a straight face because I knew she was going to jump all over that proposition.

We were interrupted once again when our food was placed in front of us. Things were quiet as we both devoured the delectable cuisine. Summer was drinking the wine as if it was Kool-Aid, but I didn't care. I wanted her to be good and tipsy so she could be nasty as she wanted to be, without thinking about cheating on that fuck nigga. I sipped the wine and water simultaneously because I wanted to be in my right state of mind. Hell, I had to drive too.

Breaking the silence, Summer put her fork down but held onto the glass in her hand. "This is too good to be true. You mean to tell me you still want to fuck with me, even though I have a man?" I nodded my head in agreeance and kept eating. "There has to be some type of stipulations. Lay everything on the table right now."

"There's nothing to lay on the table. You have a man, cool. Whenever I call, make sure you're available. It won't be frequently because I don't want that nigga putting his hands on you. Then he will die if I find out. What you have going on with him is the shit you're used to. With me, it will be a whole new ballgame. In other words, your escape."

She sat pondering the words I'd hit her with, I knew she was all in. It would be a matter of time before she would lead me right to Heat's grimy ass. After Summer finished off the bottle of wine, I paid the tab and left a hefty tip. Standing up, I stood next to her and held my hand out.

"I had a great time with you tonight. We're gonna have to do this again soon," I said as we walked outside and headed to valet.

"You making it seem as if this is it," she pouted. "The night is still young. I'm not ready to go home."

Handing the valet driver my ticket, I turned and looked down at her. I ran my thumb down the side of her face and down to her cleavage. "You trying to roll with me, Summer?" I asked seductively.

"Since I'm not ready to go home, I guess so," she smiled.

"I hope you're ready for my hospitality. It's going to be a long night for both of us."

My car arrived and the valet attendant waited patiently as I gazed in Summer's eyes while she turned into putty on the low. She was the first to break the connection and grasped my hand, leading me to the car. Summer got in and I closed the door softly as the attendant stepped back. I greased his palm with a few bills and jumped in the whip.

I pulled off and headed a few blocks away to the decoy hotel I booked for the night. Summer's eyes were low, but she was swaying back and forth to the music that was playing on the radio. Tank was swooning and gave her the foreplay she was going to need when she was finally alone with me. As I pulled into the driveway of the hotel, Summer reached over and cupped my dick through my pants. Glancing over at her, I smirked. The alcohol had to be flowing through her bloodstream, because she wasn't holding back.

"I see what you on, baby girl, but hold that thought," I said, removing her hand as I opened the door, getting out of the car. Handing my keys to the valet driver, I once again rounded the car to help Summer out. She stumbled and fell against my muscular body, letting out a small giggle.

"That wine is running through me, Savon. I need to get to a bathroom fast."

"I got you. Can you walk?" I asked, looking down at her.

"Yeah, but you can carry me if you like," she said seductively.

Instead of picking her up, I led the way into the hotel, making sure I held her body close to mine as we headed for the elevators. The doors opened soon as we approached one of the cars and I inserted my key for the penthouse suite. Jazz music played lowly, causing Summer to sway in my arms. Her movements became erotic and before I knew it, she dropped to her knees while fumbling with my belt. As much as I wanted her to swallow my man whole, I was still a gentleman at heart.

"I can't let you handle that in an elevator, love. We have all night for you show me what that mouth do. It won't be too much longer, be easy," I laughed, pulling her up from the position she was in. Summer started dancing around like a two-year-old and I was glad the doors opened. "The bathroom is right through those doors in the bedroom."

Summer dropped her purse on the table and raced in the direction I pointed. Walking toward the bay window, I heard a phone ringing behind me. I followed the sound and noticed it was coming from Summer's purse. Not wanting to invade her privacy, I continued to the window and took in the scenery.

I smelled the scent of her *Soleil Blanc* by Tom Ford and knew she was behind me without turning around. Summer pressed her breasts against my back and wrapped her arms around my waist. Not missing a beat, her right hand traveled to the spot I didn't let her explore while we were in the elevator. Summer wanted the dick, and she wanted it now. Instead of stopping her, I guided her hand to the lump of coal she desired. The way she was massaging my shit made my eyes close slowly, because it had been a while since I'd had any type of sexual relations since Angel.

When she removed my joint and it sprang out like a boa constrictor, she moaned into my back. I smiled at the shivers that flowed through her body. The precum oozed out of the tip of my shit and she rubbed it into my skin.

"Can I taste some of this?" Summer asked, referring to my cum.

I couldn't find my voice and my dick was hard as a brick. Nodding my head, she walked to the front of the window, and I backed up to give her space. Summer dropped to her knees while licking her lips. She looked up at me with a smile and flicked her tongue. The way the wetness of her muscle made contact with my pipe, it slightly jumped, smacking her in the mouth.

"Oooooo, I'm about to have fun with this. He looks delicious too."

Soon as she ran her tongue along my shaft, her phone started blaring from her purse. Ignoring it, she swallowed my pipe in one gulp and my body fell forward. I had to reach out and plant my hands against the window. The muscles in her throat constricted, pulling me in like that damn fish did the snake on a video I saw on social media. My toes balled up in my shoes and I could've sworn they cracked with every suction of her jaws.

"Shit. Damn. Suck that shit," I grunted as I palmed the back of her head with one of my hands.

Summer smacked my hand away and gripped my shaft as she sucked away. Her saliva slid down to my balls and my nut was building quickly. Backing away from her killer jaws, I looked down at her as if she was a demon. I'd never had a bitch suck my shit like that before. No wonder Heat was questioning her ass about the cufflinks. He didn't want another muthafucka to get the treatment she provided.

"Where you going? You promised I could taste that good shit that was about to glide down my throat," she said, wiping the corners of her mouth.

"Nah, I'm not ready for that. You almost had a nigga cummin' before I could get the chance to bless that sweet tunnel of yours."

Her phone started ringing again and she groaned in frustration before rising to her feet. Stalking across the room, she snatched the phone from her purse and shook her head. "I have to take this. I'll be right back, so get ready for me, handsome."

Summer made a dash into the bedroom and closed the door. I took that opportunity to retrieve my phone from my pocket and went right to the app because I knew Heat was calling to check on her. Just as I thought, Heat's phone came up and he was at Summer's address. This was the chance I needed to get at his ass. I backed out of the app and sent Scony a message. He had the connects in Atlanta that would help me out.

Me: Aye, I got a hit on Heat. He's here in Atlanta. Get in touch with yo' people. He's at his bitch Summer's crib. Here's the address.

I sent the address and waited for him to respond, but Summer had stepped out of the bedroom. She was naked as the day she was born, and her ass was stacked. Scony better handle that shit, because I was about to get balls deep in some pussy.

Chapter 8

Khaos

I took Kayla to PetSmart to shop for Snow. I had to do something to keep my mind off Layla being in the hospital. When I talked to Phantom the day before, he was adamant about me not going back to the hospital. Instead, I stayed with Kayla and Snow for the rest of the night. The moment me and Kayla entered her home, she put Snow down and he took off running. The lil nigga acted as if he lived there all his life and it hadn't even been a whole day. Kayla had me sit all his food on the kitchen table and everything else on the floor. I watched as she went through all the bags. I didn't think she would be so happy to have a dog and I took a chance, but she was in love at first sight.

"Khaos, thank you so much for buying all the essentials for Snow. I wouldn't have known what to buy if you weren't there." Kayla beamed from ear to ear as she placed all the items on the table.

"I got you, babe—"

"Snow, I know the fuck you didn't!" Kayla screamed as she dropped everything she held in her hands on the table and ran out of the kitchen. "This what you not gon' do around this mutha-fucka!"

"What the hell happened?" I asked confused as I followed her into the hall.

"His ass cocked his leg up and pissed on my wall! That's what the fuck happened. You will be taking his ass with you, because he can't stay here doing this shit!"

Snow took off running into the living room and huddled under the coffee table as Kayla continued to rant. She stormed toward the bathroom and Snow ran right to me, hopping on his hind legs. I picked him up and he damn near crawled over my shoulder as Kayla entered the room, carrying a bucket with a strong aroma of bleach following her.

"Go put his ass in your car along with all his shit!" she said, dropping to her knees. "I didn't sign up to be Cinderella in here behind a damn dog! If I wanted to do this shit, I would've had a child by now."

"It's never too late to practice for a kid, Kayla. Whenever you're ready, let a nigga know. But for now, you gon' practice with Snow," I smirked as she rolled her eyes. "He's just getting used to the house. Plus, he's still just a baby, Kayla." The look she gave me told me all I needed to know. "Come on, lil homie. We're going outside before your mama kills us both."

I put Snow on the floor and walked toward the patio door. He followed behind me but slowed down as he neared Kayla. Sniffing her underarm, he moved around and nudged her face. She couldn't even be mad at him too much longer, because she smiled from ear to ear.

"Snow, let's go," I said, opening the patio door. I stood there for a few seconds before I whistled loudly because his ass was still over there lovin' on my woman. He whipped his head in my direction but hesitated to follow my command. I had to show his ass he had two masters in that muthafucka.

"Snow, get yo' ass over here now!"

The bass in my voice had him moving faster than the speed of lightning. Snow slid to a sudden stop when he realized the ledge was high off the ground. I stepped over his small body and bent down to his level. Snow started whimpering and I wasn't having that soft shit. I wouldn't be like those niggas on social media talking about the dog they wanted but ended up with a chihuahua in a pitbull's body.

"Cut that punk ass shit out!" I snarled grabbing him by the skin on the back of his neck, giving him a strong shake. "Step down!"

Snow stared me down, squared his shoulders, and hopped down like he wasn't just scared to move his little paws. He sized me up as if he could talk. "Fuck you, nigga," would've been his choice of words. Snow took off running after a squirrel and I couldn't do nothing but laugh. My phone vibrated on my hip and Scony's name appeared on the display soon as I looked at it.

"Yeah, what's up?"

"Get to Summer's crib now! Stone got a hit on Heat and that's where he is. Don't kill that nigga, take his ass somewhere and call me when he is locked up tight."

"Say less. I'm on it."

Jogging to the other side of the yard where Snow was yelping at the squirrel that got away from him, I scooped him up and headed back into the house. Kayla was in the kitchen when I entered, and she looked up.

"What's wrong?" she asked.

"I have to make a run. I'll be back soon as I can."

"Where are you going? We have to go back to the hospital to check on Layla."

"Your brother called and there's something he wants me to check out. I won't be long," I said, walking briskly to the front door.

"You going after Heat, aren't you? I'm going with you," she said, hurrying to put Snow in his cage.

"Nah, Kayla. Stay here and bond with Snow. I'll fill you in when I get back."

Not waiting for her to reply, I left the house and hurried to my whip. Kayla was screaming but I couldn't make out what she was saying. I would listen to her bitch when I returned, I didn't have time for that shit right then. Driving fast as I could to make my way to the other side of town, I entered the highway in record time.

When I turned down Summer's street, I parked several houses away. Jumping out of my whip, I snatched my Glock off my hip and held it by my side as I walked briskly toward Summer's house. There was no activity on the street and no sign of Heat anywhere. The driveway was empty of all cars, so I eased along the side of the house as I peeked into one of the windows. The lights were off and there was no sign of anyone being inside, but I didn't leave based on that thought alone.

Meesha

I made my way to the back door and jimmied the lock with one of my credit cards. The lock wasn't a very good one, so it didn't take much for me to get inside the property. It was quiet as hell inside as I moved around slowly with my tool aimed. Going room to room, I came up empty on my search. Leaving out the same way I came in, I returned to my car and still, no Heat. I was pissed because I came out on a blank mission. I didn't appreciate that shit at all.

Wasting no time calling Stone, I waited for him to answer but when he didn't, it only pissed me off more. I immediately dialed Scony, because both of them niggas needed to get their shit together if we were planning to get at Heat. Obviously, this nigga was slithering through the cracks of whatever they had in place for his ass.

"Did you get his ass?" Scony asked.

"Hell nawl. Ain't nobody over in this bitch! What the fuck is y'all on?" I didn't even try to mask how frustrated I was.

"What do you mean? Stone said the tracker showed he was there."

"Just what the fuck I said! Stone should've been tracking his every muthafuckin' move instead of sending me on a blank mission. Is he the only one with eyes on this damn tracking device? If so, that shit ain't working! Hit me up when y'all on one accord, because I won't be roaming around blind. This is bullshit, Scony."

"I feel where you're coming from, Khaos. I'll holla at Stone about this tracking shit. I appreciate you jumping on it without hesitation. Keep yo' line open and I will be in touch. It will be solid next time. Mark my words."

"Yeah, aight."

I hung up from Scony and headed back to Kayla's, so I could hear whatever she had to say about me leaving without her. Not allowing her to tag along wasn't worth the argument that was sure to come once I stepped inside her house. As I prepared to turn into Kayla's driveway, I noticed her car was no longer in the driveway.

Shaking my head, I didn't bother pulling in, she wasn't there. I dialed her phone, and it rang until the voicemail picked up.

"Kayla, I don't know where the fuck you went, but I want you to at least tell me where you are. Leaving the house without letting me know where you were going was not cool. Be careful. I'm on my way to the hospital to check on Layla."

Driving in silence, I was mad as hell because Kayla knew what the fuck was going on in the streets. For her to leave without a word, was plain stupid. She thought the shit was going to have me chasing her, but she was sadly mistaken. Nothing better happen to her though. If it does, I'm whoopin' her ass whenever I found her.

I drove into the hospital's parking lot and didn't even notice how fast it took me to get there. My mind was on Kayla. I had to shake that shit off because Layla was my main focus at that time. After obtaining a pass and the number to the room Layla was in, I made my way upstairs. The halls were quiet, and a few nurses sat behind the desk talking lowly. When I walked slowly past the nurse's station, all chatter ceased, and all eyes were on me.

"Heyyyy, how you doing?" one of the nurses sang with a smile. I nodded and kept walking, but I guess that wasn't enough for her. "That nigga is fine. He seems kind of arrogant though. I guess he wants a bitch to sweat his ass."

Laughing as I neared Layla's room, I was glad Kayla wasn't with me because that hoe would've gotten snatched over the counter. I tapped lightly on the door and walked into the dimly lit room. Layla was sleeping soundly in the bed and Phantom was seated next to her in a chair. My cousin was watching his daughter like a hawk. He glanced up at me with his hand positioned at his waist. When he saw it was me coming in, he relaxed and leaned back in the chair.

"You just missed yo' mama. She told me to tell you to get yo' head out of that woman's ass and call her. She hasn't heard from you in a few days, and you know she ain't about to come second to no damn body."

"That woman is a trip. She's lowkey blockin' and I'm gon' tell her about that shit. Now I see why I haven't been with nobody in a while, it's her hating ass."

"You're the one that's neglecting her. Auntie Kimille isn't used to you not calling to see how she's doing. Tighten up, Cuz, and don't be coming for her like that. She will beat yo' ass and you know it," Phantom laughed.

I automatically started laughing with him because I knew there was no lies detected about what he said. Me and my mama was closer than shoestrings and I'd been neglecting her, not purposely though. I would make it up to her one way or another.

"How's my Lil Homie?" I asked, sitting on the edge of the hospital bed as I eyed the slings that housed Layla's legs.

"Her right leg has the lesser of the two injuries. Layla sustained a break called a shaft fracture. That's when the small bone that runs along the outer part of the leg is broken. It will heal with the cast in a couple weeks but the injury to her left leg is so much worse. It will be six months to a year before that bone heals fully. She has a major fracture in her left femur bone, which is her thigh bone. The doctor had to reset the bone, and has to keep a close watch on Layla, because there's a chance of her having complications that can be life threatening."

Reaching out to grasp my little cousin's hand, I gave it a tiny squeeze just to let her know I was there by her side. "What's the complications she's facing, Cuz?" I choked out.

My emotions were getting the best of me because I couldn't stomach seeing her laying there helpless like that. Layla was the little girl that loved to run around playing, dancing, and having fun in general. It was going to take time for her to do any of the shit she was used to doing. I breathed slowly as I waited for Phantom to tell me what I wanted to know.

Phantom took a deep breath as he rubbed his hand slowly down his face. "The inability of my baby ever walking again is my main concern. Swelling can set in, which is not good. We must pay attention to any fevers, sweats, chills, and excessive fatigue. Physical therapy will start tomorrow if there's no signs of complications. The doctor explained that early movement can help prevent blood clots and any of the other complications. Cuz, I just want my baby to be straight again."

The tears in my cousin's eyes I'm quite sure matched the ones welled in mine. All that shit turned to anger when I thought about how Layla ended up in the hospital in the first place. Tiffany wasn't going to have a second to explain why she did the heinous act against her own daughter. I didn't want to hear a damn thing she had to say. The only sound I was looking forward to hearing was the sound of her taking her last breath.

Layla squeezed my hand and a lone tear fell from my eye. She didn't move another inch, but I knew she was going to be alright. The Bennett's were fighters and Layla was going to be a warrior with the therapy shit. She had a whole team behind her. We were all going to be in the race to recovery with her.

"The physical therapy is going to be difficult with the weight of the casts. The early start is necessary, in order to build the muscle mass in her legs. It's going to be a painful experience, but I'll be right here with my baby, pushing her through. When I tell you, Cuz, if I could trade places with her, I would in a millisecond."

"Phantom, I'm right there with you on that shit. Layla don't deserve to be in this predicament. Let me know what time her session is, and I will be here to cheer her on too," I said, staring at my lil homie as she slept while rubbing the top of her hand.

"Where's Kayla?" Phantom asked, bringing me out of my thoughts.

"I don't know. She's mad at me because I didn't let her go with me to check out a lead Scony had on Heat."

"Y'all got that nigga?"

"Nah, it was a blank muthafuckin' mission. I'm waiting for Scony to hit me back because that nigga Stone didn't answer his fuckin' phone. He has some type of device on Summer's phone. He can track Heat's movements when he contacts her ass. Obviously, the shit ain't no help for us if Stone's not watching the shit properly. I've already told Scony they need another plan in motion, because I'm not feeling the one they have in place."

"I feel you, fam. Heat is going to—"

"Daddy," Layla cried out without opening her eyes.

"I'm right here, baby," Phantom said, sitting on the other side of the bed.

"My legs hurt." Seeing the tears fall from her eyes onto the pillow, messed with my emotions. I looked down and pushed the button for the nurse as Phantom tried his best to console Layla. Instead of responding to the call, a nurse entered the room.

"What can I help you with, Mr. Bennett?" she asked with a smile.

"Layla is hurting. Is it time for her dose of pain medication?"

"I was actually getting her dosage together when you rang. The doctor wants her to try and eat something first, though. I ordered a tray for her, and it should be here any minute." There was a knock on the door and the nurse opened it and moved back. "I was just talking about that tray. Nice timing," the nurse laughed.

The kitchen aide placed the tray on the portable table and left the way he came. I pulled the table closer to the bed and removed my hand from Layla's. Lifting the lid to the container, I scrunched up my nose because the food didn't look appealing at all. Layla wasn't going to eat any of that shit. The nurse came back, and I stood and whispered in her ear.

"Does she have to eat what was brought in? That shit looks like dog food."

"No. She's not on a strict diet. If you want to go out and grab something she's going to eat, then that's fine. She has to eat something in order to get the medication."

"Okay, thanks," I said, turning around toward the bed. "Layla, do you want Chipotle?"

"Uncle K, what kind of question is that? Of course. I want a burrito bowl with extra steak, chicken, lettuce, tomato, cheese, and sour cream. Hurry back because I'm kind of hungry. Thank you and I love you." The mention of her favorite restaurant dried those tears right up, but I could still see the signs of pain on her face, even though she tried her best to hide it.

"Before I leave, how are you feeling?" I asked.

"Like I've been hit by a car. Whatever that feels like, that's how I feel. Now gone and get my food, Big Homie."

"You got it, Sweetness. Anything for you. Phantom, I'll be back in five." Walking to the door, Layla called out to me.

"Uncle K! Call Kenzie and tell her to come see me, please."

"I'm on it, baby girl. Chipotle and Kenzie, coming right up."

Phantom shook his head as I rushed out to get my lil homie what she asked for. As I waited on the elevator, I dialed Kenzie's number and waited for her to answer.

Meesha

Chapter 9

MaKayla

Khaos leaving without letting me go with him really pissed me off. He of all people knew how bad I wanted to fuck Heat up and he left to deal with that nigga on his own. After he left, I put Snow's food and water dish in the kitchen next to the pantry and set his cage and bed up in the spare bedroom next to mine. Snow followed me everywhere I went, except up the stairs. His whimpering was so pitiful, I felt sorry for the little guy.

I spent about an hour teaching him how to climb the stairs but found myself lifting him up, because he wouldn't even try on his own. I gave up and carried his ass upstairs and placed him at the top of the stairs. Walking into my bedroom, I sat on the side of my bed and called my brother. As I waited for him to answer the phone, I realized I still hadn't heard from my twin.

"What up, Kay?"

"Where the fuck did you send Khaos?" I snapped.

"Kayla, don't call me with that bullshit," Scony said too calmly for my liking. "If your man didn't tell you, neither will I. Tone that shit down, sis. It's business."

"Business? I thought I was part of this operation. Heat did something he's not getting away with and I want in. Why y'all trying to keep me on the sideline is something I don't understand, but the shit is fucked up. I never thought you would hold anything from me, bro."

"I'm not holding nothing from you. The mission I sent Khaos on did not require your presence. When I have something for you and Kenzie, I'll let you know. Is there anything else?"

"Aht-aht, you will not blow me off like I'm nothing, Scony! Heat murdered Will and did something to Nicassy, and you want me to sit around waiting! You got me fucked up!"

I hung up on his ass and headed for the door. Hurrying down the stairs, the sound of Snow's small cries caught my attention. I ran back up the stairs and scooped his lil ass up. Walking into the guest bedroom, I put a puppy pad in the cage and chucked him inside and pushed the latch in place. Locking my home after running back downstairs, I hopped in my car and made my way to my sister's house. There was no way I could keep what my brother and Khaos was trying to pull to myself.

When I parked my car in Kenzie's driveway, I didn't even cut the ignition good, before I grabbed my purse and hopped out. Without knocking or ringing the doorbell, I used the key to enter. "Kenzie! Where you at?" I screamed at the top of my lungs, throwing my purse in a nearby chair.

"Why the hell you coming in my shit hollering? Where's the muthafuckin' fire?" she asked, standing at the top of the stairs.

"Your brother is on some good bullshit today, sis," I huffed, stomping towards her. "He sent Khaos after Heat and won't tell me what's going on!" Kenzie stared at me like I was speaking a foreign language and threw her hand at me before going back into her bedroom.

"Girl, stop throwing a temper tantrum. This one wasn't for us, I'm sure. When everything is in order and they know for sure Heat's ass will be caught, we will be one of the first to know about it. Until then, be cool. You can help me track down Tiffany's ass in the meantime."

"What do you mean, track her down?" I asked, kicking off my shoes and climbing in the middle of her bed.

"After I turned off from behind you and Khaos yesterday, I went straight to that hoe's house. She wasn't there. I went through her shit and found this box full of shit, and I'm sifting through it to get a general idea of where she could be. That's why I'm not worried about Heat. Stone has that covered for the most part."

Looking around at some of the items and papers Kenzie had sprawled over the bed, my eyes landed on some photos of Layla and Phantom. Most of the pictures were only of the two of them, never any pictures with Tiffany included. One of the pictures caught my eye and I cringed.

"What the fuck is this?" I asked, holding the picture up for Kenzie to see. It was an image of Layla and Phantom, but the heart around Phantom's face and the tombstone around Layla's was what worried me. Kenzie chuckled but it was wicked.

"It's obvious, Tiffany has been pretending to love Layla for years. That picture tells a story of its own. Anybody can see she never liked her child. Her love for the thought of someday having that man back in her life, made her act like she gave a fuck. The bitch's true colors revealed itself with the bullshit she pulled yesterday though."

My sister was talking calm as hell and her cool demeanor would've frightened the shit out of the average person. I, on the other hand, knew there was nothing but murder on her mind. She was going to search until she located Tiffany and the end result wasn't going to be pretty. I was going to be right by her side, helping her fill that hoe with hot slugs.

Kenzie pulled a purple hardback book from the box and started rifling through the pages as she skimmed fast through the content. Pausing, her eyebrows crinkled together before she laughed out loud. "This bitch been plotting for years. Listen to what she wrote four years ago," she said, sitting on the edge of the bed.

"I called Xavier to bring this lil bitch some pull-ups just so I could see his sexy ass. The only time he would answer his phone was if Layla needed something. Other than that, he would hang up in my face. I put on lingerie and when he arrived, I tried to seduce him. Xavier walked right past me without giving me an ounce of attention and went straight to Layla's room. When he came out, I tried to get him to let me suck his dick. He cursed me out and left. I went into his daughter's room and held a pillow in my hand, contemplating smothering her ass, but something inside me wouldn't allow me to go through with it."

Hearing the words Kenzie read bewildered me. There was no way Tiffany documented that shit. I snatched the book from Kenzie and read the entry myself and true enough, there it was in black and white. Every entry afterwards was about how much she loved Phantom, but he didn't love her in return. I felt bad for her because she got with the Butch dude because she thought it would make Phantom jealous, but it did the complete opposite and only pissed her off more.

I was about to close the book because reading about how Butch was beating her ass was depressing as fuck. I turned the page one last time and my heart dropped. Tiffany once again incriminated herself and the proof was in the palm of my hands.

"Listen to this shit, sis. Brace yourself. This happened about a year ago." I was scared to read the words before me out loud, but I had to.

"*Last night I got up because Butch wasn't in our bed. I got up and put my robe on and went looking for him. After searching the entire house, I was heading back to my bedroom when something told me to go check on Layla. When I opened her bedroom door, Butch was standing over her with his dick in his hand. Layla's nightgown was pulled above her waist, but she was sleeping. That nasty muthafucka was rubbing one out while lusting over my baby.*

I backed away and turned to leave, but I bumped into the wall, causing him to quickly step away. The fire in his eyes made him look like the devil. Butch beat me so bad that I have black and blue bruises all over my body. He spared my face this time, which I'm grateful for. Butch fucked me in all three holes while moaning out my daughter's name. Hell, I didn't deserve that ass whooping because I was trying to give him privacy to carry out his fantasy."

That's enough! Don't read no more of that shit!" Kenzie yelled as her phone rang from across the room. She got up and stomped her way to the dresser, answering without looking at the screen. "What?" she barked into the phone. "Khaos, I'm sorry."

At the mention of his name, I got up and went into the bathroom. I heard Kenzie say my name and I knew Khaos asked if I was there. I closed the door and handled my business, leaving my sister to finish her phone call. While washing my hands, Kenzie knocked on the door and pushed it open.

"I'm about to go to the hospital. I'll finish looking though this shit later. You coming with me?" she asked. "There's no way I'm keeping the shit in that book a secret from Phantom. I swear, she is digging her grave deeper with every breath she continues to take."

"Yeah, I'll go with you. We don't need to be riding around alone. Khaos is already gonna talk shit because I left the house without letting anybody know where I was going. May as well get it over with."

"What, you letting that nigga call the shots?" Kenzie smirked. "That dick got yo' ass being all submissive and shit."

"Fuck you, Kenzie. Don't start with me," I huffed as I left her ass standing in the doorway.

"Yo' ass even walk differently. Yeah, he put that act-right in yo' life," she laughed.

"Wait 'til Phantom hit you with that death stroke Tiffany proudly talked about in that book. Yo' ass gon' be trying to kill every bitch that utter his name. Trying to play hard to get and setting yourself up to fall in love," I shot back.

"What the fuck is love?"

"That shit you running from." Her muthafuckin' ass didn't have a comeback for that shit. Shut her up every time, but she met her match when she started fuckin' with Xavier Bennett, and thought she was going to move around after she was finished with him.

***

Kenzie was fuming the entire commute to the hospital. I was holding the handle to the door with all my might, because she was swerving around cars like a madwoman. I was in fear of my life. Tiffany's journal slipped from my lap and there was no way I would attempt to retrieve it while the car was in motion. When I saw our exit up ahead, I thanked God because the ride was almost over.

Kenzie whipped her car into the parking lot of the hospital, and I sprang from the seatbelt nervously. My fingers were cramped from holding on for dear life while she drove. I'd never been so scared in my life while riding with her behind the wheel.

"What the fuck is your problem?"

Meesha

"Kenzie, you could've killed us driving like you're crazy!" I screamed, reaching down to get the journal and chucked it at her.

"Yo scary ass got here safely, didn't you? That's all that matters. Get out my damn car and get ready to get chewed out for not checkin' in," she laughed, getting out. I opened the door and slammed it shut with force. "Kayla, you know I don't play those games when it comes to my whip. Don't slam my shit like that, hoe."

"Keep your snide remarks to yourself then. I don't check in with nobody and you know this. Khaos better find him some business."

"That's what your mouth say," she laughed. "We're about to see in a few minutes. Now, bring yo' ass on, Little Miss Submissive."

My sister could be an asshole at times and a pain in my ass, but I still loved her. We entered the hospital and the thought of Phantom's lawyer being there came to mind out of the blue. I truly hoped she wasn't present, because Kenzie was bound to attack if she opened her mouth and said the wrong thing. After what Kenzie told me about her, I was preparing myself to hold Phantom back so she could wear her ass out.

I was relieved when we entered the room and only Phantom and Khaos was sitting with Layla. Layla was smiling with her eyes low as if she was fighting sleep. It was good seeing her doing better, I just didn't like seeing her lying there with her legs in casts.

"Kenzie!" Layla came to life fast as hell. The medicine didn't have shit on the energy she mustered up when she saw my sister. "Thank you for coming! And thank you for calling for me, Big Homie."

"Hey, pretty girl. How are you?"

"Now that you're here, I feel wonderfantabulous! I can't wait until I can go home, because I want you to take care of me. Will you be here for my first therapy session? I really need you here with me, Kenzie."

88

Kenzie looked uncomfortable and avoided Phantom's gaze at all costs. Layla put her on the spot. There was no way Kenzie would be able to tell her she couldn't take care of her. Phantom sat back in the chair he was sitting in with a slight smile on his face. I stared at the side of my sister's face as she struggled with what to say. I turned my head slightly and Khaos was shooting daggers at me. I purposely didn't say anything to him when I came in and didn't have any intentions to start anytime soon.

"We'll see what I can do when the time comes for you to go home, baby. I'll be there much as I can. As for your therapy session, I'll be here with bells on. You know I have to be by your side because we are going to get through this together," Kenzie said, sitting on the side of the bed as she hugged Layla.

The smile fell from Phantom's face. "Nah, that's not gon' work. Layla, Kenzie will be at the house with you every day."

He crossed his arms over his chest, daring Kenzie to protest what he said in front of his daughter. Kenzie opened her mouth but closed it just as fast when Phantom glared at her from the other side of the bed. Layla was glad Kenzie would be part of the team helping during her recovery. She gleamed brightly, staring between her daddy and Kenzie. Layla started laughing and talking about everything under the sun. That removed the elephant from the room, and I was relieved the two of them didn't carry on in front of her.

"Let me holla at you in the hall."

Khaos' breath on the back of my neck sent a shiver down my spine. His deep baritone jumped started my yoni, but I cussed that hoe out in my head. He tried to mask his anger, but I heard that shit loud and clear. Taking a deep breath, I told Layla I would be right back. Kenzie looked over at me and chuckled. I couldn't stand her instigating ass. Khaos guided me in the direction of the door by my elbow.

"Kayla, are you going to marry my Big Homie? I like seeing y'all together, because he always smiles when you're around. His last girlfriend—"

"Layla," Phantom said sternly.

89

"Okay. Zip it. I got it. Stay in a child's place," she said, doing the hand movement to her mouth.

I couldn't hold my laughter as I left the room. The minute the door closed behind us, Khaos looked up and down the hall before he went to the nurse's station. When one of the nurses looked up, her face lit up when she saw him, but it fell when she saw he was holding onto me for dear life.

"What can I help you with, sir?" she asked snidely.

"Where's the bathroom?"

"The family bathrooms are down the hall to your left. You will need this key." She handed Khaos a single key and he led me in the direction she gave down the hall.

This muthafucka wanted to really be in private when he called himself going off on me, huh? Well, I guess I'd be able to smack the fuck out of him when he opened his mouth with the bullshit. Watching him unlock the door and push it open, he practically shoved me inside before stepping in behind me.

"Why do you insist on playing with me, Kayla? I was worried about you when I went back to yo' crib and you weren't there."

"Was I supposed to sit back and wait for you to come back? I think not," I sneered. "All you had to do was let me go with you."

"I'm not trying to hear that shit yo' hardheaded ass talking about. I told you what it was but you all in your muthafuckin' feelings. What if something happened to you? While you running around, not letting nobody know where you going."

"Khaos, I'm grown! I haven't checked in with anybody since my grandmother was alive and well. I won't be starting that shit back up to appease you or nobody else. I can take care of myself!"

His hand went around my neck and my body met the wall with the force he put behind the push he gave me. We were face-to-face as his breath caressed my neck. Khaos brought his lips to the base of my throat after lifting my head upward.

"I see you need a dose of act-right. I told you when you gave yourself to me, there was no turning back. That meant all of you, not just the pussy. You got me fucked up and I'm about to show yo' tough ass just what I mean."

Khaos slid his hand into the front of my leggings and strummed my pearl. My eyes closed and my knees became weak as overcooked Ramen noodles. I fought hard not to moan, but I lost that battle when he parted my lips and slid two fingers into my love box. It took seconds for my juices to start flowing at a rapid pace. When he put his hand around my neck, I had a small trickle, but the river was flowing now that he was playing in my sacred garden.

"We are in a fuckin' public bathroom, Khaos. You know I don't like to use these nasty ass toilets, let alone fuck in one."

"Shut yo' ass up," he growled. "You won't be sitting, lying, or squatting on shit in this muthafucka. You about to take this dick and maybe you will learn to listen when a real nigga say something to you."

He snatched my pants down and dropped to his knees. Khaos reached down and took my shoe from my foot and slipped my leg out of the leggings before placing it on his shoulder. His tongue connected with my clit, and I damn near slid down the wall. I had to grab his head to keep my balance. He sucked on my shit hard, and I squirted all my secretions down his throat.

"Oh my God!" I moaned lowly as I grinded into his mouth. He pulled away and looked up at me.

"God ain't got shit to do with this, Kay. This is all me," he said, going back in with a vengeance.

Trying to suppress my cries was hard but I found a way to keep it cute. The slurping sound that bounced off the walls had my stomach clinching once again and the waterfall came down quickly and he caught every drop. Rising to his feet, he unbuckled his pants and let them fall to the floor. My eyes closed slowly, and I felt the tip of mushroom head at my entrance. He pushed his way in, and I gasped. I felt my body being lifted against the wall and his dick making its way to my uterus walls. The way his pipe roamed my tunnel, I couldn't do nothing except claw at his shirt, because he was moving all my organs out of the way, at least that's what it felt like.

"Fuck! This is not what we came in here for," I cried out. "That feels so gooooood."

"This is exactly what I came in here to do. I had to give you the kryptonite you were craving. Now, cum on this dick."

The strokes he delivered had my back thumping against the wall. His veins were protruding in his arms from holding my little ass up while putting in work. I held on tightly to his head and threw my pussy at him, matching his rhythm. We were fucking like jack rabbits in the bathroom of Emory Hospital.

My juices were sloshing loudly. I held my bottom lip with my teeth until I tasted blood. Tears filled my eyes from the euphoric orgasm I felt building within me. Khaos started growling lowly and I knew he was about to bust any minute.

"Don't cum in me, Kannon," I moaned as I continued to bounce on his dick.

"I'm about to cum, baby. Shit. Aaahhh!" He bit down on my neck and dug his nails into my ass cheeks.

"Fuck! Yes! Oooooooooo, shit!" I screamed, forgetting where I was as my orgasm took over my body. Khaos' strokes slowed and realization set in. "I know you didn't just drop yo' kids off in my got damn incubator!"

"I told you earlier we were going to practice. What, you thought I was just talking? I just shot yo' shit up and I put ten bands on it, my seed is marinating as we speak."

I was mad as fuck that he came in me after I told him not to. This wasn't a fuckin' game, I wasn't ready to be a mother to anybody's child. Wiggling out of his hold, his dick slid out of my cave, and I pushed him in his chest until he put me down on my feet. I walked to the sink, turned on the faucet and snatched some paper towels from the dispenser.

As I wiped our juices from between my legs, the thought of Khaos impregnating me pissed me off. The streets were calling me, and his ass wanted to be a father, when all I wanted was to shoot up any and everybody that brought trouble our way. If down the line I was with child, his ass wouldn't know until everything we needed to do was taken care of.

Chapter 10

Phantom

Kenzie and Layla chopped it up as I sat watching the two of them from the chair beside the bed. Layla told Kenzie she wanted her to be the first to sign her casts and it brought a smile to my face. Tiffany came to mind and my mood shifted as I thought about where she could be. When Kenzie said she didn't find Tiff at her crib, I was relieved because killing the mother of his child was something he wanted to do himself. Taking his phone from his pocket, he texted one person that might know where Tiff was hiding out.

Phantom: Hey, fam. I need a favor. Can you ask Sweetz if she has heard anything from Tiffany?

He watched as Kenzie signed Layla's cast when the door opened and Khaos entered the room with Kayla frowning behind him. His cousin sat in the chair next to Layla's bed while eyeing Kayla from afar. Phantom knew Khaos said some shit to her about wandering around without telling him. Knowing his cousin, he bent her over somewhere to prove a point. Phantom couldn't help laughing and drew attention his way.

"What's so funny, Phantom?" Kenzie asked, holding the marker over Layla's leg.

"Nothing, man. Keep doing what you doing over there." My phone chimed and I had a text from Tim. I hoped like hell he had news for me.

Tim: What up, Phan? Sweetz haven't heard from that broad. I'll see if Jeff knows where she is. What did her bum ass do now?

Phantom: The bitch ran Lay over with her car. My baby is laid up in the hospital with casts on both of her legs. I'm going to put a hurting on her ass when I catch her."

Tim: I know you muthafuckin' lying! That hoe got a death wish, huh? Did you check her mama house?

Phantom: I didn't even think about them since I know they haven't dealt with Tiff in years. I'll go by there when I leave the hospital. If you hear anything, don't hesitate to hit my line. Thanks for responding.

Tim: No problem. One more thing, have y'all cleared that other situation, yet?

Phantom: Nah, that shit is still in the works. I have other muthafuckas working on that while I take care of Layla. You know when we get a drop on his ass, you will be called to come through.

Tim: I'm coming up in a few days because you seem to need my help now. Concentrate on baby girl and me and Khaos can deal with the rest. I'm always going to be there to take the stress off your shoulders. I'll hit you when I touch down and we'll go from there.

Phantom: Fo sho. Good looking.

Looking up from my phone, Kenzie stared at me evilly and I couldn't do anything but shake my head. For someone that didn't want shit to do with a nigga, she sure as hell wore her jealousy on her sleeve. I placed my phone on the nightstand and smiled at Layla as she admired the message Kenzie wrote on her purple cast. I leaned over and read it myself and I was touched.

You are strong and confident. Love yourself. Your voice matters. You don't need to be perfect. You can reach your dreams. You are important. And you are truly loved. Layla, remember, we will get through this together and you will bounce back stronger than ever. I will always be by your side whenever you need me. Just pick up the phone and I'll come running. Love Always, Kenzie.

There's no doubt in my mind that Kenzie loved my daughter. I just wish she had the same love for my ass, because I was ready to give her everything. Kenzie was stubborn and wasn't trying to let me love her until she was ready. Patience was key, but I didn't have that shit in me.

"Can I talk to you in the hall for a minute?" Kenzie didn't wait for me to reply, she grabbed a book she'd brought with her, and left out of the room with Kayla behind her.

"Stay in here with Layla for a minute, Cuz. I'll be right back."

"You didn't have to tell me that. What you can do is tell Kayla to bring her raggedy ass back in here though."

I laughed at his ass because he was serious as a heart attack. Leaving the room after making sure Layla was comfortable, I looked up and down the hall for Kenzie, but she was nowhere to be found. My phone chimed with a text. I read the notification on the lock screen from Kenzie.

Kenzie: We're in the parking lot. Come down

As I made my way to the elevator, I wondered what she could possibly have to talk to me about that required her to leave the building. Not wasting anymore time, I opted to take the stairs instead of waiting for the elevator. Soon as I stepped out of the doors of the hospital, I spotted Kenzie and Kayla standing outside along the wall. The way her ass formed in the leggings she wore had my dick hard as fuck. I wanted to sneak off to my crib to bend her fine ass over, but I knew her stubborn tail wouldn't fall for the bait.

"What's so important that you had to bring me outside?" I asked walking up. "Oh, Kayla. Cuz said bring yo' ass back to the room."

"Khaos can kiss my ass. He don't run shit but his mouth." Kayla rolled her eyes, taking a blunt from her purse.

"Come on so we can walk and smoke. The last thing I need is one of these pink folks talking shit. My attitude is not the best right now and anybody can get this heat that's building inside of me."

"Kenzie, I know you are mad about Tiff. We talked about that already. What you mad for now?"

"The same shit! Yo' bitch ass baby mama! How the hell you didn't know how much Tiffany hated your daughter until now?"

"Huh? Tiff may not have been the best mother in the world, but she did not hate my daughter. Where did you get that shit from?"

Kenzie could come to the conclusion that Tiffany hated Layla because she hit her with a car, but there were no signs other than that. Layla was always with her mother. I was the one that had to make an appointment to see my daughter. Which wasn't hard, because Tiffany knew I didn't play that bullshit.

"She definitely had a sour spot for Layla. I know you probably figure since I'm new to the equation, I don't know what I'm talking about. Take a look at this and see for yourself." Kenzie handed me the purple book and I was confused. "I found this, along with some other things in Tiffany's closet, after going through her shit since I couldn't whoop her ass. The contents of that book are going to make your blood boil, so brace yourself."

I sifted through the book slowly and scanned the pages. The beginning entries which started the day after Layla was born, made me smile. Tiffany was a proud first-time mom, and our daughter was the light of her life. Reading how she planned to care for Layla brought back so many memories and fun times we had as a couple. Those entries lasted until the day of Layla's first birthday. I went all out for that party. It was also the day Tiffany became just my baby's mama.

Today is Layla's first birthday. A rejoiceful day turned sour about an hour into the party. Xavier came in with so many gifts and it seemed as if he shopped for the entire neighborhood. Layla didn't even know what to do with all the things he'd brought into our home. The way he gushed over her as if she was his woman, made me gag. All the love he gave her should've been directed towards me.

I had a whole attitude from the way Layla squealed while dancing to Baby Shark. My sisters and their kids were present, as well as some of the kids from the daycare. Xavier hadn't said three words to me, let alone showed me any type of affection during that time. I was pretty fed up with being ignored, so I started an argument and smashed cake in his face. Embarrassing him in front of all the guests.

Xavier played it cool by going into the bathroom and cleaning himself up. He never missed a beat with Layla and the party continued. My sisters and cousins got on me about my actions, but I didn't give a damn what they had to say. After Layla opened her gifts, she played for a while and fell asleep in the middle of the

Savage Storms 3

floor. Karla picked her granddaughter up and took her upstairs. Xavier and his aunt Kimille passed out candy bags and the party was officially over.

We argued and I told him I should've gotten as much attention as Layla had. My man told me I sounded stupid as fuck because he had just spoiled me two months prior on my birthday. I laughed, because if it wasn't for me, her little ass wouldn't be in the world. This motherfucker had the nerve to tell me to get out of his house as if I was actually going to leave.

I laughed out loud after reading that shit because I remembered that day like it was yesterday. Tiffany may not have left the house that night, but she slept her ass on the floor in Layla's room. When she woke her ass up, all her shit was packed at the door. Tiffany thought she was about to take Layla with her. Nope, wasn't happening. I sent her ass back to her parent's house by her damn self.

"You need to get to the good part because that smile is going to fade away slowly," Kenzie quipped. "As a matter of fact, let me help you out." She walked over and took the book from me, turning the pages vigorously.

She handed the book back and I started reading the entry she wanted me to read. My heart started pounding and an image of me putting a bullet between Tiffany's eyes replaced the words before me. I couldn't believe the hatred Tiff displayed to herself. I never saw this side of her, and I was mad at myself for not peeping the shit before it was brought to my attention. Layla was in harm's way from the beginning. All because I wouldn't be in a relationship with her mother.

"That's not the tip of the iceberg. Actually, this is where I had to close the book and I don't know what else is in there."

It was hard for me to read the next entry, but I pushed through. Butch had already died by my hands and his bitch was next in line whenever I caught up to her. This nasty ass nigga was lusting over my baby and there was no telling if he had gone further than that. I'd asked Layla if he had ever touched her and she told me no, I believed her. That didn't let her mammy off the hook, because she knew his nasty ass was looking at my daughter and never opened her mouth. According to her words, she was hoping the shit would've happened. So, that alone gave me the right to split her wig in two.

"Kenzie, stay with Layla until I come back. I have to find this bitch before she gets too far away. It's not too many places she can hide. Tiffany fucked up."

I didn't wait for her to respond, before I stalked across the parking lot to my car. Throwing the book in the back seat, I started the car and burned rubber out of the space. Flashes of what I thought took place behind my back played before my eyes. Blinking to clear my vision, I slammed on my brakes in record time. I almost rammed the back of someone's car with the bullshit that plagued my mind.

"You better do everything you plan to do now, because I'm fuckin' you up."

Driving like a madman toward Tiffany's parents' house, I was on ten. She was out of her mind leaving out of the room so that nigga could do whatever he wanted to my daughter. Not only did she hit Layla with a damn car, but she subjected her to some foul shit. My phone rang and Tim's name popped up on the dash.

"What you got for me, Tee?"

"You will be wasting your time, fam. Tiffany's people moved to Junction, Kansas, a minute ago. How the hell you didn't know this?"

"Tiffany don't share anything about her parents with me. When they cut her off, they cut off contact with me. The only time I would speak with them was when they called Layla and even then, it was a dry ass hello."

"I'll see if I can get an address on them and get back with you. We will never know, maybe she took the chance of going back to them just to get away from Georgia. Get your head into the game, Phan. Everything's gonna be alright."

Tim and I said our goodbyes and I drove around aimlessly. My stomach growled, reminding me I hadn't eaten anything. All of a sudden, I had a taste for a burger and ended up going in the direction of Five Guys. Pulling into the parking lot, I spotted Rocko talking to a female and immediately drove past them, hopping he hadn't spotted me. I parked further into the lot and snatched my Glock from under the seat before getting out of my ride.

Rocko glanced up with a smile on his face, but it soon fell when his eyes met mine. Without a second thought, his bitch ass took off running and I was right on his ass. He had been missing in action since Heat fell off the scene and I knew he was guilty of something, because he was hauling ass before I could utter a word to him. Rocko was running faster than the niggas in the Olympic trials as he dodged cars on the busy street.

Cutting into a neighboring yard on the other side of the road, I kept my sight on him because I had fallen behind a little bit. As I approached the yard, the owner was yelling at Rocko's retreating back. I ran in the direction Rocko went and tripped. My gun fell from my hand, and I reached out and retrieved it promptly before jumping back to my feet.

"You thugs are going to get out of this neighborhood! You don't belong here!" the Caucasian man screamed at the top of his lungs.

Without giving it any thought, I pointed my Glock in his face and his eyes bulged out his head. I was tired of these Karen's and Ken's thinking the world revolved around them. His pale ass picked the wrong day to tell my black ass where the fuck I didn't belong.

"How about you tell me where exactly it is I belong? Last time I checked, this was a free muthafuckin' country and I can go wherever the fuck I want." The muthafucka lost his voice because he opened his mouth, but no words came out. "I can't hear you. Where's all that bullshit you were talking a few seconds ago? I'll blow your muthafuckin' head off, bitch. Watch what the fuck you say to black people because we not standing down to y'all. You were spared today, but you may not be so lucky next time."

I turned to walk away, but all the shit that had been happening to my people wouldn't let me. Doubling back to Ken's bitch ass, I hit him in the mouth with the butt of my Glock. He fell to the ground holding his face. "Tell yo' homies it's open season for you crackas. Stop playing with us!" I stalked back in the direction of my car without looking back. I wasn't worried about him coming after me. His ass wasn't stupid by a long shot. He better stay his ass right where he is, trying to get his teeth out of his throat.

Rocko ran but he wouldn't be able to slide through the cracks too many times. He and Heat was going to feel my wrath and it wasn't going to be pretty. With all the pent-up frustration I had built up, I didn't even want to hear any explanations from either of them. Going into Five Guys, I still got my muthafuckin burger and fries before I headed back to the hospital.

Chapter 11

Nicassy

The story Heat told me had so many holes in it, I didn't believe any of that shit. I went into the room he set me up in and tried my best to piece everything together. When he knocked on the door, I purposely didn't answer because I didn't have anything to say to his lying ass. The relationship Kenzie and I had back in the day was strong as fuck. The things Heat said didn't sit well with me and I just couldn't believe any of it. I was having a hard time with my memory, but I was far from stupid.

I hadn't said anything to him other than good morning. Sitting in the room, I thought about all I'd done while being in Heat's presence. I regretted having sex with his conniving ass the more I thought about things. I sat racking my brain, trying to remember someone's number, but the only one that came to mind was his. My eyes started burning because I was fighting hard not to allow the tears to fall. Running the conversation back in my mind, I grabbed a notebook and a pen to write down everything Heat had said to me.

The one thing that stood out to me was the information he gave me about the man I was supposedly sent to kill. Writing the name Stone at the top of the page, I chewed on the tip of the pen, trying to remember anything I could on him but I came up empty. Scribbling Club Onyx on the next line, I closed my eyes and Houston, Texas, echoed in my ears. Adding the city and state to the list, I then wrote owner underneath.

Maybe Stone would be able to give me some type of information, because I needed to get to the bottom of all this shit. I'd have to talk fast to tell him about Heat, but I had to take my chances. I refused to be kept in hiding and I didn't know exactly why. Heat was keeping me close for more reasons than he's telling. Standing up from the bed, I searched for the bag my personal items were in from the hospital. When I found it, my phone wasn't there, and I was pissed.

"I need to find a way to investigate. Fuck!" I screamed in my head.

There was a knock on the door, and I knew it wasn't anyone except Heat. Closing the notebook I was writing in, I placed it under the pillow. Ignoring his constant knocks and went into the bathroom to relieve my bladder. Heat started beating on the door, but I still didn't give him an ounce of attention. As I washed my hands, the sound of the wood breaking and the door slamming against the wall startled me. Heat rushed into the bathroom with fire in his eyes.

"Why the fuck you didn't just open the damn door, Nicassy? You heard me knocking because I could hear yo' ass walking around in this muthafucka!"

"Who you think you're talking to? Your best bet is to watch how you speak to me. I'm not a child nor your bitch, so you will respect me!"

Before I knew what was happening, Heat grabbed me by the throat, squeezing tightly. "Nah, you got the game fucked up! You gon' respect me! Don't you ever in your life talk to me like that."

Heat shook me like a rag doll, and I saw small dots dancing in front of me. I could barely breathe, so I couldn't do anything except claw at his hands, which didn't help at all because his grip only became tighter. He finally shoved me into the countertop and my back banged against it. I winced in pain, doubling over. I took a couple deep breaths as I fought the urge to cry out.

"I brought yo' ungrateful ass here to heal and you want to stand here talking to me like I'm a lil nigga. I will fuck you up, bitch!"

I didn't understand why he was so hostile towards me. I didn't ask him to do anything for me. After getting my breathing back to normal, I could see Heat's feet right in front of me and I knew he was too close. Rising up slowly, I punched his ass in the dick with all of my might. The howl he released sounded like a wounded dog that had been hit by a car and left for dead.

"Argggghhh!" he yelped while grabbing his genitals with both hands.

I tried to run past him and fell face-first when he punched me in the back of my head. Heat hit me repeatedly in the head and I blacked out. Flashes of light appeared behind my eyelids with every hit that landed. Heat stopped punching me at some point and left me lying on the carpeted floor.

Scenes entered my mind and I saw everyone Heat said had a problem with me. I heard Kenzie's voice and she told me we would catch up when I touched down in Atlanta. Then I heard Scony's voice, telling me to get out of Houston and don't tell Stone the truth. A man she assumed was Stone stood in a doorway, pointing a gun at me.

"Sit the fuck down before I fill yo' ass with some hot shit! Fuck all that other shit, who sent you to come for me?"

"Heat! I work as a hit woman for a guy named Romero "Heat" Ramirez. He sent me to kill you because he said you were a pedophile and liked to mess with little girls. I took the job because I hate a man that likes to fondle kids. I'm sorry, Stone. I really am and I've learned over time, you aren't the man Heat perceived you to be."

"Heat sent you to kill me?" he laughed. "I'm the muthafucka that gives him the jobs to send his team on! That nigga on some fuck shit and sent a female to do his dirty work. I understand where this is coming from now. Get yo' shit and get out of my muthafuckin' house, bitch! I don't deal with sneaky muthafuckas of any kind. Usually, you would be dead by now, swimming in a pool of water waiting to be discovered. By the time I come back, I want you and yo' shit outta my crib." Stone stuck his gun back in the small of his back and left the room, pulling his shirt down to hide it.

"One more thing," Stone said, appearing in the doorway. "Don't take shit outta here my money bought. Take whatever you came in this bitch with. Call your boss and let him know he fucked up comin' for me."

The incident played back in my mind, and I swear it sounded as if Stone didn't know me from a can of paint before I approached him. So, that meant he didn't know about Kenzie either.

That confirmed the story Heat told me was a bold-faced lie. I struggled to open my eyes, but they wouldn't budge. Lying where I was, darkness consumed me as I slowly faded away.

My head was pounding when I was finally able to open my eyes. Looking toward the window, I noticed the sun had set and wondered how long I'd been out. Heat must've gathered a heart from somewhere and put me in the bed. He was a bitch nigga for putting his hands on me, but I was going to have my get-back moment in due time.

Turning on the lamp on the side of the bed, there was a bottle of Tylenol along with a bottled water, waiting for me to consume. "Stupid nigga knew knocking me upside the head was going to cause a headache. I know he don't think this damn medicine is going to make shit right."

I was mumbling to myself as I struggled to open the bottle of pills. Soon as I placed two tablets in my hand, the door opened. Heat stood in the doorway looking pitiful. Once again, I ignored his presence because I had nothing to say to him.

"How are you feeling?" he asked.

"Get out of my face, Heat. Where the hell are we? Take me home," I said, popping the pills in my mouth and chasing them with water.

"You are safe. As far as you going home, that's not going to happen. If I take you back, you will be dead within a day."

"I'll take my chances because apparently, I'm not safe in this muthafucka either!" I yelled in his direction. "You punched me like a man on the street and you want me to believe you're protecting me. Let me out of this damn house! I trusted you because you said there's people out to kill me, but hell, you can kill me yourself and no one would even come looking for my ass!"

"I'm sorry for what I did to you, Nicassy. I've been checking on you like clockwork all evening. I was wrong for taking my frustrations out on you. That shit should've stayed outside the door when I entered. How can I make it right?"

"You can't," I said, standing to my feet. "Since you won't let me go, I would like for you to stay away from me until you make up your mind about what you're gonna do with me."

A lone tear escaped my eye and I quickly swiped it away. On the outside I was showing weakness, but on the inside, I wanted to tear his fuckin' head off his shoulders if I had the equipment to do so. Closing my eyes, a vision of a house flashed before my eyes, and I realized my memory was coming back slowly. I opened my eyes at the sound of Heat's voice.

"Are you hungry? I can go out and get something for you to eat."

"I don't want anything from you. All I want is to be left alone. Is that hard for you to do?" I asked, walking into the bathroom.

Heat left without trying to say anything more. The sound of the door closing allowed me to let out the air I'd been holding in my lungs. I had to play the role of victim so he wouldn't know I was on to him. The time would present itself for me to break away from the prison life he had subjected me to. Even though I was starving, I refused to allow him to feed me. I'd survive without him.

Chapter 12

Rocko

When I spotted Phantom walking toward me, my first thought was to get the fuck out of Dodge. I saw the gun in his hand and took off like Sha'Carri Richardson. I did a cool hundred and never looked back. I glanced over my shoulder and saw he was no longer behind me, and I waited a few minutes before I doubled back and jumped in my whip. I took the chance coming back to the area for some muthafuckin' pussy and I should've known to watch my surroundings.

My phone rang and I looked to see who was calling before answering. "Where you at?"

"Nigga, how the fuck you gon' leave me out here like a sitting duck?"

"Look, Kim, I'm about to scoop you up. Where you at, man?"

"Don't worry about it. Take your scary ass on somewhere. I can't even see myself loving a fuck nigga. I was about to pop that muthafucka, but you took off before I could blink. Lame ass."

Kim hung up on me and I felt small as shit. The bad part about it, she was right. I had my burner on me and didn't even think to pull it. Phantom wasn't somebody one wanted to square up with when it came to busting that thang. He and Khaos wasn't Heat's best hittas for nothing. I was surprised he didn't shoot me in the back of my head. Obviously, he wanted me alive whenever he caught up with me. Listening to my phone ring, I was praying Heat picked up. I was about to hang up when the call finally connected.

"Rock, what's going on?" Heat asked.

"Man, that nigga Phantom just came at my head. We have to come up with a game plan, because his ass is out for blood. We've been sitting long enough, it's time to take action."

"I was just thinking the same thing. I'm coming back tonight so we can open the club back up, I'm missing out on money. Plus, Summer is on bullshit, and I have to see what the fuck she's been up to. I won't let these muthafuckas run me off a day longer. Meet me at the club about nine and we can get shit in motion."

"Bet. See you at the club."

Heat ended the call, and I felt a little bit better as I pulled to a stop at the red light. I hit the power button and Pooh Shiesty's "Back in Blood" blared through the speakers. The light turned green, and I slowly pulled off. Out of my peripheral, I saw a car pull up on the right side of me and I turned my head just as the window lowered. I pushed the pedal to the floor just as the first shot rang out. My back passenger window exploded, and small shards of glass hit the back of my neck. Ducking low as I sped through the streets, my only mission was to shake whoever the fuck was trying to kill my ass.

Bullets were hitting the side of my whip like they were trying to turn my shit into Swiss cheese. Rounding the corner on two wheels, I barely missed an old lady crossing the street. My heart was beating a mile a minute when my rear window was shot out, causing me to duck my head. The bullet lodged in the radio, cutting the power.

"Fuck! I gotta get out of this jam!" I screamed as I navigated through the cars in front of me.

Looking in the rearview mirror, I noticed the car was speeding up beside me on the left side. Reaching for my burner, I cocked that muthafucka, ready to blast. Soon as I saw the front end, I extended my arm out the window and let my shit ride. I popped the driver and the car swerved into a mailbox and came to a complete stop. Taking the opportunity, I floored the gas and headed to Heat's guy Tony's chop shop.

"The Black Kings is out for blood! I hope I killed that nigga. Better him than me though," I laughed as I hit the corner and sped to my destination.

When I smoked Brando, it was in self-defense in my book. He was about to kill my nigga and that shit wasn't going down like that. If I hadn't come on the scene, Heat wouldn't even be breathing. It pissed me off that he left me to fend for myself while he hid under the radar. Now these muthafuckas was out to take my fuckin' head off.

Not only that, I had to watch my back with Phantom and the rest of the team. They must've found out Will was dead and wanted to know what I knew about his demise. Running only made me look guilty, when all I should've done was lie about not knowing shit. All this back-and-forth shit was tiring. I had never run for my life like I've been doing in since the day I saved Heat's ass.

***

After dropping my car off for Tony to get rid of, one of his workers took me to the crib. I had plenty of time to rest before I had to meet up with Heat. The first place I went was to the shower. My ass was funky as hell from all the excitement I'd been through. The hot water hit my body and I leaned into that shit. All the years of working for Heat, I'd never been as nervous as I was in that moment. Whenever I was on a job, Will was always by my side. Now, here I was, dodging multiple muthafuckas and there was no plan in motion. A nigga was out by himself, blind as fuck.

Drying off and throwing on a pair of basketball shorts, I slipped my feet into my house shoes and headed for the kitchen. I hadn't eaten all day and my stomach was in my back. I opened the refrigerator and decided to prepare a ham and turkey sandwich with a side of Doritos. That was the quickest shit I could come up with. Moments like the one I was having is when I wished I had a steady woman, because I rarely had a homecooked meal. The closest I'd ever got to one was by going to a soul food spot.

I ate the two sandwiches and washed them down with a can of Pepsi. Throwing the paper plate in the garbage, along with the empty can, I went to my room and got in the bed. Sleep claimed my body before I could close my eyes good.

Waking up, I was groggy as hell. I snatched my phone off the nightstand, and it was already seven thirty. Jumping up, I went into the bathroom and took care of my hygiene. Stepping into the closet, I took out a black button-down shirt and a pair of black jeans. Going to the club, I wanted to be ready for whatever the fuck was in store if something jumped off. So, all black everything was my preference for the night. After tucking my heat in the back of my pants, I snatched my keys and wallet from the dresser. Stepping out the bedroom door, I doubled back and scooped up my phone.

Finally, I was able to leave the crib and jumped in my truck. It pissed me off that my damn car got fucked up, because money had slowed down drastically, and I had to cop another one. That shit was going to wait because I had to start stacking again. I was far from broke, but I had to do what was right before doing what I wanted. Heat fucked it up for everybody when he messed over Brando.

"Killer" had me rockin' to the beat as I cruised through the Atlanta streets. Looking around me as I waited at the light, my head bobbed and I was feeling the cut. Pulling off, I thought about the day I had to wax my nigga Will. That shit wasn't supposed to even go down the way it did. He waited 'til we made it to Stone's crib to try and bail out. Will kept saying he wasn't for killing Nicassy because of how much she meant to him. I agreed she would get away scot-free so he would at least help get at Stone.

Once he jimmied the lock and opened the door, Will walked in and I grabbed him around the neck and pulled his head back. Slicing deeply into his throat with the knife I had ready, I cut him from ear to ear and pushed his ass to the side. I knew it was kill or be killed because he was standing on not killing the bitch, so he decided his fate when he went against the original plan.

Thinking about how his blood squirted onto the sleeve of the black hoodie I wore, sent shivers up my spine. Going against Heat was something I didn't want to do. Killing the nigga that stood beside me on every job we went on together was harder than a muthafucka—but had to be done. I missed that nigga on some real shit, and he let me know every time I closed my eyes that he was waiting for me on the other side to kill me again.

I was about five minutes from the club, and I could see a dark cloud of smoke in the air. "Somebody's shit is burning like a muthafucka," I said lowly. As I got closer, I noticed fire trucks and police vehicles lining the street. An officer was directing traffic away from the scene. I let my window down as I approached her and asked, "What's going on, Officer?"

"That club, what's it called, Heat? It's burning to the ground. Get out of here because they can't control the fire at this time."

"Thank you." I turned left and leaned over to get my phone. Hearing that shit, I had to call Heat. I listened to the phone ring then his voicemail picked up. It then dawned on me that Heat was probably in the fuckin' club. One thing he was always serious about was promptness, so his ass was always early as fuck. He felt if you were on time, you were late. Glancing at the clock, it was eight fifteen and my heart dropped to my stomach. I redialed Heat's number and prayed he'd answer.

"What's up, Rock? I'm running behind schedule, and I'll be at the club right about nine," Heat said when the call connected.

Letting out a deep breath, I thanked the man upstairs that this nigga was okay. "When you get to the club, we won't be going in to talk business. The whole fire department is over there, trying to distinguish your shit as we speak."

"Huh, what the fuck you talking about?"

"The club is on fire! Somebody set yo' shit ablaze, my nigga. You might as well make your way now. I couldn't get through because the street is blocked off."

"This is fucked up! That was my place of business!" Heat screamed. "I don't even know which way this shit came from. It could be Spike's bitch ass and his crew, or that damn Phantom! Fuck it, I'm going after all them niggas!"

I was thinking the same thing but the incident that happened earlier had me going with Brando's brother Spike. It was one of his niggas that busted at me. "I think it was Spike. One of his cronies shot at me today. I think I killed his ass too."

"Why the fuck I'm just hearing about this shit? Muthafuckas getting bold now. If they thought this was going to bring me out of

111

hiding and get my attention, they got it. It's about to be an eye for an eye type shit from this point on. I'm on my way to the club, I know these damn pigs gon' think I did this shit for insurance money. Damn!" Heat said frustratedly. "I'll call you back. Go to the crib and lay low. I'll be over there soon as I take care of this bullshit."

Heat hung up and I hit the highway and headed home to wait for him to come through. It was going to be a long night and I needed a drink to be prepared for whatever he had planned to settle this shit once and for all.

Pulling onto my street, I felt an eerie feeling I'd never experienced before. I shook that shit off and turned into my driveway. As I reached to push the button to cut my truck off, muthafuckas ran up and started busting from both sides of my shit. The bullets riddled my body, causing me to shake uncontrollably. Hot piss escaped my body, and every part of my body became numb. The driver's side door opened as my heartbeat slowed down tremendously.

"You thought you were going to get away with shooting at me, nigga? Somebody should've taught your ass to make sure the muthafucka you shoot is dead. Just like this."

POW

Nothing but darkness consumed me as I took my last breath. I didn't even feel the shot that took my life, but the first thing I saw when I opened my eyes was Will, with an evil grin on his face. The shit scared the fuck outta me for a split second, but I took the shit for what it was, I was a dead muthafucka.

"Welcome to hell, nigga. Anything goes down here, and you will suffer for eternity, bitch."

Chapter 13

MaKenzie

I took the highway by storm, zipping through traffic, trying to get to the area the club was located. Parking a block away from the scene, there was still a lot of action with the firefighters, and they still hadn't put the fire out completely. Whoever took a torch to that muthafucka wanted Romero to feel the heat, literally. The club burning down was a major hit to that nigga's pockets and I was laughing my ass off just thinking about it as I made my way down the street.

Not telling Phantom about what was going on would come back to bite me in the ass, but I was preparing myself mentally to deal with it when the time presented itself. At the moment, I just wanted to see the look in Heat's eyes as he watched everything. He worked hard to get the club to where it was, just to watch it crumble right in front of him. Knowing him, Heat was crying on the inside wondering if his safe survived the fire.

Once I blended in with the crowd across the street, I scanned the many faces, trying to scope out the man himself. I'd finally spotted him a few minutes later, talking to a police officer who looked as if he was hanging onto Heat's every word. There was mixture of hurt and anger displayed on his face, and I loved it. Feeling a presence approach on my left, I glanced over when the nigga's shoulder brushed the side of my head.

He was a young cat that stood at least six foot three, dark as night with a low fade, edged up razor sharp. Wearing designer from head to toe, the nigga smelled good as hell too. That's how close he was on my ass. I was irritated as fuck because he was invading my personal space and I didn't like that shit at all.

"Um, you want to give me six feet or nah?" I scoffed.

"Damn, my bad, lil mama," he said, stepping back a little bit. "This shit crazy. Ain't no mo' coming to the Heat to turn up. This was my spot!"

His random rant was really irritating my soul because I didn't give a fuck about none of that shit he was talking. Shooting him a side eye glare with a frown to match, I peeped the dude staring me down lustfully while licking his lips. The small shorts and halter top helped bring his attention to me, and I hated when a muthafucka did that shit. No matter what a woman decided to wear for the day, respect her as if she was your mama. That shit gave off creep vibes, especially if the female wasn't checking for his slimy ass in return.

"I already know this shit is hard for you. I've seen you a couple times working the floor in that muthafucka. It's a good thing you got the experience and can be a bottle girl at any club."

Bottle girl? I laughed heartily when he said that shit because he was dead wrong. Not now, nor has thee MaKenzie "Storm" Jones ever been a bottle girl. Hell, if anything, I tipped them bitches better than his ass probably did. But I let him think he had his facts straight.

"If you need help finding a job, I can plug you in at a couple spots." When I didn't respond verbally, he kept going as if I was actually one of those thirsty ass bitches that worked at Club Heat. "Here's my card, ma. Hit me up," he said, holding out what I assumed was a business card. I laughed again because the shit looked like he cut up a cereal box and added his contact information on it.

I took it so he would leave me the fuck alone, but when I saw plain as day "Black Kings" displayed at the top, I smiled sinisterly, because this was my chance to get some payback from the niggas that shot at me and Kayla not too long ago. Looking up at his face, I noticed Lox, which was his name on the card, was fine as shit and he knew it. So, I played that shit to my advantage.

"Thank you," I said sweetly. No longer was Heat on my radar, it was the perfect opportunity for me to send a message of my own. Since this nigga thought I was a bottle girl, I was ready to make him believe that shit too. "I'm really going to get at you because my pockets been dry as hell, since that nigga Heat closed down the club and disappeared. With him doing that shit, I think his ass really did have something to do with that Brando dude getting knocked off." I had his attention at that precise moment because his head tilted to the side.

"I don't know nothing about Brando or his people, but I hope they catch that bitch nigga. Anyway, do you own a club?" I asked, knowing damn well he didn't own shit but the clothes on his back.

"Nah, but a know a lot of people in big places. Tell me this, ma. Do you know about the Black Kings?" he asked.

"The who?" I asked, looking back at the card. "Oh, that must be your business name. What type of business you got?" He looked around and I followed the direction he was looking and if looks could kill, Heat would've been dead from a distance. "Is that Heat? Let me go holla at that nigga about my money," I said, stepping off the curb. Before I could get far, Lox grabbed my arm gently, halting my steps.

"Nah, beautiful. Fuck that nigga and his money. I'll double what he owes you if you come rap with me, away from here."

"Rap to you about what?" I asked curiously. "I don't even know you to be going anywhere alone with you. I could be walking into a setup because I'm affiliated by association with Heat." I pulled out of the hold he had on my arm and backed up.

"It's not even like that, shorty. It's too many people out here for me to talk freely. We can talk over dinner, my treat," Lox said, licking his lips.

I stood as if I was truly thinking about going with him, when I knew exactly what I had in store for his ass. Putting the makeshift card in my purse, I felt around to make sure my bitch was in place. And she was, which I already knew, because I never left home without her. Lox better hope he went as hard as his name did in rap songs because he was in for a treat, and that shit was going to be sweet for me, not so much for his ass.

"Aight, but I'll follow you. I parked on the next block," I finally said, pointing in the direction of my car.

"Okay. I parked that way too."

I walked swiftly down the street with Lox behind me. If I was to look over my shoulder, I would bet money that nigga was gawking at my ass. He was probably thinking of ways to sit it on his face. If I felt generous after dinner, he might get his wish before he met his maker.

"This me right here," he said, standing in front of an older model Charger. Nigga clothes cost more than the ride he was trying to flex in. I smirked as I took out my phone and snapped a picture of his license plate. "Hold up, what the fuck you doing?" he snapped.

"Nigga, like I said before... I. Don't. Know. You. I need to send this shit to my sister, just in case you decide to be on bullshit," I said, snapping a picture of his ass too. "I have to protect me, and I'm taking a chance going with your ass anyway. Believe me, if anything happens to me, your ass will get caught by law enforcement."

Sending the images to Kayla with a caption that read, "Don't tell Khaos shit!" I kind of regretted that shit soon as I sent it.

"Aight. Do what you gotta do so we can get out of here. Where's your car?" Lox asked.

I felt ashamed for his ass because his lil whip didn't have shit on my ride. I pointed to my Benz and his eyes bulged. Chuckling lowly, I snuck another peek at his ride before heading to my car, which was parked two cars away from his. Seeing what he was rolling in, I knew the nigga wasn't capable of giving me double shit I'd ever made with Heat.

"That's how you doing shit?" he asked. "I see you, shorty. Wait 'til you see what I roll in on a regular."

Laughing while I continued to strut down the street, the way he said that shit let me know his regular ass wasn't rolling in shit but that damn outdated ass Charger. Soon as I put my seatbelt on, my phone started ringing from my purse. Hurrying to grab it, I checked the display and saw Kayla calling. I laughed hard as hell because Lox had his foot on his brakes, and one of the brake lights were out. He was one of the scrubs TLC rapped about and it showed.

"What the fuck you laughing about, and who the fuck is that nigga in the picture you sent me?" she bellowed out.

Gathering myself as I pulled away from the curb and stopped next to the car behind Lox, I finally responded to my Inspector Gadget ass sister. "That's this nigga named Lox. He just signed his own death certificate."

"Kenzie, what the fuck are you talking about?"

"I was at the hospital when I saw on the news Club Heat was on fire. I told Phantom I was going home and came downtown so I could follow Heat. But this nigga I later learned was part of the Black Kings, approached me. The muthafucka thought I was a bottle girl and that alone pissed me off. Figuring I'd leave Heat to Phantom, like he wanted anyway, I decided to get my lick back from them Black King niggas that was gunning for us."

"Kenzie, I have to tell Khaos! You are on a mission alone and them niggas ain't to be fucked with," Kayla screeched.

"Since when have you known me to *need* back-up? Don't tell Khaos shit! You hear me? I got this shit, sis."

"You are not a superhero! Send me your fuckin' location, now!"

Hearing Kayla mention my location, I hung up on her ass and turned my location off immediately. She had reminded me that Phantom was able to track my shit and I was going through with my plan whether Kayla liked it or not. My phone rang again, and I shut that bitch off and tossed it in my purse. Lox finally pulled out of the parking spot, and I followed behind him while "Blackout" by DMX featuring Jay Z and the Lox kept me company.

I reached into the glove department as I switched out my nine for the .38 snub. I was trying to be ready, just like the bars Jadakiss spat on the track. See, I was a woman that was able to live the same way the niggas rapped about. The lame nigga driving the hooptie in front of me, had no clue what type of hell he was walking into.

Lox was leading the way out of the downtown area by taking the street versus the expressway. We passed many restaurants, but he didn't attempt to stop. The way my stomach churned as I continued to drive, would've been enough for another bitch to turn off on his ass and go the fuck where they paid bills. Not me though. The saying "curiosity killed the cat," was all I heard in my head, but that muthafucka was gon' have to catch me because I wasn't backing down. Reaching in the armrest, I grabbed a blunt filled with the finest weed and blazed that bitch up. Lox was fuckin' with the right one because by the time we made it to his destination, Storm would be out in full force to join the party.

If you love the money, then prepare to die for it
Niggas done started something
You can lay in the flames, or hug the sky for it
Niggas done started something
Don't come at me with no bullshit, use caution
Cause when I wet shit, I dead shit, like abortions
For bigger portions, of extortion and racketeering
Got niggas fearing, fuck whatchu heard, this what you hearing
How much darker must it get, how much harder must it hit
See if your hardest nigga flip, when I start a bunch of shit

DMX's verse on "Niggas Done Started Something," brought the deadliest bitch alive out the cage. Lox thought he was pulling a fast one, but he just didn't know I was part of the *Fast and the Furious* cast, Chicago style. My trigger finger was itching like a muthafucka because in the forefront of my mind, dude thought he was about to take advantage of the petite killer he was lusting over.

About ten minutes later, I noticed we were in Edgewood, and I reached over to make sure my doors were locked. The neighborhood wasn't shit to fuck with and I tried my best to stay the fuck away from out there. Lox turned right onto Ozone Street Southwest and parked in front of a raggedy ass house. The block was quiet, and I couldn't wait until he came to my car so I could question his actions. Parking my ride, I didn't move an inch.

"What you waiting on, ma?" he asked when I let the window down.

"This don't look like a restaurant. I thought we were going to talk over dinner," I said, rolling my eyes. "I only agreed because we would be out publicly. I'm not feeling this secluded shit you trying to pull right now. Especially not in this neighborhood."

"You're safe with me, I promise. Nothing's going to happen to you over here. I thought you were down with whatever, because you never stopped following a nigga. I can go up and get your bread and you can leave if you think I'm on bullshit. The last thing I want is for you to be scared."

Biting my bottom lip as I portrayed myself as a nervous female, my eyes bounced back and forth in their sockets as I pretended to survey my surroundings. Lox stood back calmly as he allowed me time to make up my mind. Taking a couple deep breaths, I reached over and grabbed my purse from the passenger seat, before pushing the button to shut my car off.

"Didn't you send my shit to your sister?" I nodded my head, but still showed signs of uncertainty. "You good then. I'm quite sure you turned on your location too," he chortled. "That's what most females that's smart do, and you look like you're very intelligent."

Lox had a point, but he underestimated a real one. Even if he didn't have any intent to do anything malicious, he wouldn't live to take another breath of air after I was done. He could blame his counterparts for the bullshit they pulled when they came for me and mine. Easing the door open, I still played the part of being scared and Lox stepped back as I climbed out.

"You don't have nothing to worry about long as you with me. Come on, so I can get you inside. Plus, I got to get on this food since I promised you dinner."

He led the way to the front door of his house and unlocked the door. When I stepped foot inside, I wanted to walk the fuck back out. It looked like a fuckin' squatter house and I started to feel uneasy for real. The first thing I thought was I'd actually stepped into a death trap. There was no way Lox didn't know who I was when he saw me downtown, because he couldn't possibly be living in filth when he was dressed to the nines.

"Have a seat, I'll be right back."

If he thought I was about to sit down on that piss-stained ass couch, he thought wrong. I looked around and saw a lawn chair that sat in the corner. Dragging it close to the door I sat down with my hand buried deep inside my purse. Lox came back and looked at me like he had a major problem. It wasn't my fault his house was nastier than a muthafucka.

"I'm going in the kitchen, you gon' sit in here?"

"Nah, I'm going to come with you," I said, quickly jumping to my feet.

We walked through the living room, if that's what you wanted to call it. There were clothes littering the floor and I could've sworn a mouse peeked out of a black bag when Lox hit the light switch. My skin crawled with every step I took. It took everything in me not to shoot his ass from the filth alone. When we got to the kitchen, Lox flipped the switch on the wall and bile traveled up my throat, but I forcefully swallowed that shit. The roaches scattered in every direction and crawled over any and everything from the sink to the stove. I'd made up my mind when I first walked in that I wasn't eating shit he cooked.

"So, I figured we could get at this nigga Heat together," Lox said, bringing me back from watching his house guests run around without worry. "He fucked you over with your bread and he killed my nigga. He won't be looking for you to go against him. All I need you to do is lead that nigga to me. You will call and tell him that you got your ass beat or some shit. I don't give a fuck what story you come up with, but I need you to make it believable. Can you do that? I will give you five stacks for that alone and we won't forget about the paper I promised for lost wages."

"Yeah, that's easy. I used to fuck with Heat, sexually. I'm sure he will come to me if I call on him. I'll just have to keep my anger in check, because he hasn't reached out during his entire disappearing act."

I didn't totally lie, there was a time Heat would be at my beck and call. Since I was one of the people after his head, he knew better than to dial my shit. Lox nodded as he opened one of the cabinets and a rain of roaches were happy to get out. My neck started itching and I swiped at my shit, hoping one of his many pets wasn't on me.

"So, Brando was your boy?" I asked, looking around the kitchen. "You ready to go to war for what happened to him, huh?" I was going to pick his brain for whatever I could get out of him while he was still able to tell me. This was the only shot we had to learn what type of problem Heat had with the Black Kings.

"Brando was more than my boy. He was like my brother, and we did everything together, from the mud 'til his death. I was out of town the day he died. Had I been with him, it would've been ya boss' body found in that park." Lox's back stiffened as his head fell to his chest. "That nigga owe my man half a mil. He had been skimming off the money he was supposed to wash. Brando was on his ass but wanted to see how far the greedy muthafucka was gon' go. When he brought it to Heat, he started duckin' and dodgin' a nigga. So, Brando ran down on his ass. I wish he would've waited until I got back in town. My nigga wasn't with the right muthafucka to pull that shit off."

He pulled a skillet from the sink and rinsed it off and put it on the stove. When he took what looked like steak out of the fridge, he took it out the package and placed it on the counter, after knocking a few of his roach friends out the way. "I know you fuckin' lying!" I screamed to myself. This nigga had to have salmonellosis, poliomyelitis, leprosy, cholera, typhoid fever and breathing problems. Lox was living the real-life version of the movie, "Joe's Apartment."

"The Black Kings, and I'm just asking out of curiosity, killed Loco and his bitch? That shit was a hit if I've ever seen one." Lox turned around with a menacing expression on his face. "Calm down, killa. I'm working with you now, anything we talk about in here, stays here. You don't have to worry about me opening my mouth to any damn body. I'm taking a chance setting up Heat, but I want to see him pay for what he did too."

"You right," the stupid muthafucka said before he went back to seasoning his contaminated ass meat. "Yeah, I was the one that took care of that smart mouthed nigga. If he wasn't trying to save his hoe, she probably would've lived. I'm going after bad ass Phantom next. All them niggas gotta see me."

I may have been hating on Phantom at the moment, but I'd be damned if this bastard got the opportunity to do anything to that nigga right there. Lox gave me another reason to leave his ass stankin' in this dirty ass place he called home. He had a little while longer to express himself before I deliver the gift of death to him.

"Damn, to be honest, I don't think Phantom had anything to do with any of what's going on with y'all. They quit long before that shit with Brando."

"I don't give a fuck about none of that!" he exclaimed, slamming the seasoning salt container on the counter. He turned around fast as hell and the nigga was foaming at the mouth. "I'm going after their whole team. Including the bitches I heard killed my other niggas."

Throwing my hands in the air in surrender, my pussy throbbed after hearing him admit he and his people in fact had a hand in shooting at me. "Aight, do what you feel you have to do. I want you to know, Heat got some straight shooters on his team."

"Loco didn't get the chance to pull shit when I ran up on his ass. Spontaneous shit is what I'm always on. When I'm coming for a muthafucka, I never miss my target. I stay alert at all times, and I never underestimate nobody."

Until now, asshole. I nodded my head letting him know I understood everything he said. Lox turned his back, and I went to work screwing my silencer on my nigga Mike. That's the name I gave my .38 after Scony gave it to me for my nineteenth birthday. I was staring daggers in his back, imagining the big-ass hole I was going to make after putting something hot in his ass.

Changing the subject, I had one more interrogation question for him before I put in work. "How are we going to set this up with Heat? It wouldn't be wise for you to come to me, so I think I should meet you somewhere in your territory."

"I'm going to run it by my niggas and more than likely, I'll have you meet me at our main spot at 923 Drummond Street," he said, looking over his shoulder. "It's not too far from here so, you should be able to get there with no problem. Just in case, you may want to write all this down. I won't be repeating myself. My cellphone number is, (404) 555-1211."

I typed the address in the notes on my phone because that was going to lead us to other parties in the Black Kings organization. "I have one final question, Lox. How did it feel to shoot Loco, and send niggas to do your dirty work?" My voice changed drastically, and I was tired of listening to this nigga basically brag about what he and his crew had done. "I mean, have any of that shit made you feel like a real man, or what?"

I'd stood to my feet and sat my phone on the chair by the time I said anything because I knew Lox was going to jump bad. Me and Mike was ready for him when he turned around with fire in his eyes. My arm came up automatically with my finger on the trigger, waiting for him to make a sudden move. Seeing me with a gun in my hand, the fire sizzled out of eyes, and I saw a sign of fear replace it instantly.

"What the fuck, shorty?" he asked nervously. "I just put you on to everything we've been up to. That should've told you I ain't on bullshit. Put the gun down." Lox wasn't pleading with me verbally, but his eyes were.

"Nah, the problem with you is, you revealed the shit to the wrong muthafucka. Didn't your parents ever teach you to not talk to strangers? I'm the bitch you sent ya boys to take care of and they didn't quite make it out. Now, you have to pay," I sneered sinisterly.

Lox lunged in my direction, and I let off a round that hit his ass in the right shoulder, making him fall over slightly. He caught the edge of the counter, refusing to fall to the floor. That was cool with me because I needed to get the rust off my boy Mike, it's been a while. The blood oozed out of the gaping hole, but that wasn't good enough.

"You not 123 ragging now, huh? Where's all that shit you were talkin', Lox? I do things kind of differently," I laughed. "I like to see my prey suffer and feel everything I dish out. That quick shit is for times when I got shit to do and today, my nigga, I got time."

"Look, I'm sorry about all that—"

"No, no, no! You bet not apologize! Own up to the shit you did. For the past half hour or so, you were the big bad wolf around this muthafucka. Keep that same energy and take these slugs with ya chin up, so I can tell your boys you went out like the G you claim to be."

"Fuck you, bitch!" Lox looked like he was about to pass out from the lil gunshot wound I delivered to his weak ass.

A mouse ran over my foot, and I jumped and screeched at the same time. Lox mustered up strength while I had my eye on the rodent and pounced on me. He grabbed my right hand that held the pistol and headbutted me. Small lights flashed behind my eyelids, but I refused to let him take the gun from me. Fighting with everything in me, Lox was strong, and I had nothing on his strength. Pushing me backwards, he was too close for me to do anything to get him off me.

"That shot wasn't fatal and that's where your pretty ass fucked up," Lox sneered. "I'm gon' kill yo' ass in this muthafucka."

The murderous stare he shot at me only caused me to brace myself for the blow to my back when I hit the wall hard. This nigga was dancing with the devil and didn't even know, but I was ready to send him straight to hell. Lifting my left hand, I planted my thumb into the bullet hole and pushed with all my might.

"Aaaarrrrrgggghhh!"

He screamed out at the top of his lungs and released my arm in the process. Wrong move because I was done playin' with his bitch ass. Side stepping away from him, I aimed at his head and waited for him to stand up straight. Holding on to his shoulder, he looked up and opened his mouth. I didn't want to hear shit else and sent some hot shit right in his mouth. The back of his head splattered onto the refrigerator and the roaches had a field day with that shit.

I moved around Lox's body and hated the thought of grabbing the towel on the counter to wipe down everything I'd touched. I didn't have a choice and did what needed to be done. After grabbing my phone and dropping it my purse, I decided to leave out the back door instead of going back out the front. With my nigga still clutched in my hand, I walked through the alley and back around the block to my whip. Letting out a sigh of relief, I started my shit and made my way back to the side of town I was accustomed to with that nasty nigga's dish rag in my hand.

Meesha

Chapter 14

Heat

Seeing all I worked hard to achieve burn to the ground had a nigga ready to fall down on my knees. The bad part about it all, the muthafuckin' pigs think I did this shit on my own. Why the fuck would I burn my own establishment down, when I make more in a month than the insurance policy is worth. That's the stupidest shit I've ever heard in my life? Once I finished listening to the bullshit thrown at me, I went straight to Rocko's crib to set up a plan.

I thought about how we were going to get back at everybody that was against us the entire way to my destination. There was too much shit happening to me in such a short span and all I could think about was all the dirty shit I'd done in my lifetime. That bitch named Karma had me by the balls with a tight grip. Everything I'd done was coming back on me and burying me alive.

I'd sacrificed so many people and the Grim Reaper was stalking my ass to take me to his kingdom. The nigga was going to have to be quick with his shit, because there was no way I was surrendering to death. I had too much life to live to die anytime soon. Me and Rocko was basically the last of a dying breed and giving up wasn't part of the plan.

As I attempted to turn down the street Rocko lived on, there were a slew of red and blue lights up and down the street. A patrol car was blocking both ends, preventing anyone from entering and leaving. I pulled my car along the curb at the end of the block and got out and started walking toward the actions.

As I got closer to the middle of the block, my stomach balled up in knots. Rocko's truck was encircled by red crime tape, and it was riddled with bullets. The holes were big as fuck and there was a tarp thrown over the top, letting me know my nigga was still inside that muthafucka. The only reason they would cover the shit up is if my dawg died viciously, and they didn't want any of the neighbors to see that shit.

Meesha

Standing still, I felt the tears fall down my face. I shouldn't have told Rocko to go home after he'd told me them niggas from the Black Kings had just shot at him on the way to the club. A nigga was hurt and mad at the same muthafuckin' time. There was no way I'm going to be able to take out two teams of niggas gunning for me. I backed up and headed back to my whip as a tow truck was let through the barricade. Yeah, shit was bad for the homie and all this shit was my fault.

I drove around for a hot minute, trying to figure out where I would lay my head for the night. Going home was out of the question, because I knew them niggas probably had somebody waiting for my ass. I didn't want to go back to the crib with Nicassy, because the anger I felt would only be unleashed on her if she said the wrong thing to me. And I couldn't go to Summer, because I didn't want to put her in the midst of the bullshit I was involved in. Even though she wasn't fucking with me, I didn't want to put her life in jeopardy.

How I got back downtown was something I would never be able to figure out. It didn't matter long as I got out of the streets of Atlanta. Parking my ride in the parking lot of the Sheraton hotel, I grabbed the bottle from the trunk and made my way inside and paid for a room. After obtaining the key, I rode the elevator to the fourteenth floor and went to the couch and sat down. Placing my head in my hands, I cried for Rocko as I tried to drink the events of the night away. After drinking half a bottle of Don Julio 1942, I passed out on the couch.

I woke up still thinking about Rocko and the scene at his crib. As much as I wanted it to be a dream, I knew it wasn't. That shit was real, and I needed to avenge my nigga's death. Looking at the clock on the wall, it was after ten in the morning. Jumping to my feet, I rushed out of the room to the elevator. Something told me I needed to get back to the house as I got in my car and drove out of the parking lot. Speeding through traffic, I knew I needed to get back to the house with Nicassy. I'd never left her alone overnight and hoped like hell I hadn't made a mistake with doing so.

She'd been a lot flipper at the mouth since I slapped her ass up and that kind of worried me. Nicasssy was tired of being in the house and I believe she hadn't believed none of the shit I'd told her about Kenzie and why she was even in hiding. The last thing I needed her to do was leave and roam around without a clue.

It took me about twenty minutes to pull up to the house. There weren't any signs of movement at the window of the bedroom she slept in. Most of the time, Nicassy would peek out to see who was pulling into the driveway. There were no signs of her that time around. I got out of my car and made my way to the front door and stopped abruptly because the muthafucka was slightly open. Removing my Glock from behind my back, I pushed the door and stepped inside. The house was quiet and that could be good or bad. I damn sure wasn't taking any chances thinking everything was okay.

As I moved through the lower level, I paused in front of my office and listened at the door. When I was sure no sound was coming from within, I pushed the door open and scanned the room. There was no one inside and I backed out, heading up the stairs quietly. By the time I got to the top of the staircase, I knew right away Nicassy wasn't there. The bedroom was empty, and I rushed back down the steps to check the backyard.

"Fuck! Where the fuck are you, bitch?" I yelled out, pacing back and forth.

I was back to my car fast as my legs could carry me and I drove slowly through the neighborhood, hoping I would spot her. Driving around thirty minutes, I gave up and went back to the house. No one knew Nicassy was alive, so I couldn't inquire about her to anyone. Leaving her alone throughout the night was the wrong move, and I was regretting the shit with every minute she was out of my sight.

Walking back into my office when I got back to the house, I noticed the top right drawer was slightly ajar. That's where I left the money I would empty from my pockets at times. There was a couple thousand in the drawer last time I checked, but the money was gone and so was Nicassy's phone. I kept it from her purposely but didn't lock the muthafucka.

"Stupid! Stupid! Stupid!"

Gathering my laptop and anything else I might need, I left the house and headed back to my home in the city. There was no reason for me to run any longer. I was going to face whatever came my way with all the fight in me. It was time to face everybody head-on. Summer came to mind, and I needed to check on her. Pulling into her driveway, I checked my surroundings and got out of the car. When I entered, she was laughing on the phone in the kitchen and my ears perked up. There was something about the way she was giggling like a schoolgirl that caught my attention.

"No, that's not even what it's about," she said, chewing loudly.

I stood back quietly, listening to her obviously talking to some nigga. I was waiting for her to say something wrong so I could knock her head between the wall and the refrigerator. Being gone gave her a chance to do exactly what I told her ass not to do. And that was get involved with someone else.

"Come on now, you always saying something off the wall," she laughed. "What did you tell me though?"

I couldn't stand idle a minute longer, my presence needed to be known. "I'll be in the bedroom when you finish akee keein' with the next muthafucka."

Summer spun around fast at the sound of my voice. As I walked away, I vaguely heard her whisper, "I'll call you back." I shook my head and went right where I told her I'd be. Standing propped on the dresser as I waited for her to scurry her ass upstairs, it didn't take long at all. Summer appeared in the doorway with a scowl on her face.

"Why are you poppin' up at my house, Heat? I thought we had an understanding when I told you I was done."

"You said that shit and didn't believe it when you said it out your mouth. Stop fuckin' playing with me and cut off whoever the nigga is tonight!" I snapped.

"See, you're always jumping the gun to another nigga, because you're feeling quite guilty from laying up with a bitch for weeks. Don't bring that shit to me, Heat."

"There's no way you were giggling on the phone with a female. I don't know why you're standing there trying to play me for a fool." Summer had guilt written over her face, but she still wanted to play the tough role.

"Fuck you! What if it was a nigga? I'm tired of you coming in and out of my life at your convenience. That shit is dead, Heat, and I'm tired of playing the role of side chick to your ass. As I said before, I'm done with all of this."

Stood with my arms folded over my chest for a minute, before opening my mouth. Summer wasn't having it and beat me to the punch. Which pissed me off more than I already was.

"I don't want to hear nothing else you have to say. This is what you wanted, Romero! I don't know how long you thought I was going to be stupid for you, but your time is up. Go back to wherever you've been and leave my keys on the dresser. It's your fault for leaving room for me to hop on the next dick."

The words left her lips a millisecond before I had slapped the fuck out of her. Summer's arms flared wildly as she tried her best to return hits. Catching her mid-swing, I wrapped one hand around her neck and squeezed. She was out of her mind, telling me she fucked another nigga as if I wasn't going to react. Yeah, I was out getting my dick wet, but she couldn't do what the fuck I did. She was about to learn the hard way though.

"I've invested a lot into the pussy you hold between your legs. How many times have I told yo' stupid ass to stop worrying about what the fuck I'm doing when I'm not with you? This is one of the times you gon' wish you had taken heed to what I've constantly told you. There's no coming back from deception, bitch. Fuckin' another nigga is a major slap in the face."

Summer's eyes rolled to the back of her head as she clawed at my hands. The skin rolled under her fingernails with every scratch she made. Letting her fall to the floor, I pulled her up by her hair and punched her in the right eye. Summer was getting all the frustration from my club burning down, Rocko getting wet up, and Nicassy running away from me taken out on her. Oh well, she should've kept the information she put out into the universe to herself.

"I'm sorry! Please stop hitting me," she cried out as I continued punching her.

I punched her in the nose, causing blood to squirt all over the beige carpeted floor. Summer's face was a mess and I felt like shit after what I'd done. Never been the one to put my hands on a woman enough to hurt them in the manner I'd done to Nicassy, then Summer, I stepped back and left the room before I killed her ass. I knew taking care of everybody after me was the only solution to everything that was going on.

Walking down the stairs, Summer's cries followed me all the way to the door. Instead of going back to console her, I left and hopped in my ride. As I backed out of the driveway there was a vehicle coming down the street, fast. Not giving the car a chance to get any closer, I whipped out and took off in the opposite direction. Passing the vehicle, I looked over and was staring in the face of Savon "Stone" Cole.

The menacing glare he shot my way before raising his tool was all it took for me to step on the gas. I glanced in the rearview mirror, and he had turned into a driveway and was coming for me full throttle. Cutting the first corner I approached, I was doing fifty on a residential street and I prayed there were no kids out, because they were going to get hit if they were in my way.

Stone was on my bumper as if we were racing for the finish line in the Indianapolis 500. It was the middle of the day and traffic was thick as hell. I drove out into the ongoing traffic and barely missed a van as I turned in front of it. The blaring of the horn startled me for a moment, but I steadied the wheel as I searched for an opening to get away from the nigga that was out for blood.

There was no doubt in my mind Stone was the nigga on the phone with Summer. How else would he know to come to her crib at that precise moment? Her gullible ass was sleeping with the enemy, trying to get back at me because she was mad. She's lucky he didn't kill her stupid ass, but his plan worked because he had me in his sights and the nigga was trying to do damage.

"Move the fuck out the way!" I yelled at the muthafuckas driving too slow for my liking. If they knew like I knew, they would get the fuck on.

I was driving like a mad man and heard sirens in the distance. It wouldn't surprise me if one of these scary assholes called the law because of the erratic driving me and Stone was doing on the road. Concentrating on getting away from his ass, I glanced in the rearview mirror and didn't see his ass behind me. I let out a sigh of relief and eased off the gas a bit, relaxing my hands on the steering wheel. What a mistake. Before I knew what was happening, a stream of bullets entered my whip from the passenger side, and tore into my body with force.

Losing control of the car, I veered into a car on my left as I watched Stone's car speed ahead and cut the corner. The last thing I remembered was jumping the curb, ramming the front end of my car into a pole, and the airbag deploying in my face before everything went black.

Meesha

Chapter 15

Phantom

I'd been calling Kenzie since she left the hospital the night before, saying she was going home. Thinking nothing of it, I sat back chilling with Layla until Dreux called, telling me to turn to Fox 5 news. When I saw the image of Heat's club on the screen, I started putting two and two together, getting pissed. Kenzie knew about that shit all along and I should've known something was up when she was watching fuckin' cartoons. I let her believe she'd pulled one over on me for the remainder of the night, since her phone kept going straight to voicemail. But the minute my aunt Kimille walked into Layla's room to take over for me, I was out the door with the quickness.

Kenzie's car was sitting perfectly in her driveway when I pulled up. I jumped out and jogged up the steps two at a time, as I rang the doorbell and pounded on the door at the same time. The sound of her shuffling on the other side of the door turned me into a madman, because she didn't attempt to open the muthafucka, so I started kickin' that bitch. I was getting in one way or another. She must've come to her senses because the door swung open just as I was about to kick the door off the hinges.

"What the hell is wrong with you, Phantom? It's too early for your shit!"

Kenzie stood before me in a shirt that barely covered her ass, with a bonnet on her head. The way her lips pouted was sexy as fuck and I wanted to bend her lil ass over where she stood, but I didn't come over to dig in her guts. My brain reminded me about her sneaking off to go downtown looking for Heat. See, I knew her better than she knew herself. One of these days she was going to learn that shit.

"No, what the fuck is wrong with you turning your phone off last night? You didn't learn your lesson from the last time when some niggas rolled up shooting at yo' goofy ass? I'm trying to save you from getting hurt, but you out here trying to fight everybody by yo'self! Yeah, aight, Billy Bad Ass!"

"Are you done? I was sleeping and want to get back to it," Kenzie asked sarcastically. I looked at her ass like she was a polar bear in a bathing suit, and she tried to close the door in my face after I didn't respond. Catching the knob, I pushed it back just enough to make entry causing her eyebrows to furrow. "Get the fuck out of my house, Phantom."

"I'm not going nowhere, MaKenzie! Why the fuck didn't you just tell me what was going on last night? What's with the sneaky shit, huh? I know you didn't come to this damn house when you left the hospital."

"Xavier, it's not your business where I went. I don't know how many times I gotta tell you to stop worrying about me. I'm not your woman! Go question Chanel about her whereabouts and leave me the fuck alone!"

Kenzie turned her back to walk away from me and I knew exactly why she was acting the way she was at the moment. The seriousness of why I came over went out the window, especially when her ass cheeks swayed under the shirt in a way that made my dick brick up without thought. Play time was over and she was going to learn to stop playing with me.

I let her walk into the kitchen before I stalked right behind her. Lifting her in the air, I pinned her ass high on the wall and her legs automatically wrapped around my neck. Burying my head between her legs, I ran my tongue repeatedly over her clit before sucking it into my mouth.

"Oh, shit!" she moaned as she grinded her love box into my mouth.

I missed the taste of her nectar, and I needed the fix just as much as she claimed she didn't. The way she'd been acting as if she didn't want to fuck with me, her pussy was telling a different story. It was the main reason she had an attitude every time she saw me, but all that shit was going to change after I fucked her ass like I loved her. Which I actually did, and she was going to know it.

"Stop! That's enough," Kenzie screamed, pushing my head back.

My neck was stronger than a sixty-pound dumbbell and wasn't shit she could do to unlatch the grip I had on her pearl. Cum was running down my chin, moisturizing the beard I'd grown out. Lapping up every drop, I went in for the kill, fucking her with the stiffness of my tongue while bouncing her ass on it roughly.

"Yes, oh God, yes!"

The grip she had on my head as she pushed it further into her snatch had me fighting for air. I didn't give a fuck because I wasn't backing away from what was between her legs, until she made it rain on a nigga. Running my tongue from her pussy to her asshole, the tremors in her legs told me she was on the brink of cummin'. Making her wear her feet as earmuffs, I balled her up until all her secrets were on display in front of me. Her juices glistened in the light and that shit looked scrumptious. Running my tongue through her folds, I rubbed my face over her mound a few times then sucked hard on her bud.

"I'm about to cum! Phantom, wait! Wait! Don't stop! Right there."

I had her ass confused than a muthafucka and it made me laugh without removing my mouth. The vibrations from my tongue had her climbing the wall. Literally. The way she dug her nails in my scalp let me know she was fighting the damn orgasm threatening to erupt any second. My tongue was going a mile a minute and her clit hardened. Bracing myself for what I knew was coming, I pushed her legs further back, so she was secured in place.

"Oh, fuck! Here it come! Yes, yes, yessssssss!"

"That's what the fuck I'm talking about," I said to myself, but moaned into her pussy.

Her cum shot down my throat and I had to spit most of it out because I almost choked. That didn't stop me from sucking on that fat muthafucka though. Kenzie was trying hard to catch her breath, but little did she know, I was just getting started. I didn't come for sex, but I didn't come to play with her ass either.

Placing her feet on the floor, I propped her up against the counter and her head fell onto her arms. I took that opportunity to release my demon from the joggers I wore and eased up behind her. Kneading her cheeks in my hands, Kenzie pushed them away lazily. I didn't need my hands to guide my man where he belonged. There was no way I would allow her to deprive him of the warmth he was seeking.

I parted her legs with my knees then guided myself inside her warm tunnel. My back went rigid as her muscles constricted around my dick and sucked him deeper inside with every pulse. I gripped her hips and pulled her back into me, pumping in and out of her wetness. My mouth hung open and my eyes closed, because I'd forgotten how good she felt, since it had been so long since I'd been inside. She was tighter than a muthafucka and I was in heaven.

"We're not supposed to be doing this," she moaned.

"Nah, you were preventing this shit, Kenzie. This my pussy and I'm back to claim it." Fucking her into submission was my plan and I was going to reach my goal. "Yo' hardheaded ass gone take this dick because from here on out, this will be your punishment. I'd rather fuck you than bury you, Kenzie."

My choice of words must've hit a soft spot because she threw that ass back and cocked her leg up, giving me the go ahead to fuck her harder. Flesh against flesh was the only sound echoing off the walls of the kitchen. The way she gripped the counter with her left hand told me I was pushing the right buttons. The tip of my wood bounced off her G-spot with every stroke. The tingle of my balls let me know I wasn't going to last too much longer in her love cove.

"Fuck, Kenzie," I growled as I dug my toes deeper into the cushion of my shoes.

"Give it all to me, Phantom," she coached as her cheeks bounced.

"I'm about to cum," I grunted in her ear.

"Me too, but don't cum in me!"

I wasn't trying to hear none of that shit. I'd been beating my dick for the longest and I was gon' get the nut I was seeking right in her hot spot. My pullout game was weak as hell when it came to Kenzie, and I wasn't trying to practice. I wanted the full session. The kind where my python spit out all its venom, relaxing afterwards.

"Arggggghhhhh, shit! Fuckkkkk!"

I busted hard as hell and saw small lights flashing before my eyes. Kenzie squeezed my man as she came with me, causing my stroke to slow down. Backing out of her warm box, I was smiling as if I won the Mega Millions jackpot, but Kenzie wasn't feeling the victory as I pulled up my pants.

"I know you didn't cum in me, Xavier!"

"Oops. I forgot to pull out," I smirked. "Maybe if I put a baby in your ass, you'll sit the fuck down somewhere. Now, come on so we can go to sleep." I walked out the kitchen, not hearing her behind me so I paused. "Bring yo' ass on, Kenzie!" Storming past to go upstairs, I smacked her on the ass and it jiggled like Jello. "And you will answer all my questions soon as we sleep off this euphoric high we're both on."

Kenzie rolled her eyes and climbed the stairs without looking back. She was probably mad about me dropping my kids off in her daycare, but she was satisfied with my performance. I could tell by the funny way she was walking. I tore that ass up!

***

Kenzie was snoring as if she hadn't slept in years. I slept for about an hour before I woke up and just laid in her bed watching her sleep. Seeing her in the flesh was soothing to my mental because the night before, I was scared out of my mind, worrying about where she was and if she was alright. Every time I called her phone, my heart would thump hard as hell each time I received the voicemail.

When Dreux called and told me what was going on, I had him slide down to the scene to see if Kenzie was there. By the time he got downtown, everything was done and only the arson investigators were present. I felt as if something bad happened to her. When I called Khaos, he questioned Kayla and she came out with what she knew. Kenzie went to talk to some nigga named Lox that was affiliated with the Black Kings. Hearing that shit had me heated because once again, she was on some superhero-type shit.

Using the alone time I had, I thought about Layla being in the hospital, and how Tiffany needed to be found ASAP. Not knowing her parents moved was news to me and I was kicking myself for not keeping up with them. I'd tried calling both of their numbers and they no longer belonged to them. I was waiting on Tim to get back with me with an address, because I was rolling out soon as I got the information. Kenzie broke my train of thought when she rolled over in her sleep. I looked over at her and she was staring back at me sleepily.

"Hey, sleepyhead."

"Phantom, why are you still here?" she asked, adjusting the pillow under her head.

"I told you to be ready to talk to me when you woke up. That should've told you I wasn't leaving anytime soon," I said calmly. I wasn't trying to argue with her, so I was trying to take a different approach. "I know about you going with Lox last night. I don't know the nigga, but you know that shit was dangerous, ma." Kenzie bit her lip and closed her eyes. Gathering her in my arms, I kissed the top of her head as I hugged her tight.

"Walk me through what happened."

She attempted to move out of my arms, but I held on for dear life. The feeling of her being so close felt good and I wanted her to stay right where she was. She stopped trying to get away and just closed her eyes as she sighed. Clearing her throat, Kenzie ran her finger down my chest, causing my spine to shiver.

"The dude Lox approached me while I was watching the firemen put out the fire at Heat's club. He noticed me from the club and thought I was a bottle girl. I let him think what he wanted and went with the flow. When he gave me a business card and it said Black Kings, I knew right away that was my chance to get some payback for them shooting at me. Lox mentioned Heat killing Brando and piqued my interest. To make a long story short, the nigga is laying stankin' in his dirty ass crib after saying what he planned to do to you."

Kenzie let it out the bag that she felt some type of way when the nigga brought me in the mix. I smirked and kissed her on the lips, and she slipped her tongue in my mouth. Her reaction was getting to me, and I cut that shit short.

"So, you killing muthafuckas for me now?" I laughed when she ducked her head, hiding her face. I lifted her chin so she could look me in the face. "I appreciate you doing what you had to do, but I need you to stop acting on impulse. These niggas don't give a fuck that you are a female, Kenzie. I know you can hold your own, you don't have to say that shit. I need you to think about your wellbeing, just as I am."

Nodding her head in agreeance, Kenzie zoned out for a second. "Wait, how did you know about Lox?" she asked. Without giving me a chance to response, she sat up and shook her head. "That damn Kayla. She's getting soft under Khaos' ass. I have to get my sister away from him. He's fuckin' my shit up."

"No, Kayla was actually scared after you turned the fuckin' phone off. I have an idea why you did that shit too. Yo' ass knew I was going to track your shit and come guns blazing."

"You're right. I took care of that problem with no problem. I didn't need help. They don't call me Storm for nothing. This is what I do, baby," Kenzie gloated.

"Well, make it your last time. From this point on, you will roll with me to get your fix. How that sound?"

"As long as I'm in the loop, I don't care if I go out on a job with Yogi Bear, I need to be out there."

The mention of cartoon characters had me laughing hard as hell, because Kenzie pulled a fast one on my ass with that SpongeBob bullshit. She was looking at me as if I'd lost my mind when the doorbell rang. We both grabbed clothes to throw on and grabbed our tools as we headed for the door. That shit was sexy as fuck to me. Kenzie was more like me than any woman I'd ever encountered, and I loved it. We moved faster as the doorbell sounded repeatedly, and I snatched the door open. Kenzie gasped, falling against the doorframe as she stared blankly at the woman standing before her.

Chapter 16

Nicassy

Heat didn't come back to the house, and I went to work going through everything I could find in his office. Going through his desk, I copped four thousand dollars and my cellphone. As I searched, I charged my device and started searching the paperwork on anything I could find on Kenzie and Kayla. When I found what I was looking for, I also spotted my own address in the process. Running upstairs to find something decent to put on, I left my phone charging.

    I prayed harder than ever Heat didn't show up by the time I left. Taking my chances fifteen minutes later, I left the house with my phone and everything in hand. I walked until I got to a gas station. There was an older lady pumping gas and I walked over to her, explaining I was kidnapped and practically begged her to take me to my sister's home. My sobs had her looking around nervously and I needed her help. So, I had to tug at her heart.

    "Please call the police, but you have to help me get away from here! He's going to kill me if I'm left here! I have money. Just help me!" I cried hysterically.

    The woman glanced back at the gas pump and eventually hit the locks on her doors. "Get in. I'm going to help you, just let me finish getting gas."

    A few minutes later, she was in the car hitting the road. Putting the address in her GPS, she drove the car, but kept looking over at me every so often. A few miles into the commute, she finally conjured up a conversation.

    "So, what's your name, baby?"

    "Nicassy. Thank you so much for helping me."

    "No thanks needed. I'm Bernadine. I knew I had to do what was right, because folks aren't taking this trafficking shit for what it is. You're one of the lucky ones because you got away. This is getting out of control, and I knew you weren't lying because the proof is in the bruising around your neck and on your face. I wish there were other's that would help more, but I get it. The world isn't the same anymore and it's hard to trust anyone, male or females nowadays. You're safe now and that's all that matters."

The animated voice of the GPS indicated in three miles, the destination would be on the right. I didn't really recognize the neighborhood, but I would find out if Kenzie lived there before long. Bernadine pulled into the driveway and sat in front of a beautiful two-story home. Still, I didn't recognize where I was, causing fear to take over my body. I had to take my chances and hope for the best. Reaching in my pocket, I felt around until I had three bills between my fingers.

"Thank you so much, Bernadine. I appreciate your help," I said, handing her three hundred dollars.

"Keep your money, Nicassy. Call the police and tell them everything you know, so that son of a bitch won't do this to another woman. I saved you, now save someone else. We have to get the word out and make people aware that this shit is really happening. It's not a myth, there are people going through this every hour of the day. Take care of yourself and don't let this break you. Grow from it, learn from it, and help fight it."

Bernadine hugged me and I broke down in her arms. The weight had finally lifted from my shoulders from being in that house, knowing Heat lied about everything. Even though my situation had nothing to do with trafficking, there were cases out there being overlooked. Bernadine still saved me from a situation I didn't ask to be in.

Getting out of the car, I tossed the money on the seat and made my way to the front door of the residence. I rang the doorbell once and looked over my shoulder. Bernadine was still waiting for me to gain entry, so I pushed the bell as if my life depended on it. The door swung open and Kenzie and a man both stood before me with guns drawn. She fell into the door, and I thought she was about to faint by the look on her face. Lowering her gun, Kenzie was shocked to see me, and it showed. The guy wasn't taking any chances, because his gun was aimed directly at my head.

"Baby girl, you gon' be okay?" Bernadine asked with her head leaned out the window. I answered yes in my head, but didn't realize I hadn't opened my mouth, until Bernadine said next, "I'm calling the police!"

Turning quickly, I said, "No, no. I will call the police once I'm inside. I'm safe here. Thank you again. I'm safe, I promise." I reassured her, and she sat staring at us for a while before backing out onto the street and driving off.

My body was shaking because I didn't know if Kenzie was going to beat my ass or not. Deciding to face whatever head-on, I turned to address Kenzie and saw the tears rolling down her cheeks.

"Who the fuck is you and what do you want?" the guy sneered.

"I—" I started to say before Kenzie cut me off.

"We thought he killed you," she sobbed, wrapping her arms around me. "I'm so sorry for whatever I did to you. All that shit is water under the bridge. You are back with us and that's all that matters." Kenzie let me go and snatched me inside, leading me to a chair in the dining room. "You hungry?" I shook my head no and wiped my own tears from my eyes.

I didn't know what Kenzie was talking about, but obviously something went on between us I didn't remember. Before I could respond to her, Phantom was worried about her mindset. The way he looked at her showed nothing but love, and I was happy Kenzie had finally found someone to love her for the woman she was. She deserved it.

"Kenzie, baby, what's going on?"

"Phantom, this is Nicassy. Tornado," Kenzie said, never taking her eyes off me. Once she told Phantom who I was, he finally put his gun on the counter and stood with his arms folded. The way he was looking at me gave the impression he didn't trust me as far as he could see. I wondered what story he heard about me, because it couldn't have been a good one.

"I need you to tell me where that nigga had you at and who was the old bitch that dropped you off?" Phantom asked with much authority.

"To be honest, I don't know the address to where he had me—"

"That's bullshit and you know it! Heat had you in his presence for weeks and you didn't think to go outside and look at the address on the side of the house?" Phantom snapped, cutting me off.

"If you would let me finish, I don't know the address, but I took a picture of the house, the number on it and a street sign. Heat left me in the house all night and I got the chance to leave this morning when I noticed he still wasn't back. The only reason I'm here is because I found the addresses in his office for Kenzie and Kayla. My phone was in one of his drawers, so I took that too and charged it just enough so I could leave," I explained in a rush.

"Bernadine was a lady pumping gas at the gas station that helped me when I told her I was kidnapped. I promised her I would call the police once I was safe. You are standing there grilling me as if I wanted to stay with Heat and that's not close to the truth. That man fed me a bunch of lies and told me I couldn't get in touch with Kenzie if I wanted to live."

"What the hell was he insinuating, I was going to kill you or some shit?" Kenzie asked with her face balled up.

"That's exactly what he said, I know there's no truth to what he said but I want to hear it from you. Were you the one that told the Stone person I was sent to kill him and had his house blown up?"

"Hell, nawl! Heat was the one that sent Rocko and Will to kill you and Stone. Rocko in turn, killed Will in the process, because he probably didn't want to go through with Heat's plan. That nigga lied through his teeth and soon as I catch up with him, he's dead. Let me see the address."

Kenzie was heated and I didn't see any deception in her actions at all. I went to my camera roll and found the pictures I'd taken. She took my phone and went upstairs. Phantom stood guard while she was gone and watched me like a hawk. I could tell he was looking at the bruises I'd sustained from Heat, and I subconsciously rubbed my neck.

"That nigga was putting his hands on you?" he asked.

"The other day was the first. He got mad when I called him out on his bullshit, but it's okay."

"We were told you lost your memory. Is anything coming back to you?"

"I've had flashbacks from the last time I saw Stone. I don't know anything before the day I was almost killed, but it still worries me that the only thing I could recall was Heat's number." I shook my head, trying hard to think back. It still didn't work. "I knew Kenzie and Kayla were like my sisters, but I didn't know anything about Kenzie being mad at me for messing with Heat. He made sure to fill me in on it though. I feel like shit, knowing Kenzie caught me in bed with her man."

I was fiddling with my hands because I was ashamed and couldn't look Phantom in his face. Kenzie was willing to let that shit go. I didn't think it would ever be that easy for me. Sleeping with a man that was involved with anyone within a circle, was foul as fuck. We made vows not to allow any nigga to come between us and I did just that. Kenzie made her presence known and marched into the kitchen with her phone up to her ear.

"Hold on," she said to whomever she was talking to. "What the hell you talking about, Nicassy? I ain't never walked in on you and Heat in bed together! We didn't fall out over him. We fell out because your ass felt you weren't getting the attention you deserved. It had nothing to do with you fuckin' that muthafucka. Far as I know, you didn't even look at him in that manner and would never fuck him, knowing I used to."

My head dropped to my chest and fell from my eyes. There was no reason to keep silent about what went on in that house. I might as well go ahead and tell the whole truth.

"Kenzie, I'm sorry. I've slept with Heat a few times while I was with him. When he said you caught us together, I felt bad. The thought of you sending someone to kill me, had me thinking, fuck it. I didn't know he was lying to me, and he wouldn't call so I could talk to you myself."

"Nicassy, that's the least of our worries. Heat is a fuck nigga and I believe he would fuck whoever gon' give him the pussy. As you can see, I don't give two shits about him. There's a whole man in my crib, but we have other things to handle, and Heat getting his ass handed to him is on the top of the list."

I felt like a fool because Heat blew so much smoke up my ass and I believed it all, until he knocked me upside my head. Kenzie was looking at me with disgust while she talked on the phone. When she said Scony's name, my head whipped around quickly, almost causing whiplash.

"Scony, she's sitting right here. That nigga beat her ass. Other than that, she looks fine to me. Heat had her thinking the worst of me and I cleared it up best I could by telling her I wasn't the enemy." Kenzie listened to what Scony was saying before shaking her head. "I don't think that's a good idea, bro. I mean, Nicassy did go to Houston to kill that man. The last thing I need is for him to come here and kill her for what transpired." She paused again before taking a deep breath. "Okay, I'll be waiting, and I'll see you when you get here."

Ending the call, Kenzie turned to me with a grim expression. "Nicassy, Stone is on his way here. I don't know what his state of mind will be when he arrives, but you have to take whatever he dishes out. I mean, you did go on a job to kill him, and he may not feel too good about seeing you."

"I remember the last conversation we had, and he wasn't happy then either. The only thing I can say is, he didn't want me dead. Stone told me to get out of his house. I can still see the anger mixed with hurt in his eyes after I told him why I was sent to Houston. Kenzie, I swear Heat shitted on that man's name, and Stone did none of the things I was told he did. I fucked up when I fell in love with the mark." I was crying as the relationship I had with Stone filled my mind. Everything we did together was real, and I enjoyed every minute of being with him.

"As I thought of ways to end his life, Stone treated me with nothing but respect. There was no way I could kill him after all the ways he treated and catered to me."

Kenzie walked over and wrapped her arms around me. She reached to grab something from the table, causing my body to stiffen. Stepping back, Kenzie handed me a pair of leggings, a shirt, and towels.

"Don't worry about any of that. Go upstairs to the left and take a shower. I'll come up to get you when Stone arrives. Scony will be here tomorrow and I'm going to call Kayla to come over as well. You are back with your family now. Heat will get what's coming to him. The sooner we take care of him and all the bullshit he's brought our way, the sooner we can get back to living. Nicassy, I want you to know, there's nothing that would ever come between the bond we have. Was I pissed at you? Yes, I was. I'm not mad anymore and we will get through this. I'm happy to know you are still amongst the living and we're about to tear some shit up."

Hearing Kenzie say those things eased my mind a lot, but I was nervous as hell, wondering what Stone would say or do when he laid eyes on me. I wasn't able to find the words to say in return to Kenzie, so I just nodded my head. Getting up, I followed her directions and went to take care of my hygiene. I'd been through so much and I was tired. Whatever my life was before all of this, was coming to an end after we got through with Heat. I wanted to live a normal life because the line of work I was involved with, wasn't something I wanted to do anymore.

Meesha

Chapter 17

Stone

"Celeste, you good though?" Stone asked his sister as he laid back on his bed.

"Yeah, I'm okay. This baby is kicking my ass. The morning sickness is the worse though. My doctor suggested medication for it, but I don't want to take anything because I'm scared it could harm the baby. I've made sure I stay hydrated and eat right. It's getting better, but I'm so ready for this baby to come out."

"I know, sis, and I'll be there soon as I can. There are a few things I have to take care of, and it's been taking me a little longer to get to the bottom of it. Where that nigga at?"

"He's in there somewhere, surprisingly," Celeste said lowly.

"Why the fuck you whispering?" Stone asked. "That muthafucka still talking to you crazy?"

"Savon, I'm okay. Just leave it alone," Celeste said nervously.

"I'm gon' have a talk with his ass when I get back. I don't like how you are cowering and tiptoeing around that nigga. You know you can always go to Mama and Daddy's, or even to my house. I understand why you haven't gon' to Sam's house, but I'm not getting into that." Stone laughed. "Celeste, I want to know if Joe is putting his hands on you. Please don't let me find out from a third party or see the scars."

"I will tell you if that ever happens. I promise, I'm fine."

The phone beeped and I had another call coming in. Telling Celeste I loved her, I clicked over and answered the call before it went to voicemail. If Scony was calling, there had to be some type of action in effect.

"Tell me something good, Scony."

"Aye, I need you to get to Kenzie's crib. Nicassy showed up to her house out of the blue."

The words Scony spoke had a nigga stuck, because I'd been trying to figure out where Nicassy was. Now that I knew, I didn't know how to feel about it. When I thought she was dead, it crushed me. After the doctor said she was discharged, I was relieved and wanted to find her. But now that the opportunity came about to see her, I was scared because on one hand, the urge to strangle her ass was strong, for portraying herself to be something she wasn't and causing me to fall in love with her. On the other, I wanted to hug her tight and kiss all the pain away. In other words, I was stuck between a rock and a hard place and needed to figure out which hand I would choose.

"Did you hear what I said, nigga?" Scony bellowed out.

"Yeah, yeah I heard you," I said, taking a deep breath. "Is she alright?"

"According to Kenzie, she's confused and feels bad about the shit Heat had her believing. He beat her ass and left her bruised up, but other than that, she's okay." Scony explained. "Stone, I don't want you going over there pulling yo' gun and shit. You already know how the fuck she came into your life. Don't hold that shit against her. Say what you have to say and end that shit the right way. Plain and simple. Nicassy was wrong, we know this. But you also know how the business works. I want you to remember one thing, she's still my muthafuckin' sister. You already know where I'm going with this shit."

"I hear you, Scony. I'm going to take care of it. I'll let you know how it goes."

"No need. I'll be there in a few hours. I told Kenzie I'd be there tomorrow, but I changed my mind. Knowing your ass, I need to be there to fuck you up before you can get too far away."

Stone laughed because Scony was exaggerating like a muthafucka. "I'll still be in Atlanta, regardless of what I do or don't do to Angel. You scare other niggas, not me."

"Her name ain't—"

"Shut the fuck up and get off my phone. I got moves to make and you holding me up."

After banging on his ass, I flopped back on the bed and remembered what happened with Heat earlier that morning. I called his ass back and told him about that shit.

"Is the nigga dead?" Scony asked.

"I don't know. I couldn't make sure because the police rolled through fast as hell. I lit his ass up though. If he survived, he's a lucky muthafucka because you know I aim to kill."

"Well, if he pulls through, he just breathing for the duration of time. He won't make it too long around that muthafucka. I'm going to get my people on it to see where that muthafucka laid up at. He's going to have an accident in whatever hospital he's admitted in. I'm going to need you to reach out to his bitch. She's most likely his emergency contact and will lead us right to him. It's time to put some heat under her ass too."

"I'm two steps ahead of you. I hit her up soon as I got home, and she was happy to hear from a nigga. I know she hasn't heard anything because she didn't sound distraught. It doesn't matter how much dick I put in her life, Summer loves that nigga and won't leave him alone. I'm going to put my Glock in her mouth and make her ass sing like Mariah Carey though."

"You a fool," Scony laughed. "I'll see you in a few hours."

"Aight, bet."

Hanging up from Scony, I just laid in the bed for a minute before I ended up taking a nap to get my mind off what I had to head out and do, come face-to-face with Angel. Trying to figure out how I was going to handle the situation had tired me out. I woke up maybe an hour or so later and got myself together. Throwing on some clothes, I grabbed my keys and left the hotel without a thought.

I shot Kenzie a text, letting her know I was on my way. When I pulled up, I couldn't will myself to get out of the car. It took Kenzie coming out and standing on the porch to put a pep in my step. Putting my Glock in the small of my back, I got out and climbed the steps.

"It took you long enough," she said, giving me a quick hug.

"I was coming earlier but I had to get my head right. I'm not trying to come over here on no type of drama, so I had to let out all the negative shit I was thinking. In other words, I had to prepare myself to see the woman who was sent to end my life. The shit ain't easy, Kenzie."

"As long as you got the evil out of your system, you should be good. Nicassy been through hell and back. We have to guide her on this road to recovery. She may not remember a lot of things, and this is just as hard for her too."

Kenzie was right and I took everything she said into consideration. For her to be years younger than me, she spoke very logically and beyond her years. I had a lot of respect for her and Kayla, because they go hard in whatever they set out to do. Leading the way into the house, I was left in the living room while Kenzie went upstairs to get Nicassy. Phantom walked in and we dapped up before he sat across from me.

"Any word on Heat?" he asked.

"I hope his ass is dead. I caught him leaving Summer's crib earlier and put some hot shit in him. Twelve pulled up fast as fuck because nine times out of ten, a muthafucka called them because of how reckless we were driving. Shit pissed me off, because I couldn't make sure he wasn't breathing."

"Man, I wish you would've called for back-up. I need that nigga dead like yesterday. With all this shit going on, I want it to be over and done with, because Kenzie is going out of her damn mind. We have to settle this shit now."

"I'm right there with you on that. It's been going on far too long."

My train of thought vanished as the sound of footsteps caught my attention. Angel stood at the bottom of the steps, while Kenzie summoned Phantom with a nod of her head. They disappeared upstairs, leaving me and Angel alone. She walked slowly to the loveseat Phantom had vacated and I followed her every move.

Blinking repeatedly, I couldn't believe I was looking at the woman I'd come to love. Many may think I was crazy for wanting to wrap her in my arms after she openly admitted she was sent to end my life. At the moment, that was neither here nor there. I hadn't cried and stressed myself out wondering if she was actually dead for nothing. Those sleepless nights weren't going to be in vain.

"Are you alright, Angel?" The look of surprise showed in her eyes at the mention of the name I addressed her by.

"How do you know about that name? No one has called me that since my grandmother," she asked, taking a seat on the loveseat further away from me. I took a seat across from her, preparing myself to answer her question.

"That's the name you gave me when we first met. I know now your real name is Nicassy though."

I purposely kept the stoic expression so she wouldn't know how I was feeling being in her presence. She was nervous because she was fidgeting in her seat, and she looked everywhere but at me. We were silent for at least five minutes before I got up and went into the kitchen. I had to get something to drink because my throat felt as if cotton balls were lodged in it. Grabbing two bottles of water, I made my way back into the living room. Angel peered at me as I sat and hesitated when I offered the water. Finally accepting it, she muttered a thank you and took a long sip. She sat the bottle on the table and sat back with a huff.

"Stone, I want to apologize for putting you through all of this. The flashbacks that's been running through my head allowed me to see the love I truly had for you was real."

"I don't want to hear that shit! It don't even matter because you are here now." My voice came down a few octaves. My heart was beating fast in my chest, and I had to take a few deep breaths in order to go on.

"You were everything I wanted in a woman, Angel. Heat sent you to kill me off under false pretenses, and you were only doing what you were being paid to do. I can't fault you for that. I'm not gon' lie, I wanted to tear your muthafuckin' head off after you told me why you scoped me out at the club. My love for you is the reason you made it. If it was anyone else, they would be dead right now."

Tears rolled down her cheeks and I sat, admiring her beauty before getting up to comfort her. Lifting her as if she was a newborn baby, I sat down and cradled her in my arms. For several weeks I'd envisioned that very moment and my wish came true.

Examining the bruises on her neck and face, I ran my finger over each one and the image of Heat crashing after I shot him replayed behind my eyelids.

"Stone—"

"Savon. I don't want you to call me Stone anymore." She smiled and nodded her head.

"Okay, Savon. It seems as if you are willing to forgive me for what I set out to do to you. To be honest, I think it's too easy. Deep down, I believe you don't trust me, and I wouldn't blame you. There isn't any way you will fully forgive me for what I've done. We can't go back to what we had because technically, it doesn't exist. The relationship we had was based on lies and deception."

Thinking about what she said, I let it marinate for a minute and I had to agree. Even though I spent countless days and nights laughing, sexing, and enjoying her every being for damn near a year, her entire persona was a façade. I fell in love with Tornado the assassin, not Nicassy Avers the woman.

"I have to make everything right with you and I know your family hates me right about now. It wouldn't be okay for me to come around as if I hadn't deceived you in the worst way."

"You remember my family, Angel?" I asked, lifting her head.

"No, but I'm quite sure they know what I've done."

I talked about my family to try and jar her memory about them. Angel and my sisters were close. It was the reason I didn't go into the dynamics of our relationship with them. Tarnishing her name was something I'd never do to her. If that was the case, that would mean I didn't give a fuck about her at all.

"I haven't told them you're alive as of yet. I wanted to find out where you were, before getting their hopes up like I'd done with myself. They're aware your body wasn't in the house when it exploded though. Celeste is more worried than Sam, but they're both hurt just the same. Believe me, they will welcome you back with open arms, because they can't scrutinize what they don't have knowledge of. Your hitman tendencies are safe with me."

She recanted what went on while she was with Heat and Angel became emotional as she revealed that she slept with the nigga. I couldn't be mad because her mindset only processed what he'd told her. Plus, I'd smashed Summer during the ordeal too, so we were even. She didn't need to know that tad bit of information though.

When Angel got to the end of her tale, I sat holding her in my lap until she fell asleep. Kenzie peeked around the wall of the staircase, and I laughed lowly because she probably thought I killed her sister. It was extremely quiet in the room and all I was doing was thinking, as I held the woman I thought was long gone in my arms. Kenzie led me to the room Angel was using and I laid her down, kissing her temple. After turning off the light, I pulled the door closed, just as my phone rang. Kenzie was waiting to talk, but I held up one finger and took the call.

"What up?"

"I'll be pulling up at the airport in about forty-five minutes. Get at Phantom and tell him to get in touch with Khaos and Dreux. I should have word on Heat soon, but in the meantime, we going after the Black Kings to make their entourage a little smaller," Scony said.

"Sounds good. I'm at Kenzie's now and so is Phantom. I'll let him know what's up and we'll be there to scoop you up. It's time to put an end to all this bullshit."

"You ain't never lied. I'm tired of running in circles. I haven't done this shit since I had to search high and low for this nigga named Kelvin. That muthafucka got what he deserved, and we made that shit happen. This time won't be no different, except the bloodshed is about to be ten times worse." Scony disconnected the call and Kenzie was right there hanging on to every word.

"What's going on?"

"Scony will be landing soon, and he wants to meet up and talk about some shit."

"I'm going too—"

"Nah, stay here with Angel. We're not getting into anything today. I'm quite sure Scony will fill you and Kayla in on the plan," I said, cutting her off.

Phantom walked out the room at the end of the hall already dressed. Kenzie rolled her eyes and stomped off to the same room Phantom exited. She slammed the door and shook the pictures on the wall. I laughed because I'd never seen a woman throw a tantrum because she couldn't pull the trigger on a muthafucka.

"She'll be alright. She better sit her Mrs. 007 ass down somewhere. Her days of killing is coming to an end, she just don't know it yet," Phantom said, tucking his Glock behind his back. "I heard you telling her what's up. I'm ready when you are."

I hopped in the truck with Phantom, and he hit up Khaos as we backed out of the driveway, but Dreux's phone went straight to voicemail. We would try to hit him up as time went on. Until then, we had shit to do, and a nigga was ready to put in work.

Chapter 18

Dreux

Kenzie called, informing me about Nicassy showing up on her doorstep. That was the best news I'd heard in a long time. I was at the barbershop when I got the call and stood to leave, but Micah my barber stopped me by saying he would be getting at me next. Figuring there was no rush, I sat back down, because I needed my haircut.

I'd been searching the streets for Heat and ran into a dead end at every turn. When I saw his establishment burning to the ground on the news, I broke my neck to the scene. Fuck the fire, I was going for Heat's ass so I could follow him to his hideout. The nigga had been hiding out better than Casper's little ass, but I knew he was far from friendly. Luck wasn't on my side that night either, because he was nowhere to be found.

"Man, I finally got to gut out Anastasia. She got some pussy that's out of this world!"

Tuned in on the conversation going on around me, I laughed at the lil homie. He had been talking about getting with this woman for at least five months, and many warned him to stay away from her because she wasn't right. Obviously, he didn't listen and by the expressions on the faces around the shop, they were about to go in on his hardheaded ass.

"Trey, didn't I tell yo' ass not to touch that damn woman? You better get to the nearest clinic because you need a shot in your ass," Micah laughed.

"A shot? That nigga won't be fuckin' no more once the word spread about him getting down with Antibiotic Anastasia," another cat added.

"Aye yo, Trey. Is your dick burning yet? She done had every STD known to man. The worse I've heard was herpes. That shit never goes away, fam. We tried to tell you not to do it, but I guess that tingle in your pants pushed you forward. I feel so sorry for you, boy."

Trey sat back, mad as hell, because they weren't going to let him live that shit down. The smile he had on his face when he was bragging, vanished fast as hell. His fist was balled up tighter than that Arthur meme on social media.

"Look at him over there pissed off. I bet you fell in love with that sick ass pussy too. Didn't you, Trey?"

The whole shop was laughing. "Fuck you hatin' ass niggas!" Trey growled as he got up and left. I felt bad for dude, because they made him feel low as fuck after they finished roasting his ass. All I could do was shake my head because these youngins always thought somebody was hating on them. But in this situation, he was given the rules and he ignored every play. Now he was upset because he was lusting over the neighborhood hoe.

Micah was ready for me, and I got in the chair so he could work his magic. We were chopping it up while he cut my hair, when the door to the shop opened. A light-skinned cat walked in, and everybody got quiet because they'd never seen him before. With all the bullshit going on in the city, that alone put niggas on guard. Underneath the cape I had my tool in my hand, with a finger on the trigger just in case.

"What up, man? What I can I do for you?" Micah asked.

"I'm not from around here and just so happened to see this barbershop. You do walk-ins?"

"Yeah, it's gon' be a lil minute, 'cause I got three after this one."

"I'm free after I'm done over here," Frank called out. "I'll hook you up, homie."

"Nah, I'll wait on him. he seems like the popular one," he said, hiking up his jeans before sitting in an empty chair.

It was something about the nigga's mannerism that had my bullshit radar going a mile a minute. I couldn't put my finger on it, but there was something fishy about his ass. From the way his eyes were shifting around the room, to him tapping away on his phone, that shit had me watching him very closely. Micah was probably thinking the same because I could feel the hesitancy in his movements while cutting my hair.

"That muthafucka up to something, Dreux. His vibe ain't right. He's in the right place for that bullshit though," Micah whispered, without missing a beat with the clippers.

"Mm-hmm. I'm on it."

I watched him lowkey like a hawk, until he got a call and tried his best to keep his voice low, before getting up going outside. All eyes were on him until the door closed with a bang. There was small chatter about the mysterious man going around the shop.

"I think I've seen that dude somewhere before. I could be wrong though," Frank said to no one in particular.

The shit wasn't important to me because I wasn't worried about his ass. Ten minutes later, I was paying Micah for the cut, satisfied as usual. Saying my goodbyes, I headed for the door as Micah yelled out, "Be careful out there, bro. These niggas don't give a fuck about life anymore."

"You got that shit right, but they know who the fuck to try that shit with though. I'll be good," I said, tucking my heat in my pants before leaving.

Walking across the lot to my whip, I kept my eye on the dude that was still on his phone. I was focused on the wrong shit because a silver Monte Carlo cut in front of me, and I couldn't move fast enough before bullets were flying. Reaching for my heat wasn't possible. The hot slugs were penetrating multiple parts of my body as I fell to the ground, hitting my head on the pavement.

It sounded like there was a war going on before the sound of screeching tires were heard, then there was nothing but screams and loud talking filling my eardrums. My head was lifted into someone's lap, and I closed my eyes.

"Dreux, open your muthafuckin' eyes, my nigga! You gon' be aight. Stay with me, dammit!" Gripping my jaws and giving them a firm shake, Micah wasn't going to let me give up without a fight. "You not going out like this, bro. You gotta stay with me. Where the fuck is the ambulance!"

The quake in Micah's voice had tears cascading down my face. I couldn't feel the pain from the gunshots, but I felt every bit of the pain he felt, seeing me in the position I was in. Micah and I went way back. We'd been through so much together coming up in the hood. Our mothers were best friends, and we grew up like brothers. So, to see me down, I already knew he was fucked up behind it.

"I got that muthafucka, fam. Blew his shit back. I should've followed my first mind because I knew he was on some shit." I opened my mouth and felt blood slide down my chin. My eyes fluttered closed and Micah got to shaking my shit again. "Open yo' eyes! Do that shit for me, Dreux! I'm not gon' be the one to tell yo' mama you died in my fuckin' arms. The ambulance is coming. I promise they're coming!"

Looking up at my long-time friend, the tears were flowing down his face, and I tried hard as hell to keep my eyes open, but it was a losing battle. I was getting weaker with every passing second. Blood was seeping through my shirt, and I knew them niggas got me good. I laughed on the inside because they caught a real nigga slipping. No longer able to keep my eyes open, they closed slowly, and Micah begged and pled for me to stay with him. The sirens were loud as hell but in my mind, I knew they were a little too late to save me.

The EMT's were barking out orders but their voices were fading fast. I felt them put the oxygen mask over my face after lifting me on the stretcher. When I was loaded in the ambulance, I stopped breathing.

"He's coding!"

My shirt was ripped open, and I felt the electric current flowing into my heart. My body jolted with every hit of the defibrillator, and I was watching everything from the sideline. Whoever shot me made sure they didn't miss. I had at least five bullet holes in my torso, and I was hit in the left arm and thigh from what I could see. A nigga was fucked up. If I was watching these people work to get my heart going, that meant I was good as dead, right?

Chapter 19

Tiffany

I'd been in Junction for days and still hadn't been by my parents' house. With Phantom's reach, he'd probably found them already and I was scared to show my face. Instead, I'd shopped and laid low until that day. There was no way I was going to continue spending money on a hotel when I could go sleep at my parents' home. They were going to talk shit, I knew, but I didn't give a damn.

Getting out of the shower, I combed my hair into a ponytail and slipped my feet into my Nike slides. Just in case I had to slap the hell out of my mama, I was going to be ready. Checking the room to make sure I wasn't leaving anything, I grabbed my bag and headed out. After checking out, I got into my car and made my way to the last place I wanted to be.

I changed my number after all the threats Phantom had made. I didn't blame him for wanting to kill me for what I'd done to Layla, but what's done was done. There was no way I could take that shit back. It was his muthafuckin fault anyway, so he needed to sit back and think about the part he'd played in it all.

The closer I got to my destination, the more frazzled my nerves became. I didn't even know why I was going to the house because there was no good going to come from it. Mainly because I came without the one person they cared the most about, Layla. Nobody gave a fuck about Tiffany. Everybody cared about that lil muthafucka though.

Soon as I parked in front of the house, I groaned because I thought there would be a moment for me to gather myself beforehand. Oh, I was wrong. My mama was out front on her knees, tending to her rose bushes. When she turned around, I could see the deep scowl on her face, and I shook my head knowing shit was going to go downhill fast. Standing to her feet, she wiped her hands on the apron she wore and walked slowly toward my vehicle. I took a deep breath before turning off the car and got out. Peering into the backseat, I knew who she was looking for.

"Where is Layla?" she asked.

"She's with her father. Is it a problem that I came to see my mama and daddy without your precious granddaughter? Where is my hello? Are you going to ask how I'm doing?" I snapped. Ignoring everything I had said, she went on to interrogate me more as if I had to answer any of that shit.

"Why are you here? Let's start there. And I'm not trying to hear no bullshit about wanting to see me."

"Dang, I haven't seen y'all in a while. What's with the twenty questions?" I asked, getting irritated as fuck.

"I haven't talked to my grandchild in months, and you didn't think to bring her along for the ride. You're running from something, and I don't want the shit at my doorstep. Go back to your problems, Tiffany, because I won't be saving you this time."

"I didn't need you to save me before and I won't need you this time around either! Why the fuck do you hate me so much?" My father walked out of the house and my eyes lit up.

"What's going on out here? Tiffany, baby, when did you get here? Is Layla in the car?"

Trying my best not to snap on him about asking about *their* granddaughter, I plastered a smile on my face. "No, she's not with me. It's Phantom's week to have her. How are you, Daddy?" Doing just as his wife, he ignored the pleasantries and concentrated on the subject of Layla.

"When is our week? I mean, she will be starting school soon and we haven't even talked to her. As a matter of fact, I tried calling but your number isn't working. What's going on, Tiffany? Talk to me. Are you in trouble?"

"Daddy, I'm not in trouble and I had to change my number. You and *Kathy* is digging too deep and I'm not feeling the insinuations that's going through y'all head. I don't have to be in trouble to visit my parents!"

"Now, you know better than to call me anything other than your mother. After all the shit I've put up with you, give me the respect I deserve! You must be running from that Butch guy. Is he whooping your ass again, Tiffany?"

Bringing up Butch took me over the edge, because my mother always assumed everything was about him. Little did she know, he was never going to put his hands on me again, thanks to Phantom. I didn't bother responding and used their tactic in return. "Can I come in and take a nap for a couple hours before I get back on the road?"

"Go to sleep for a couple hours so you can leave? I thought you said you came here to see us. How the hell you just want to sleep? You didn't drive fourteen hours just to rest and take off. Who are you running from?" My daddy was no better than his wife with all the questions, and he didn't do anything except ignite my anger even more.

"I'm not going through all this with y'all. I'm out of here. I'll take my chances getting a damn room."

I rushed to the driver side of my car with my daddy on my heels. He grabbed me by the arm, preventing me from opening the door. I was done with all the back and forth questioning and was just ready to get away from them. Instead of saying anything, my daddy just hugged me tightly, told me he loved me and walked back to the house. I didn't know what to gather from his actions, so I just took it for what it was. His goodbye. My mother, on the other hand, had already gone back to tending to the muthafuckin' plants in her front yard. Stupid ass bitch.

Going back to Georgia wasn't what I wanted to do. It was the only place I knew. My sisters for a fact wouldn't help me because even if they agreed, by the time I made my way to them my mother would've already called, reciting how I'd spoken to her. That would be another wasted trip and I wasn't for it. Georgia was big enough for me to get lost in and that's exactly what I planned to do.

Seven hours later, I was forced to find a hotel so I could sleep. The scene in front of my parents' house played in my head the entire time and I wanted to go back and kill both of them. Knowing my mother, she was going to reach out to Phantom. It didn't bother me none because all she could tell him was, I got in my car and drove off. The nigga still wouldn't know where to start looking for me.

Pulling into the parking lot of a rundown motel, I contemplated going inside. In my mind, I knew it wasn't a safe place to lay my head, but I was tired as hell and in dire need of sleep after all the diving I'd done that day. I grabbed my bag and went inside to pay for a room. What could go wrong in a matter of a few hours? When I was settled inside the small room, I sat on the bed and checked my social media page before my eyes started burning.

I took a shower then not too long after, crawled under the covers and fell asleep immediately. Sleeping as if I hadn't slept in weeks, I was awakened by someone banging on my door. There was no way someone was looking for me because I wasn't even from the area, and no one knew I was there.

Instead of responding to the knocks, I laid back down and turned my back to the door hoping whoever it was would go away. That wasn't the case. The knocking became persistent and more irritating to me. I jumped up and pulled the shorts I was wearing out of the crack of my ass and stomped to the door. Snatching it open, ready to cuss out whomever was on the other side, was a huge mistake on my part.

"Hey, Tiff. Surprised to see me?" Tim smirked as he pushed his way into the room, followed by another man. "I know you didn't think you were going to get away with doing that shit to baby girl, did you?"

I was shaking like a hooker standing on a corner in the dead of winter. The sight of Phantom's homeboy was someone I surely wasn't expecting. While driving, I never even thought about checking to see if I was being followed. Phantom didn't even know about my parents' moving because I never told him. Tim showing up only told me that he did his homework.

"Don't worry, you don't have to answer that. I'm quite sure you already know you have to pay for that shit with yo' life. You still have until we get back to Georgia so you can think about the stupid shit you did, before I get you back to the man that insists on taking care of you himself. I feel for you, but Layla will be raised by a respectable woman that loves her."

"You muthafucka!" I yelled, smacking the shit out of him. How dare he throw the fact of that bitch Kenzie raising my daughter in my face?

Tim laughed and punched me square in the face. I fell to the floor in a daze. Using zip ties, he bound my hands and feet, then used another tie to bound them together. Opening my mouth to scream, I never got the chance to belt it out, because a piece of duct tape was slapped over my mouth. Beating myself up for not going with my first mind of going to a better hotel, I silently cried. The area I was in, nobody would question two men carrying a zip-tied woman with duct tape over her mouth to a car. My life was over, and I'd run out of time. Lying on the floor breathing in the stale scent of the carpet, I heard Tim on the phone.

"I got her," he paused. "I caught her ass leaving her parents' house after she was giving them shit. From what I observed they were more worried about Layla than her. School baby girl now to not tell her grandparents what happened to her. They can't know in order for this to work. There won't be a trace of her anywhere here, so don't worry. Everything else is up to you. I'm going to get off here because I've already said too much. I'll holla at you when I touch down."

My mind was going crazy because these niggas was about to make me vanish into thin air. I could feel my daddy's hug lingering around me, and I wished I'd returned it and told him I loved him too. As far as they knew, I was running from somebody, and I didn't even tell them Phantom was the person that had me running for my life. His ass was going to get away with killing me and not one person was going to look at him as the bad guy. Damn, I was so stupid.

Meesha

Chapter 20

Khaos

"What's up, bro-in-law?" Phantom smiled, greeting Scony.

"Get yo' ass out of here with that shit," he laughed. "Kenzie didn't get married without consulting with me first. That's the only way you will be an in-law to me, nigga. I have to give the blessing."

The look on Phantom's face told me he was about to come out his mouth with some stupid, ignorant shit. And I was right. I laughed before he even opened his mouth, but damn near pissed on myself when he finally did.

"Would I get a pass if I told you I used her uterus as a cum shop and planted my seeds inside? The load I dropped in that muthafucka, I'm sure one of them niggas made it," Phantom smirked.

Scony was stuck and didn't even know how to respond. All he could do was laugh it off as we all piled into Phantom's truck. Bringing his whip to life, Scony was sitting in the front passenger seat and reached over and slapped the back of Phantom's head. "That's for my sister because I know damn well she told yo' pussy ass to pull the fuck out. Kenzie ain't ready for no damn kids and you know this!"

"She got nine months to get ready because like I told her, oops I forgot to pull out."

Everybody in the car laughed as Phantom drove to our destination as Scony guided him with oral navigation. Before long, Phantom received a call that had him cheesing from ear to ear. He basically listened, but he was obviously pleased with whatever he was told. When he hung up, he let us know Tim had scooped up Tiffany. That shit made my day, because I couldn't wait to confront that hoe.

I sat in the back seat, with Stone sitting next to me in his own world. Nudging his ass out of his thoughts, he grilled me like I was bothering him or some shit. My phone rang and I fished it out of my pocket to see who it was. Seeing Micah's name surprised me because it wasn't time for a nigga to get shaped up.

"What it do, fam?" I asked, happy to hear from the nigga.

"Aye, K. Some shit just went down outside the shop, and I think you and Phantom may want to get to Emory University Hospital right now!"

"What the fuck going on, Micah? Spit that shit out!" I snapped.

"Some niggas wet Dreux the fuck up. Fam was in bad shape when they put him in the ambulance. I don't think he's going to make it. I just pulled up behind them and they rushed him inside. Khaos, they were still pumping on his chest, dawg. They had been doing that shit in the back of the ambulance before pulling off."

"Who the fuck did that shit? Did you get a look at the niggas?" I screamed into the phone.

"What's going on, Cuz?" Phantom asked, glancing back at me through the rearview mirror.

"Hold on a second, Micah. Cuz, I need you to go straight to Emory University Hospital. Dreux got shot and he may not make it."

Phantom looked over at Scony and he nodded his head. He took off, doing at least ninety as he hopped on the highway, hauling ass. I went back to my conversation with Micah and my blood started boiling. Telling him I would see him in a minute, I ended that shit as I snatched a blunt from Phantom's stash.

"Micah said he didn't recognize the niggas, but while they were trailing the ambulance, Frank remembered where he knew one of the niggas from. Them Black King muthafuckas has struck again. And to think we were on our way to strategize about how we were going to come for they ass."

"There's no need for that shit. We got an address to where we can find they ass and we going right in to get shit crackin'. It's all about wetting up one of the neighborhoods in Edgewood. If my nigga don't make it, they won't either. Even if he pulls through, they ass still gon' die," Phantom gritted.

"The shit is fresh and I'm not into doing this type of shit in broad daylight. Regardless of what the fuck they did, I don't jeopardize the lives of kids and women, especially the kids because I'm a father before anything. I'm all for going after these niggas for what they have done, but we will go in when nightfall hits. No sooner than that."

Scony was adamant about his decision, and I felt him on that shit. It didn't matter when we took care of it. All I knew was, the day wasn't going to end without some type of bloodshed. Phantom pulled into the parking lot and when he stopped to let a vehicle out of a spot, I jumped out and rushed the entrance to the hospital. Micah was pacing back and forth with his hands holding his head, and I immediately thought the worst.

"Fam, how he doing?" I asked, power walking toward him.

"I don't know. Nobody's been out, so I guess that's good news, right? I don't have the heart to call his mama about this shit, K."

"You have to call her, because the last thing we want to do is call Deloris to tell her he didn't make it. At least we have a glimmer of hope, and she can get here soon as possible. Make the call, fam."

I looked down at my hand and noticed I had the much-needed blunt clutched between my fingers that I didn't fire up in the whip. Not missing a beat, I flamed that muthafucka up and pulled on it hard. The smoke filled my lungs and I coughed uncontrollably as I was forced to spit into the grass. Frank walked over to me with a solemn look on his face.

"Damn, K. I wish I had figured out who that nigga was when he was still in the shop. The shit didn't come to me until after the fact and it's eating me all the way up."

"Don't worry about it. At least we know who the fuck was behind the shit, that's all that matters. Once I find out what's going on with Dreux, we gon' after them niggas tonight. I'm not taking this shit lying down. They won't get away with this, not today."

"I wanna roll too. Micah got the muthafucka that dropped the homie's location. I left the streets alone long ago, but this shit just brought me out of retirement, if only for a few hours."

Micah walked in on the tail end of Frank's statement and was ready to get in on the action too. Seeing all the blood on his clothes had me wanting to leave at that very second to kill everybody. Dreux's mom was on her way to the hospital, so we went inside to wait, and Phantom walked in a few minutes later.

"Any word on Dreux's condition?" he asked as he sat next to me.

"Nah, nobody has come out yet," I said, looking toward the door. "Where's Stone and Scony?"

"They went to scope out the spot Kenzie told me about. It's better for them to go than any of us, because them niggas gunning for us, and they don't know who the fuck running with us. When nightfall comes around, the Black Kings ain't gon' know what hit 'em."

At that very moment, Miss Deloris came crashing into the door with Dreux's brother Dino on her heels. He had a murderous scowl gracing his face. His ass looked like Method Man with his hat turned to the back. The print of his tool was visible in the front of his pants, so I knew he came to ride out too. We had more niggas to get down on these niggas without even trying to recruit. Our team was mediocre at first and we were going to do what it took regardless. Now, we were about to show them how we really got down, by letting the whole city know we were not to be fucked with. The night was going down as a bloodiest massacre in Atlanta.

"Where the fuck is my brother, Khaos?" Dino barked.

"He's somewhere in here. We haven't heard anything yet."

"What happened?"

Micah ran down what took place, and my emotions were trying to weaken a nigga as I listened to the whole story. Everything that had taken place in the past few months was taking a toll on me. Hospitals, death, deception, and bullshit was something I was tired of dealing with. After we tied up all the loose ends and put all this shit behind us, I was hanging up my guns.

As much as I loved killing muthafuckas and making good dough doing it, the shit wasn't how I wanted to live the rest of my life. Kayla was the woman for me, and it was time for me to be the man she needed and love her like the queen she was. Being out of the streets to enjoy life was how I wanted to be. Not ducking and dodging bullets and watching my back. I'd rather live peacefully watching my kids grow up.

"What's the muthafuckin' plan?" Dino asked as a doctor walked out in surgical scrubs looking around the room.

"The family of Dreux Garner?" Miss Deloris waved him over and waited until he walked to where we were. "Hello, I'm Dr. Chow. I'm the surgeon that operated on Mr. Garner."

"I'm his mother. How's my son?" Deloris asked through tears.

"Well, Mr. Garner sustained multiple gunshots. Surgery went well, but I can't predict what the outcome will be at the moment. What I can say is, he's a very lucky guy to still be breathing. Being shot six times and not succumbing to the injuries is a blessing from the man above. There were a few complications along the way. We had to remove his spleen because it was severely damaged. He has a few broken ribs on his right side along with a wound to his right arm. Mr. Garner is going to need excessive rehabilitation, because both of his legs were broken from the wounds to his thighs, and he had severe bleeding and needed to undergo a transfusion from the blood loss. Other than that, all I can say is he's very lucky to be alive."

Hearing everything Dreux endured only fueled the fire in my body. He was going to be alright, and I couldn't say the same about the niggas that put him in the situation. Retaliation was on the forefront of my mind, and I'd zoned out, missing most of what was being said around me. Someone jolted me out of my thoughts, and I blinked a couple times and turned to my left.

"You good, Cuz?" Phantom asked.

"Yeah. This shit is really fucking with me," I said as we walked away from the circle.

"Scony just text and said they were sitting watching them niggas and to meet them at Kenzie's when we're done here."

"Phantom, how the fuck we supposed to do that when you let his ass take yo' whip?"

He laughed and nodded his head. "You got a point, but that's nothing, nigga. Micha and Frank rollin' and Dino ain't letting this shit go. Believe me, we got a ride and then it's game time. When we see Dreux, we out. I'll take Kenzie's whip to go home and gear up. Tim should be here by then and that would give us two more to wreck shop. It's about to be on, nigga. Half of this shit is going to end tonight."

I heard what Phantom said, but something else came to mind and I stalked across the room. "Where you going, Cuz?" he yelled at my back but I kept going.

When I made it to the counter, the woman was typing away on the computer, looking into something for the person in front of me. A few minutes later, I was able to ask the question that plagued my mind. "Aye, I was wondering if there's a patient named Romero Ramirez here." She went back to typing into the system for Heat's name and I hoped like hell that nigga was brought into this hospital.

"No, I'm sorry. I don't see anyone with that name in our system," she said, looking up from the screen.

I smiled and thanked her for the information. It was either Heat wasn't brought to that particular hospital, or the nigga may have been in the morgue. Either way, I was going to find out in due time. If he was still breathing, Heat had one more chance to get away by the hair on his chinny chin-chin, then it would be time for him to lay down too. Phantom met me in the middle of the room with a quizzical look.

"What's going on?"

"I went to see was Heat checked in this bitch and he wasn't in the system. He may be dead or maybe not, but the key to getting at him is Summer."

"Stone is going to get as much information from her as he can. That's going to be his assignment because Heat getting his shit split should've been breaking news."

Reaching for my phone, Miss Deloris came over and told us she and Dino would be the only two to see Dreux that day. I hugged her and told her to keep me posted on my homie. Dino walked over and said hit him up with a location, because soon as he dropped his ma off, he was heading our way. They walked off as Micah and Frank came over.

"What's the move? I closed the shop and got time today." Micah was ready and I loved that shit.

"I'm about to go upstairs and check on my daughter, then we going to my girl house to figure that shit out. I'm gon' need you to drop us off though," Phantom responded.

"Nah, I got to go to the crib and change," Micah said, looking down at his bloodied clothes reaching in his pocket. "Take my whip and I'll ride with Frank. Shoot me a text and we'll be there within the hour."

"Nah, we not rolling out until nightfall, so you got time. I'll hit you up when it's time to head out. I'll bring yo' whip back within an hour. Gear up and be prepared. This one will make the news tonight, I promise."

"I'm with that shit. Let's make these muthafuckas famous," Frank chimed in.

We left the hospital and Micah pointed in the direction of his whip, walking to the next aisle of the lot. As Phantom hit the button on the key fob, Micah stopped in his tracks and yelled out. Both me and Khaos turned to hear what he had to say.

"Tear up my shit and you bought it, nigga!"

"Fuck you," Phantom laughed, looking at Micah's midnight black Camaro. "If I scratch it, nigga, I promise to buy you three more. This lil' muthafucka is in good hands like Allstate."

I couldn't stop laughing because fam didn't give a damn what he said out of his mouth. All he had to say was aight or some shit like that. Micah shook his head and went to find Frank.

Meesha

We went back inside and went up to Layla's room. It was empty and both me and Phantom panicked. Phantom stopped a nurse that was passing by and grabbed her by the arm.

"Excuse me, Miss. Where is Layla Bennett? She's not in her room."

"You must be her father," the nurse smiled. "She's on the third floor in physical therapy. Follow me, I'll take you to her."

We got on the elevator and went down to see Layla. When the nurse pointed to the room Layla was in, Phantom and I stood in the doorway watching Lay struggle through the exercise with tears running down her face. The shit hurt my heart to see my lil homie in so much pain and I wish there was something I could do to take all the pain away.

"You can do it, Layla. Just take your time," my mama said, encouraging her from a chair on the side.

"I can't do this without my daddy! He told me he would be here and he's not!" Layla screamed. Rushing into the room, Phantom was by his daughter's side with the quickness. If he was what she needed, he was going to be right there with the antidote to her recovery.

"I'm right here, baby," he said, kissing her on the top of her head.

"I'm here too, Lil Homie. We about to jam this shit out so you can get stronger. You are not a quitter, okay? Even if the people you need are not in the room with you, know that we are always in your heart. But that will never happen, because we will forever stand together, you got that?" Layla nodded her head yes and wiped at the tears on her face.

"You are strong. You are confident. You got this. Let's do it," Phantom was throwing some of the affirmations Kenzie says to Layla out loud, and a few encouraging words of his own. It worked because her little legs started raising as she lifted them slowly off the bench she was lying on.

The session lasted another thirty minutes before the therapist called it quits. "Good job, Layla. You did it. Your progress today got you a step closer to going home, but your recovery is far from over. There's so much more that needs to be done before you are back one hundred percent."

"When will these things come off?" Layla asked.

"It's gonna be a few weeks for that, munchkin." The frown on Layla's face showed just how much the accident impacted her little life. "Mr. Bennett, may I speak to you for a moment?"

The therapist and Phantom left the room. I went over to Layla and gave her a big hug. "Thanks for coming, Big Homie. I don't think I would've been able to do this without my daddy. It hurts to move my legs sometimes."

"I know. But you got this, and we will keep going until it's time to take those stupid casts off. Your legs are going to be strong as ever after this. You did real good today and I'm proud of you."

"Yes, you did, Layla. I'm proud of you too!"

"Thanks, Tee-Tee Kimille."

Layla yawned and sat back relaxing on the bench. My mama looked at me and nodded her head before getting up from the chair. I followed her and she punched my ass when we were out of earshot of Layla.

"What you hit me for?" I laughed.

"You already know I don't play around with you not calling me, Kannon. I know Xavier told you what I said the other day and I still haven't heard from your black ass."

"He told me, Ma. I was gon' call you today, but I knew you were still here with Layla, and decided to come see my favorite girl in person," I smirked.

"Yeah right, with your lying ass. What have you been up to? Kayla is getting all of your attention lately. You must really like her."

"Ma, you do know what you're doing is called hating, right?" I laughed. "The relationship I have with Kayla isn't remotely the same as the relationship I will always have with you. What I'm trying to say is this, my love for you will always trump the love I have for Kayla, but you can't get mad because I spend more time with her than you. I'm building something with Kayla, Ma. My relationship with you is solid and can't be broken. I promise I will do better with calling and coming by the house more. Kayla has pus—"

"Boy, I'll knock yo' ass into the middle of next week! I don't give a damn about that woman's private parts!"

"I was just trying to tell you why she's getting all my time," I laughed. My mama was mad as hell, and I ruffled her feathers a little bit. "Nah, for real though, I've been out trying to find out a lot of shit about what's going on in these streets. We've also been trying to find Tiffany. When everything is over and done with, I promise we are going to go away and have fun like we used to. Okay?"

"Be careful out there, Kannon. The streets are not like they used to be. There's a new species of niggas out there and I don't want anything to happen to any of you."

"I will, Ma."

A sound from the door got our attention. Transportation was there to take Layla back to her room, when Phantom and the therapist entered. Layla was knocked out by the time she was settled in the room. Both me and Phantom kissed my mother goodbye and left to go handle business. Once I was in the passenger seat of Micah's car, I called Kayla to see where she was. The phone barely rang before she answered.

"Please tell me Dreux is alright, Khaos. I can't afford to lose anyone else," she said frantically into my ear.

"Baby, he has a long road ahead of him. Get yourself together, I'm on my way to pick you up."

"I'm at Kenzie's. Scony and Stone is on their way here. Before you say anything, I'm going with y'all to get at these niggas. There won't be any back forth between us, okay?"

Instead of responding to what she said, I simply replied, "I'll be there in a minute."

Ending the call, I ran my hand over my face because I didn't want Kayla going out on this mission. The shit was definitely going to be a dangerous situation and looking out for her wouldn't be possible while trying to shoot a muthafucka. She'd already told me what it was, so there was no use trying to persuade her over the phone. I'd just wait until I was in her presence to talk face-to-face. In the meantime, I had to get my mind off the shit that was destined to have me in my feelings. I reached over and turned the radio up as I zoned out until we got to our destination.

Meesha

Chapter 21

Stone

Watching the Black King members laid back as if they had not a worry in the world was comical to me. It wasn't going to be hard trying to get at them at all. The problem was going to lie in how many of them niggas were on the inside. The fools outside would be easy targets, because their focal point was ass and titties.

Scony pulled away from the curb and slowly drove pass the trap. Heads turned but no one remotely cared about a strange car rolling down the block. That shit alone was going to help killing them that much easier. Obviously, nobody told them to stay alert at all times in the line of work they were in. It's going to be too late to learn from the mistakes they'd already made.

"This shit is going to be easy like taking candy from a baby," Scony laughed. "The nigga sitting on the porch looked like he could be the leader of that circus."

"I was thinking the same thing. There's no way my people would be sitting around after getting down on a nigga, like there wouldn't be repercussions behind the shit. That's called poor leadership and I'm ready to show them just what gunplay is all about."

"Yeah, it's time to school these rookies," Scony said as he lit the blunt while steering with his knee.

We pulled into Kenzie's driveway a half hour later, ready to set our plan in motion. Going after a whole crew with six people would be a task in itself. There was way more of them niggas, but the six of us were all shooters and I knew for a fact we could get the job done. I just didn't know if Scony was willing to bring his sisters in on the action.

Kenzie and Kayla were sitting on the couch when we entered. Kenzie jumped up and started going in on Scony right away. "Let's discuss what we're about to do with these niggas that shot Dreux. Don't tell me not to worry about it, because I will trail y'all in my own muthafuckin' car!"

"Kenzie, how many times do I have to tell you to watch how you talk to me? This will be a team effort and we're going out as one. Now, shut yo' ass up and wait for your man to get here. I may give him the go ahead to take you upstairs for a little act-right, because it seems like you need a fix."

"I don't have a man, so I don't know what you talkin' about. One thing for sure, two for certain, Phantom don't run shit over here. He has a whole daughter to chastise."

"It's ironic you knew exactly who the fuck I was talking about," Scony laughed. "I can't wait to see you talk that big bad shit when he gets here."

Kenzie huffed as she sat back in the chair, eyeballing Kayla as she babied Snow as if he was an infant. I knew she was ready to start some more shit as she turned to face her sister. "You must gon' meet us at the spot because that damn dog can't stay here. There's no way he will be roaming freely throughout my crib."

"Kenzie, don't start no shit with me. Snow will be right here until I get back. In the yard. I had no intentions of allowing him to stay inside." Kayla rolled her eyes at her sister. "Go clean yo' muthafuckin' gun or something, but you better shut up talking yo' shit."

Before Kenzie could come back with a rebuttal, the doorbell rang, causing Scony to jump up to get the door. "It's about time you got here, nigga. Ya girl is on bullshit with everybody," he said as he stepped aside to let Phantom inside.

"Scony, fuck around and get slapped, okay? You already know what I did to you at Granny's house a few years ago. I have no problem knocking your ass out again. This time there will be no hesitations shooting you in the ass."

"Kenzie, stop that shit!" Phantom scowled.

"You know what, Phantom, fuck you and that nigga!" Kenzie looked behind him and noticed Tim and a wide grin spread across her face. "What up, Tim? I didn't know you were in town." Phantom looked between his long-time friend and Kenzie in bewilderment.

"Hey, Storm. I'm here because I had to deliver a package to Phan. I'll be around until we get all this shit y'all got going on handled."

"Hell, yeah! I know I'm rollin' out now. My partner in crime is in the building and there's no way I'll get left behind. We 'bout to set shit off fa sho." Kenzie hugged Tim and the glare in Phantom's eyes prompted Tim to push Kenzie to the side and address what his friend hadn't voiced vocally.

"Yo, fam. Don't look at me like that. Me and Storm had a heart-to-heart in the Twin Cities after I caught up with her on the roof after she took out those cops. She's like a little sister to me. Nothing more, nothing less. You already know Sweetz is all the woman I'll ever need in my life."

"You cool, fam. She knows exactly what the fuck she doing, and I'll deal with that later," Phantom said, glaring at Kenzie. "Where did you take Tiff?"

Kenzie's head whipped in Phantom's direction with the mention of his baby mama. By the look on her face, I could tell she knew nothing about Phantom and Tim's game plan. "What do you mean, where did he take her? At what point was you going to tell me she was no longer in hiding?"

Phantom ignored Kenzie and that only pissed her off more, causing Scony to stand between the two of them before his sister could swing. The way her fists were balled tightly at her sides, Scony peeped the move at the same time I did. Her nose flared as she waited for Phantom to respond, but instead he stepped to the side and addressed Tim for the second time.

"Where you take her, bro?"

"I had him to take her to a crib I purchased a while ago in the city," Scony chimed in. "She can sit in that muthafucka and think about what she did to baby girl, until we handle this situation." Kenzie shook her head and stormed up the stairs with an attitude.

"What the fuck is her problem, Scony?" Phantom asked, keeping his eyes on Kenzie.

"I'm not studying her bossy ass. She wants to be in the know about every fuckin' thing and when shit don't go her way, she automatically gets mad. We don't have time to babysit her, and the mood swings she's always going through. You need to get a test to see if you knocked her spoiled ass up."

"That's not even the problem. I just put that hard shit on her the other day. I don't think my seeds traveled to its destination that quick. Anyway, I'm not ready to see Tiff, because I'll shoot her between the eyes. I need her to tell me why she did what she did to my baby. Once Layla is comfortable at home, I'll deal with that situation. Until then, fuck Tiffany."

"Do you know when they gon' let Layla go home?" Tim asked.

"She had her first physical therapy session today. I don't know when they will let her come home. Hopefully soon, because I want my baby home."

Kenzie came stomping down the stairs wearing a pair of black leggings, and a long-sleeved black shirt, with a pair of black Timberland boots. Her hair was pulled into a ponytail and her face was free of makeup. If looks could kill, Phantom would be sprawled on the floor dead.

"Kenzie, keep whatever you 'bout to say, to yo'self. You didn't give me a chance to tell you about Layla when I came in, because you were on bullshit."

"Why didn't you call me to come to the hospital? Better yet, why the fuck I didn't know about the session beforehand?"

"Aye, we need to talk about how we're about to get down on these Black King niggas. Y'all gon' have to save the back and forth between shit for another day." I wasn't for all the arguing so, I jumped down to business.

"I'm with Stone. We've wasted enough time already and it's getting late. Hell, I need some pussy." Khaos eyed Kayla seductively.

"I don't think I needed to know you're outright talking about fuckin' my little sister, but you have a point about business." The room became quiet as Scony spoke and Khaos blew Kayla a kiss from across the room. "With the information I was given by Kenzie, me and Stone went to peep the scene. It's gon' be easy as hell to roll up on them niggas and we have exactly what we need to get the job done. Females are their weakness. Every bitch that walked down the street had their attention and took their eyes off what was going on around them."

"Yeah, from what I saw, we can sneak up on them niggas from all sides of the house with the right distractions. That's where Kenzie and Kayla will come into the mix. There's an entry—"

"Wait a minute, Stone," Kenzie said, interrupting what I was saying. "My name is Storm, and I won't be used as a decoy for any damn body. There's no way I will get the attention of any man when I pull up dressed like this." Kenzie motioned toward the outfit that adorned her body. "I'm going to bust my steel, not trying to set a nigga up so y'all can have all the fuckin' fun."

"Kenzie, we need you to do this." Scony walked over to his sister and held both her hands in his. "It's not about us having fun, it has a lot to do with getting shit done by any means necessary. And if that means you and Kayla have to go upstairs and get dressed to the nines, that's what you will do." Kenzie opened her mouth, but Scony shook his head no, causing her to snap her lips closed again.

"I need you to listen for once, sis. It doesn't mean you and Kayla won't get the opportunity to body one or two of these niggas. There's enough for everybody to get shit crackin'. Don't worry about that."

Scony laid down the game plan for everybody and we all thought it was brilliant. My palm was itching badly, and I was ready for whatever. The Black Kings were about to have their last dance that night. The doorbell rang and Phantom was the closest, so he went to answer the door. The two niggas standing on the porch looked like they were ready for war.

"My niggas have arrived!" Phantom said excitedly. "Come on in." He shook up with Micah and Frank as they crossed the threshold. Before he could close the door, another figure emerged in the doorway. Phantom's hand went to his waistband, but he paused after recognizing G standing before him.

"What y'all thought, I was going to sit this one out? Nah, let's end this shit once and for all."

"G, you didn't tell me you were coming down here."

"Scony, you know damned well I will never let you go on a mission with a bunch of muthafuckas you don't know how to move with. I'll always have yo' back when it's time to put in work. Now, run the plan down to me."

Scony ran down the plan and everybody was on top of what needed to be done. It was also mentioned if there were any kids out to abort the mission, because no one was about putting anyone's kid in a dangerous position. The guy that came with Tim just had to open his mouth instead of going with the plan that was set in motion.

"Even if there's kids out, we're going forward. I came here to put in work and that's what I plan to do," the guy with Tim said boldly.

"Who the fuck are you?" Kayla asked, getting up from the couch. "We don't do kids around here. I have nieces and nephews and would hate for some shit like that to happen to them."

"I'm Killa and I live up to my name."

"Kayla is right. You out of pocket, homie. I have a daughter and I'm already about to bury a bitch for the shit she did to my seed." Phantom looked at Tim. "I fuck with you and know anyone you're affiliated with is solid. But this nigga, I'm not feeling his vibe at all. You need to holla at his ass, because I don't have a problem leaving his ass on the asphalt with the other niggas if a child gets hurt during this shit."

"Nigga, who the fuck—"

Before Killa could walk up on Phantom, everybody in the room upped pistols and pointed them in his direction. Tim had his gun trained on his friend as well and that shit let me know he was a thorough nigga. He had Phantom's back just like everyone else.

"Damn, Tim, this how you rollin'?" Killa asked astonished.

"This is my muthafuckin' family! When you say shit out the side of yo' neck and then approach one of mine like you about to do some shit, hell yeah it's us against yo' stupid ass. You just joined my team, and this was a test run, nigga. And you failed miserably. Now you gotta pay for that shit." Tim lowered his gun as he grilled Killa with hatred.

"My bad. I didn't mean shit by what I said. Look, look, we can talk this shit out."

Out of my peripheral vision, I saw Kenzie creeping behind Killa and I knew she was about to have the orgasm she'd been hoping for since Phantom walked in. Tim nodded and Kenzie shot Killa in the back of his head. Without thought, both Tim and Phantom rolled him up in the Persian rug he once stood on. Carrying Killa's lifeless body through the kitchen, they dumped his ass into one of the beaters we were going to use for the night.

When they returned, we got right back to business without missing a beat. Nobody thought about Killa getting his shit blown back a few moments prior, then the sound of the doorbell caused everyone to clutch their tools. Kenzie was the one that decided to answer the door.

"What up, Dino? How's things with Dreux?" Kenzie asked giving him a quick hug.

"He gon' make it, but my brother has a long road to recovery. My mama stayed with him because she didn't want to leave his side. Fuck that shit for now, though. Where the fuck is these niggas?"

"We were waiting on you before we set out to handle this business. Once Kenzie and Kayla finish getting dressed, we will be ready to roll. In the meantime, let me run down the plan to you," Phantom said.

That was the cue for the ladies to head upstairs, while all the men sat around talking about who would post up where when we get to those niggas' traps. About fifteen minutes later, we were ready to roll to get the party started on Drummond Street.

Meesha

Chapter 22

MaKayla

"Kenzie, why the hell are you so damn angry? I don't know what you are going through, but this isn't the time for you to be going against every damn body. We are about to go out on a mission, and we all need to be focused or shit can turn ugly quickly."

"Sis, there's nothing wrong with me. Phantom was wrong for not telling me about Layla's physical therapy session. I told her I would be there for her every step of the way, and I wasn't!"

We were in her closet trying to get dressed up to go lay niggas down. I chose one of Kenzie's black pantsuits and a pair of six-inch stilettos. Kenzie chose a pair of black wide legged pants and a sea green halter top and Balenciaga flats. We hurried to get dressed because we had been upstairs long enough. Taking her hair out of the ponytail she had it in, Kenzie's long tresses flowed down her back. Of course, my sister was beautiful, and she got it from me. I kept my hair in a high ponytail and put my feet in the heels I chose.

"Kayla, I think you need to find another type of shoe. There is a chance of us having to run and you won't be able to do that in those high ass heels."

"You're right. I'll put on these shoes, but I'm taking these heels with me because I'm going to fuck the shit out of Khaos in these muthafuckas right here," Kayla said seriously as she put on a pair of Coach sneakers.

"Make sure you bring my shit back! You know you're good for washing my clothes, and hanging them up in your closet."

"Girl, bye. I don't need your shit. Plus, you and I are one and the same. Stop trippin' with me. I'm not the one you need to be talking crazy to. I am one bitch that will throw hands with yo' ass. We are one and the same, sis, and that will be a bout that will go on and on until we are forced to stop. Now let's go, so you can let out all that aggression on the enemies."

Meesha

As the both of us descended the stairs, both Phantom and Khaos had lustful looks in their eyes. That shit was going to have to wait, because my pussy was purring for one thing, and it wasn't dick. The entire crew left the house and me and Kenzie followed suit. Scony pointed to a run-down hooptie and my sister turned her nose up at it.

"What the fuck I look like rollin' in that? I'm going to push my Benz on these niggas. I'll just swap out the license plate because I won't be going anywhere in that piece of shit. The last thing I need is to get stranded when the motor don't turn."

"Whatever you want to do is on you. We have waited long enough as is," Scony said, walking to the beater he would drive. "Follow me. Under no circumstances are you to do anything else. We have to dump this body before we head out."

After Khaos pulled the hooptie out of Kenzie's garage, she switched the plates and backed her car out with the music bumpin'. I got in and we were ready to get shit poppin'. We were following Scony like we were in a funeral procession, and I laughed at the thought. Kenzie glanced over at me, and I waved her off so she could pay attention to the road.

About twenty minutes later, we pulled into a remote area and the guys got out and threw Killa's body in the middle of the area. Scony put the rug back in the trunk and got back in his car, heading towards Edgewood. My phone rang as we got close to our destination, and it was Scony. I put the call on speaker, turning the radio down.

"What's up, bro?"

"We are going to get into position behind y'all down the street. The rest of the team is going to be up the street and behind the house. Stay on the phone with me so I can give y'all the go ahead to get out and do y'all shit."

"Okay," I said as we turned onto the street, passing Scony. We pulled up to the address as Phantom and Khaos drove past us and parked in front of the house next door. "Bro, there's nobody out here. Hell, it's quiet as hell right now."

"I'm about to go to the door and see if there's anyone in there." Kenzie got out before she could complete what she was saying.

"Kenzie, don't get yo ass out of that car!" Scony yelled, but he was screaming at his damn self, because Kenzie was already walking up to the house. "That's one hardheaded muthafucka! Kayla, keep an eye on her ass."

"I got her in my sights, bro. She good."

I pulled my bitch from my purse and checked the chamber. Staying ready so I didn't have to get ready was my motto. Hopefully, nothing bad happened while my sister was at that door. Kenzie knocked quite a few times without anyone coming to the door, so I decided to get out to stand with her. As I walked up the steps, the door opened, and a nigga stood high as a kite in the doorway.

"Why the fuck y'all banging on this door like that?"

"Well damn, ain't this the dope spot?" Kenzie sassed. "Is Lox here? I've been calling him to cop some weed but he's not answering."

"Nah, Lox ain't here. He was killed the other day, but I can help you with whatever you want."

"Damn, that was my connect. What happened to him?" Kenzie asked.

"Somebody caught him slippin'. That's part of the game. I miss my homie already though. Enough about that shit, How much you trying to get? I got you."

"I need a zip," Kenzie said, with her hand in her purse. The dude turned to leave, and she pulled her gun out of her purse.

"What are you doing? You can't kill him. Just buy the weed and we will come back another day to do this."

Scony agreed and that was the only reason Kenzie stuffed the gun back where she got it from. She removed her hand just in time because the dude came back at that precise moment with the product for us. The dude scratched his nuts through his pants and stared cautiously between both of us. He held the weed out for Kenzie and she made the exchange by slipping money in his palm.

Meesha

"Just so you know, we having a big party for Lox here next Saturday. We are going to turn up for my nigga. Y'all are welcome to come celebrate his life with us. His funeral will be private, because we don't know who the fuck did that shit to him. But the party will be open for everybody."

"We'll be here. Thanks for telling me about Lox. My condolences to his family and all of you guys. What time is the party?"

"Come through about eight in the evening. But, if you need more smoke, we will be back in business shortly after that, but here's my card, hit me up."

Kenzie took the card and we headed back to the car. Soon as we were seated, Scony's voice boomed through the speaker of my phone. "Put the car in gear and get away from here! Kenzie, you almost fucked shit up!"

"I thought the reason we came over here was to kill muthafuckas, Scony. So what, there was only one nigga in the trap. We could've got at the others at a later date."

"That shit wouldn't have worked, because then we wouldn't know where they would be, because they would've closed down shop. You have to think before you react. I'm glad I didn't hang up, because you would've botched the whole damn mission."

"Well, I didn't and now we have time to do whatever the fuck we want. I'm pushing out of this bitch and going home. I don't have time to go back and forth with you about this bullshit I just wasted my time on. Hang up on that nigga, Kay."

Kenzie turned the volume up on the radio and I looked down to see if Scony was still on the phone. He had hung up, so I knew there was going to be some shit once we got back to Kenzie's house. The rest of the ride was just us listening to music as we rode on the highway. Shit was going to hit the fan once Scony gets to her house, and I was going to get my dog and taking my ass home.

Chapter 23

MaKenzie

Kayla acted like she had an attitude about the way I spoke to her brother. There was no way I was going to let him handle me any type of way. I'm not a child and Scony needed to understand, I may be his sister, but I am far from being little. My whole take on the situation was for us to go and get back at the niggas that shot Dreux. That shit didn't happen, because the rest of them wasn't at the trap. What the fuck did that have to do with us? Not a damn thing and nothing was remotely settled, and it was a waste of my fuckin' time.

"Tell me why you really mad, sis," I said, leaning against the wall, watching Kayla stomp around collecting her shit as if I killed that damn dog of hers. It's been a minute since we'd had any type of altercation between the two of us and I was ready for all the shit.

"Your attitude! There has never been a time you've acted on impulse the way you did tonight. Kenzie, if I hadn't stopped you, everything would've gone all wrong. That was Kenzie out there because Storm would never!"

"First of all, Kenzie and Storm are one and the same. You and your brother need to get off my fuckin' back! I was ready to blow that nigga away as planned and y'all stopped that shit. Talking about they would go in hiding, humph, the muthafuckas could've been found again. Hell, if y'all would stop filtering my movements, I can find Heat and Rocko's ass, while everybody sitting twiddling their thumbs. Who's out looking for them? No damn body!"

Scony and the rest of the team walked through the door at that precise moment. By the look on my brother's face, I knew it was about to be me against all them muthafuckas. Kicking the heels off my feet, I stood firm, ready for whatever.

"How you figure nobody's looking for them niggas, Kenzie?" Scony asked with his arms crossed over his chest.

"Where are they, Scony? Nobody has said shit about them, so to me, that's still a problem lingering in the air, right?"

"If you would listen and wait for an update on what's going on, instead of jumping the gun, you would be alright with me. Stone got down on Heat earlier, but we don't know his condition, because the block got hot after the pigs showed up. He couldn't stay around to confirm if the nigga was dead or not."

"I checked at Emory University Hospital to find out if Heat was admitted, he wasn't. Believe me, we're on it," Khaos added his two cents, and I really didn't give a damn about none of that. They were trying to appear as if they were really trying to get at those fools, but I knew better. There was no action, so I wasn't moved at all.

"If Stone shot that nigga, then he should be dead. Y'all need me to get the job done because obviously, my help is needed. But no, *Kenzie, we got it covered. Stay put until we need you.* Muthafuckas, y'all need me now!"

Phantom's eyebrows furrowed as he stepped toward me. I wanted to pull my gun on his ass, but my heart wouldn't allow me to do so. As much as I fought my feelings, I could no longer deny the fact that I loved him.

"Stop this shit right now, Kenzie. You throwing a tantrum because you didn't get the opportunity to pull the trigga. This ain't no fuckin' game! Tonight, wasn't the time to make our move. We will get them, baby," Phantom said, softening his tone.

My heart fluttered and I turned to putty the minute Phantom wrapped his arms around me. I could feel every eye in the room on us and I felt vulnerable. A lonely tear fell down my face and I buried my head deeper into Phantom's chest. To be honest, I didn't even know why I was crying. The shit pissed me off all over again because I showed weakness in front of everyone in the room and that wasn't me. Pushing off Phantom, I put a mug right back on my face and turned as Dino started speaking.

"Baby girl, we will get them niggas. They're walking around on borrowed time."

"Plus, you heard dude say their whole crew would be on Drummond a week from today for Lox's celebration. That's when we will hit 'em. Until then, we can catch up with that nigga Rocko."

Usually, Kayla followed my lead, but I loved how my sister stepped up in my moment of weakness. I could act hard all day, if nobody knew it was an act, my sister surely knew. It was that thing called twin intuition and I was happy to have her by my side. No matter what took place earlier, there was never any real animosity between the two of us.

"Aye, I just got a notification about a shooting near Rocko's crib. What's that nigga's first name?" Khaos asked bringing all the attention his way.

"Darrell Flowers," both Kayla and I said at the same time.

"Man, somebody beat us to the punch. According to this news article, Rocko was shot fifteen times and was pronounced dead on the scene. The pigs are asking for any information on the crime. The way his truck looks in this picture, they lit that muthafucka up without thought. Caught his ass slippin' big time."

"Well, that leaves us with the Black Kings and Heat. Maybe they'll get his ass too," Stone laughed.

"Nah, I want in on that one," Phantom said, kissing my forehead. "In the meantime, I want you to hit up Summer and see what you can find out. Don't move on Heat without consulting with everyone first. You didn't complete that shit today, but we will all get gratification from ending his life next time around. Since there's nothing else for us to do tonight, I don't care where y'all go, but get the hell outta here. I have to make sure my woman is good."

"Nigga, you just trying to fuck! Don't give in to his ass, Kenzie. Let him have blue balls," Scony said.

Everybody laughed as they filed out of my home. Scony looked back me and winked. "I'll see yo' spoiled ass tomorrow. Lunch on me. Love you, sis."

"I love you too, Scony. Please stop coming at me like I won't fuck you up. That's my last time telling you. I won't say a word next time, I'm just gon' knock yo' head off. Now, let me know what time you're feeding me. Oh, I want seafood and steak. You got to come out of pocket for treating me like I'm the little girl you used to chastise back in the day."

Scony laughed and nodded his head. "Whatever you want, sis. I got you. Be easy, Phantom. Give her ass some act-right while you're here. She definitely needs that shit."

***

I was tired as hell after Phantom ate me from asshole to appetite. Keeping my eyes open was a chore in itself as I laid on his chest, tracing his tattoos with my fingertips. Being in an intimate environment with Phantom felt foreign to me. Since the bullshit I endured with Heat, I was never supposed to put my feelings on display for another nigga. Love isn't supposed to live within me anymore.

"What you thinking about, baby?" Phantom asked, caressing my exposed ass cheek.

"To be honest, I don't know why we're lying here as if we are a couple. This is supposed to be a fuck and move situation."

"How do you figure that?" Ph antom shifted his body so we were looking eye-to-eye.

"Phantom, I explained what I wanted in the beginning. This was never supposed to get so deep between us," I said, looking down at the small gap that separated us. He used his finger to lift my chin and forced me to look up at him.

"You are trying hard to fight what is obviously meant to be. I'm not asking you to jump into this shit head-on, Kenzie. All I want you to do is stop fighting the feelings you have for a nigga. It's not a secret that I want to be with you, but what I won't do is pressure you into anything you don't want. I'm also not about to continue to play this cat and mouse game either."

The sincerity in his voice told me his feelings were real. I was afraid to give my heart to a man that could potentially shatter it into pieces. Plus, the shit going on with him and Chanel was part of the reason I was hesitant as well. That bitch and her mouth would have her laid up stankin' somewhere, fuckin' with me.

"So, what's it gon' be? Are we going to keep playing high school ass games, or are we gon' be grown and lay this shit out on the table? I want all of you, Kenzie. Not just yo' pussy, ma. Yo' shit is Grade-A and all, but I can get that shit from any muthafuckin' where. When you came into my life, I left a lot of females alone, because I had my eyes set on yo' fine ass. You've been battling me far too long and it's either gon' stop now or we can go our separate ways. Your choice."

Phantom's phone rang before I could respond to what he said. Reaching over to retrieve his phone from the nightstand, he sighed heavily as he hit the button and placed the phone on speaker. "What is it, Chanel?" Hearing Chanel's name caused an instant attitude and I moved to get out of the bed. Phantom gripped my arm and pulled me back into him.

"I'm calling to inform you about the great news I received earlier today." The excitement in her voice didn't sit well with me and I had a terrible feeling Chanel was about to say something I really didn't want to hear. "Congratulations are in order. We are about to be parents!"

The side of my face was hot as fuck because Kenzie was sending laser like beams my way. Hearing Chanel say we were having a baby had me counting backwards in my head. There wasn't one time I didn't strap up when I was fuckin' her brain loose. I was positive there was not one mishap whatsoever.

"Stop playing, Chanel. If you pregnant, it ain't from me."

"The test doesn't lie and I'm six weeks as of yesterday. You will help provide for our child whether you want to or not, because I'm having my baby!" Chanel screamed through the phone, and that shit only made me laugh at her goofy ass. She was out of her mind if she thought I was about to be happy about a baby I know for a fact I didn't produce. Another baby was something I wanted, but not with her ass.

"Six weeks, huh? Yeah, that ain't my seed. Devin will be happy about the news though. Get the fuck off my phone with that bullshit, Chanel. It's been months since I laid down with you, and I definitely didn't leave shit behind in the process."

"This is your baby, Xavier! Stop playing in my face, nigga! What you not gon' do—"

"Nah, what you not gon' do is continue to talk to him like he's a goofy!" Kenzie said, interrupting Chanel's tirade. "You want him in your life so bad that you're willing to pin a baby on him. Shit not gon' work because I'm only playing step mama to one and that's Layla. So, if you're really pregnant, we'll see yo' ass when you ready to run that muthafuckin' test. Until then, don't hit this line no more or yo' ass will have to see me!"

I ended the call and put an abrupt stop to the back-and-forth bickering. Phantom grabbed a blunt from my stash and flamed up. I couldn't do nothing but chuckle as I wiggled out of the hold he still had on my frame. Slipping my feet into the slippers by the bed, I turned to go to the bathroom. Phantom got up and opened the window as he sat on the ottoman as he tapped his fingers on his thigh.

"This bitch got him wondering if he skeeted and shit. Blunt in the left tapping with the right and he wanna know. He don't know, he don't know. She got him out here, smoking out the window."

"That shit ain't funny, bae. That bitch crazy as fuck if she thinks I'm about to fall for the okey doke."

"It is funny because you shouldn't have been fuckin' with the bitch in the first place. Once you put a bitch in the trash bin, that's where the fuck she should've stayed. That's what you get for trying to recycle these hoes while pursuing me."

"Had you not been trying to be a whole nigga with me, maybe I'd be engaged by now," he huffed.

I entered my bedroom and saw a vein was protruding from his neck because his jaw was clenched tightly. Phantom took a long pull from the blunt and he held the smoke in his lungs for what seemed like forever. The frustration was evident in his facial features, and I felt kind of sorry for him. Not really though.

"I wasn't being anything with you. Protecting you in case you decided to play games with my heart was more like it. In case you haven't noticed, I'm a killer and I will kill your ass while riding your dick into the sunset."

Licking his lips, he looked over at me through slitted eyes while squeezing his member through his basketball shorts. "That shit just made my shit brick up. Bring yo' thuggish, sexy ass over here and demonstrate that tough shit for me."

When Phantom unleashed the dragon, all thoughts of him hurting me went right out the window along with the smoke. My pussy made the decision for me when she drooled down my inner thigh while her little ass jumped around excitedly. I couldn't lie, seeing the precum grace the tip of his dick, made my mouth water.

"Yeah, wake him all the way up. I gotta show y'all what it's like to belong to Storm. I hope you ready because this shit is about to change your life," I smirked.

Meesha

Chapter 24

Summer

"Your wound is leaking. I'll call for the nurse." Reaching over to push the call button, Heat grabbed my hand, shaking his head.

"I don't want them muthafuckas in here, Summer! They're acting like I'm dying or some shit. All I want is to go the fuck home. I'm killin' that nigga, I swear. He knows firsthand to kill or be killed!"

I'd been sitting by Heat's side since I received a call about him being admitted into Piedmont Atlanta Hospital. Wasting no time, I hauled ass to make sure he was alright. Even though he'd been on some fuck shit as of late, I still cared if something was wrong with him. After he beat the fuck outta me, one would've thought I'd leave him to fend for himself. I couldn't bring myself to turn my back on him that way. According to the doctor, he was lucky he had on a bulletproof vest. They were trying to alert the police, but Heat came up with a story about being a private investigator or some shit.

Heat was hit in the right arm and shoulder. The other four bullets were stopped by the vest and one could've gone into the side of his chest, had the vest not prevented it from going through. The way he was snapping at me, I wished whoever shot his lying ass would've hit him in the head.

"Who was shooting at you, Romero?"

"Stay out of my fuckin' business! The less you know, the better. Just know, I'm going after him and I won't miss," he snapped. "I'm tired of muthafuckas coming for me and my crew. First it was Loco, now Rocko! Nah, this shit ain't gon' fly another muthafuckin' day!"

"Rocko is dead," I muttered to myself, but obviously he heard me.

"Yeah, they killed my nigga the night my fuckin' club burned to the ground. After getting shot, I know for a fact Phantom was behind that shit."

I didn't know what Heat was into, but there was a lot he was keeping to himself. In order for him to suspect Phantom, he did something to that man and it went further than Kenzie's bitch ass. He must've forgotten muthafuckas was saying he killed Brando. That was probably a hit for that, and he was concentrating on Phantom.

"Heat, did it ever occur to you maybe it was the Brando guy's people that tried to end your life?" I was asking a serious question and the way his face scrunched up let me know he was about to be on some more disrespectful shit.

"I'm not going to tell you again to stay out of my business! Don't ask me shit else, Summer!"

Shaking my head, I sat back in the chair and pulled my phone out. I zoned out while playing bingo on an app I'd found to pass time. Opting to keep quiet, because if I responded to his mood swings, I was going to clock his ass upside his head. Heat didn't know he was skating on thin ice, and I wasn't going to be hanging around for him to treat me like I was a nobody. There were a few rapid knocks on the door before it eased open slowly. Both me and Heat's heads turned to see who was entering.

"Mr. Ramirez, how are you feeling?" Dr. Grey asked, walking further into the room with a folder in his hand. Heat mugged him as a response. "Okayyy. Well, I have a few prescriptions here for you," he said, handing the papers to me. "I also have instructions on how to care for your wounds. It's very important—"

"Are you about to send me home?" Heat barked, cutting the man off. "If so, save all that shit for the next muthafucka 'cause I'm not trying to hear it."

Dr. Grey started shifting from one foot to the other. I glared at the rude muthafucka that was now sitting on the edge of the bed. What he had done was uncalled for.

"Your discharge papers are right here. I hope you get well soon and make an appointment for a follow-up in two weeks. You can leave when you're ready."

Dr. Grey spoke fast, giving me the indication that he was nervous. Heat was wrong, but deep down, I wanted to laugh my ass off. The doctor snapped his mouth closed before turning to leave. All I could do was get up and walked across the room to get the clothes I brought for the asshole, from the cubby across the room.

"Here, get dressed since you're in such a rush to leave this damn hospital. The least you could've done was heard the man out. It was for your better good and you just had to be disrespectful. One thing you need to understand, didn't nobody put you here, except you and the nigga that shot you. You're mad at the wrong muthafuckas!"

"Summer, shut the fuck up before I put my foot in yo' ass! Don't let this discomfort I'm in fool you. I'll endure the pain and pop a pill after fuckin' you up to get back on track. I'm still the same nigga," he snarled.

"Whatever. Instead of being mean as fuck, you should be kissing my ass for even being here with you. If you don't do anything else, appreciate and respect me. If not, leave me the fuck alone and go about your way. The last thing I need is disrespect from a nigga I held down through all the bullshit brought my way!" I said, walking to the door. "I'll be out front in my car. Have one of those thirsty ass nurses to bring yo' ass down!"

I was tired of Heat's bullshit. Had my blood boiling from the way he was acting, let alone how he was talking to me. Soon as I sat in my car, a text came through on my phone and I instantly smiled when I saw Savon's name on the screen. I pulled in front of the entrance before I opened the text thread.

Savon: Hey, beautiful. What's good with you?

See, that was the exact reason Savon had my nose wide open, and why I was on the verge of leaving Heat alone for good. He always found a few seconds to simply ask how I was doing and called me beautiful every time. I didn't get that from Romero Ramirez.

Me: Nothing. Dealing with some things at the moment. How about you?

Savon: I'm chillin' Still stuck in your city dealing with business. I want to see you. Make it happen.

Meesha

My girl did a happy dance as I read his words. My mood changed when the passenger door was pulled open. I quickly closed the text and put my phone between my legs after flipping the switch to silence the device. I watched as a male nurse helped Heat into the car. The way he glared at me was an indication he was still pissed about me defending myself in the hospital room.

"You one selfish bitch," he barked once he was completely seated. "You could've got out and helped a nigga. It's all good, just take me to the crib. Don't think I didn't see you smiling all in your phone. That's why you didn't see me until I opened the muthafuckin' door."

Putting the car in gear, I didn't even bother putting him in the seatbelt before pulling off. I hit my playlist and Summer Walker's "Switch A Nigga," started playing. Savon came to mind and I sang, switching the words up to let the nigga sitting next to me know his time was up.

The drive was awkward because I didn't know if Heat would haul off and knock my shit against the window while I was driving. I turned the music up just in case he got the notion to talk shit. Best believe, I kept my eye on his ass often as possible. My phone was vibrating between my thighs, and I knew without a doubt it was Savon. "Unloyal" came on and I sang that shit with my soul.

I ain't takin' yo shit today, no
I ain't takin' yo' shit tomorrow, no
We can do it my way, so
I ain't stickin' no
No, I ain't stickin' 'round no mo
'Cause you just wanna play with my heart and, oh
I seen you with the girl at the party, oh
You think I'm just gon' stand on by
And watch you waste my time
Boy I am way too fine
So, I'm out

"Don't let Summer Walker get you fucked up. Find somebody else to play with. Whoever the nigga is that fucked you and turned yo' ass into a retard, get rid of him! There's no leaving nor replacing Heat, baby. You gon' fuck around and get that man killed. Stop playing with his life like that," he laughed as I pulled into his driveway. Heat reached for the door, and I didn't budge, because going inside wasn't part of my plans. A real nigga wanted to see me, and I was going.

"Why you still sitting there? Get the fuck out!"

"I have something to do. I'm not going—"

"You don't got shit to do! Bring yo' ass on, Summer. I won't repeat myself either," he yelled as he got out.

"Don't you need your prescription filled? I can go put it in at the pharmacy, after I get you in the house comfortably." I was trying anything possible to get away from him and into the arms of Savon.

"I already have my damn pills. They filled that shit while I was struggling to get dressed, since you left with an attitude."

"The way you talk to me is the reason you were fending for yourself. What I said still stands, you will respect me. Period!"

Turning the key to cut the engine, I opened the door and stalked to his front door. Even with me standing in his space, I refused to help him. He was the big bad fuckin' wolf, he could make that shit shake on his own. Playing with my top is something he wasn't going to keep doing. All that aggression should've been present when he was in that jam while he was getting shot at.

Heat struggled a little bit as he came up the steps. I held my hand out for his keys and he mugged the hell out of me. Chuckling lowly, I stood to the side while he fumbled with the keys, trying to insert it with his left hand. Snatching that shit out of his hand I unlocked the door and pushed it open waving him inside. Once I crossed the threshold, I stood to the side until he was completely inside the house. Heat went straight to his bedroom, and I sat on the sofa in the living room.

"Summer, come here," he called out.

I sighed and climbed the stairs very slowly. Standing in the doorway, I crossed my arms over my chest and waited for whatever he needed from me. Heat was having a hard time getting his shirt over his head and I laughed on the inside, because now his ass needed my assistance, after talking down to me. After a few minutes, I couldn't watch him struggle any longer. I walked across the room and assisted with lifting the shirt over his head and eased his arm, which was in a sling, from under it. He flinched and started breathing heavily, which caused me to dig in the bag for his medication.

"Here, take this," I said, handing him the pill I'd shaken into my hand.

"I'm not taking that shit, Summer! All I do is sleep when I take those pills, and I got shit to do." He sat on the edge of the bed and toed off his shoes. "Fix me something to eat and bring back some orange juice."

"You couldn't even pull your shirt over your head. I think you should rest for the day and go out and do whatever tomorrow."

Rolling my eyes after he didn't respond to what I said, I place the pill bottle on the nightstand and walked out the room. While his grumpy ass was trying to be the ruler over me, I was about to drop his ass off into a deep sleep. Smiling all the way to the kitchen with the Vicodin still in my hand, I went straight to the refrigerator and got his juice. Crushing the pills very fine on top of wax paper with the meat tenderizer, I poured the powdery substance into the glass and stirred slowly. He was going to take the medicine whether he wanted to or not.

I whipped up a double cheeseburger with mayo, tomato, and lettuce, with a side of seasoned fries. That would hold him over until dinner. I cut the burger in half so it would be easier for him to pick up, since his right arm was in a sling. Walking back to the room, my phone started ringing as I put the tray on Heat's lap. The food he'd demanded wasn't his focal point at that time. He was too busy shooting daggers at me as I typed out a text to Savon.

"I know muthafuckin' well you not standing in my house texting another nigga!"

"Eat yo' food so you can go wherever you're going, Romero. You're worried about the wrong shit. You should be sitting there trying to figure out how you're going to avoid getting shot again."

Taking a bite of his burger, Heat drank half of the orange juice and looked at the glass then over at me. "This juice tastes funny."

"It's probably because I didn't shake it before I poured it in the glass. Ain't nothing wrong with it."

"Come drink some then," he barked.

I got right up and went over to the side of the bed and reached out for the glass. He must've thought I was going to hesitate, but I was on to his ass. "You about to go night-night, nigga. I got a dick to ride, and it won't be yours," I said to myself.

Instead of giving me the glass, he drank the rest of it and took another bite of his burger. Within a ten-minute span, he'd yawned about six times, and I kept checking the time on my phone. It was a matter of time before he would be knocked the fuck out. Turning the TV on, I started watching *The First 48* and didn't pay him any more attention. When the first episode went off, Heat was snoring like a grizzly bear. I shouldn't have given him both pills but fuck it. Taking the plate and glass in the kitchen, I texted Savon.

Me: Where are you?

Savon: I'm still in the same hotel. You know all you need to know.

That's all I needed to hear. Checking on Heat one more time, I covered him with a sheet and grabbed my purse. I had a date with a big dick nigga, and I was going to enjoy the ride.

Meesha

Chapter 25

Stone

There was a series of soft knocks on my hotel door as I wrapped the towel around my waist. Summer texted, asking where I was, so that meant she was finished with whatever she had to do for the day. Waiting on her ass to deal with that nigga and his gunshot wounds had me on edge. I was mad as fuck because I was a thorough nigga and never missed my target. Heat was going to die, and that shit was going down that very day.

Opening the door, Summer was met with my lil nigga standing at attention under the towel. Her thirsty ass eyed my shit while licking those juicy lips of hers. She looked good in the simple fitted t-shirt and jeans, but what I had in mind for her went beyond getting my dick wet.

"Glad you could join me," I said, stepping to the side so she could enter.

"I'm sorry about the delay, I had to make sure my dude was okay before I left." Summer hugged and kissed me on the cheek before walking deeper into the room.

"Is he cool?" I asked, not really giving a fuck.

"For the most part yes. I've been sitting in the hospital with him the last two days, but he's home resting now." She laughed as she sat on the edge of the bed. "I had to dope his ass up in order to leave. I was tired of his attitude anyway. There's not much time so, can I taste the rainbow that's under that towel? He looks like he's happy to see me."

Without thought, I made my way over to where she'd assumed the position on the floor, and let the towel drop at my feet. Summer wasted no time devouring my meat and I instantly cupped the back of her head, forcing her to take him all in. Her wet mouth was soothing my member with ease and the shit felt good as fuck. Guilt of cheating on Angel surfaced and I pushed it to the back of my mind because this shit was business.

The slurping sound of Summer bobbing on my dick bounced off the walls, damn near making me bust prematurely. I stepped back and her lips popped as I took the candy away from her. She pouted and I smirked as I retrieved a condom from the nightstand drawer.

"Get naked and put that ass in the air," I said lowly.

Summer was out of her clothes quick as hell and assumed the position. Her twat glistened as I slid my thumb up and down her slit. She purred like a cat and arched her back the moment I slipped my thumb into her asshole.

"Mmmmm, yes," she moaned.

"That's what you want, beautiful?" I asked, smacking her cheek.

"I want you to fuck me, Savon."

"Say less."

I rolled the condom over my python and dove in deep. Heat wasn't hitting on shit because her pussy was tight and wet, just waiting for a nigga like me to run up in it. Gripping her thick hips, I stroked her with hard thrusts that broke her all the way down.

"Where you goin'? Bring that ass back here!" I barked, running my hand up the spine of her back. She was perspiring from the heated session we were enduring. My member tried to soften from the thoughts that ran through my mind, but I put a stop to it. I was going to enjoy this wet shit for the last muthafuckin' time.

"Come put in this work, ma."

Sitting on the edge of the bed, I waited patiently for Summer to gather the strength to come to me. She climbed right on my hardness and moved back and forth until he was able to roam freely through her sugary walls. I held her cheeks as I rocked her slowly. She tried to kiss me, and I automatically turned my head, giving her my cheek.

"Oh, shit! You feel so good, baby," Summer moaned wrapping her arms around my neck. "You trying to make me love you."

That shit wasn't going to happen. She could keep thinking it was the direction we were heading though. Summer would find out soon enough that dancing with the devil was never the solution to any of the problems she was trying to escape.

We came simultaneously together, and I allowed her to linger in my lap until her heartbeat slowed. Tapping her on the thigh, I said, "Let's get cleaned up. I want to take you somewhere special before you have to head back to your situation."

"What if I don't give a damn about him? What if I tell you I'm ready to leave to give us a try?" she asked without moving.

Her body was so relaxed in my arms and without looking I knew her eyes were closed, waiting on my response. I slipped my hand into the same drawer I kept the condoms. My hand gripped my Glock and I pressed it to the side of her head.

"Sorry, sweetie. That will never be. It was not part of my plan." She sat up abruptly with fear in her eyes.

"Wh-wha-what are you doing, Savon? What do you mean, that wasn't part of the plan?" she asked in a shaky voice.

Pushing her off my lap, Summer fell on the floor, but was back on her feet right away. Her eyes moved around the room as if she was trying to plan her escape.

"Don't try to run. I will shoot yo' ass before you fully turn. Heat is the reason I sought you out. The nigga has been hiding long enough and you about to take me to his ass."

"You used me?" Tears filled her eyes, and I didn't have an ounce of remorse for what I'd done and what I was going to do later.

"I used you with good intentions on my part. Not so much yours. Fuck it, get dressed. You don't need to wash your ass," I said, standing up. "All you got to do is lead the way and you will be free to go about your merry way. I want Heat, baby girl. No one else. If you do that without incident, you will live. Fight me in any type of way, and you will die alongside that nigga. Did you ask him if he knew who shot him?"

"I asked and he said it was Phantom."

I laughed at that shit because Heat knew exactly who shot his ass. "Nah. Phantom didn't have anything to do with that. It was all me and he knows that too. Heat tried to kill me and didn't succeed.

Meesha

I did the same and my mission wasn't accomplished, but it will be today. Put yo' muthafuckin' clothes on!" I snarled. "You will take me to this nigga, right?"

"I don't want to be involved," she cried.

"But you already smack dab in the middle of all his shit. Heat should've warned you about the niggas out here in these grimy ass streets. Especially, if he's out here doing dirt. His woman should've been protected and untouchable to a muthafucka like myself. There's no way I should've been able to get close to you. When that pussy nigga went into hiding, you should've been right beside him. Instead, he was hiding my bitch and fuckin' the shit out of her, while you were fuckin' and suckin' on me."

"He did what?" The tears dried up fast and turned to anger.

"You heard what I said. Enough of this shit. Hurry up so we can go. You can confront that nigga when we get to him."

I dressed while still holding my tool on Summer's ass. She was so mad I don't think she was scared anymore. Hearing that Heat was bangin' another bitch put the fire under her ass, and she was willing to throw him into the pits of hell herself.

"You can put the gun down. I'm going to take you to his slimy ass with no problem. I don't give a fuck what you do to him at this point."

Snatching my keys from the table, I tucked my gun and grabbed Summer by the arm and left out the door. We made it to my car, and I waited until she was strapped in, before I sent a text for someone to pick her car up and burn it. Summer wouldn't be needing any means of transportation where she was headed.

When we arrived at the two-story house, I pulled my tool, screwed on the silencer, and got out. Summer climbed the stairs, and I was right on her ass. Soon as she opened the door, that nigga's voice met her before she could get in good.

"I hope the dick you were ridin' was worth your life, bitch! Didn't I tell you not to leave this muthafucka?" Heat appeared in the hall hot as fuck. That shit changed when he was met by the barrel of my Glock.

"That's how you lost her, nigga! Your choice of words is a muthafucka," I laughed. "Get yo' ass over there with him." I pushed Summer in his direction.

"I knew this was the nigga that had yo' stupid ass under a spell!" Heat moved to his right and reached. That's as far as he got, because I hit him with some hot shit, right in his kneecap.

"Yeah, that dick had her ass losing her mind. How does it feel to be on the other end of the gun, nigga? See, I'm true about my shit. I don't need to send a flunky ass muthafucka to do my dirty work. I'm about to finish what I started the other day. I just got one question. Why bite the hand that was feeding yo' greedy ass?"

"Fuck you, Stone!" Heat said through the pain.

"Nah, Summertime already took care of me. Plus, niggas ain't never on my radar," I said, hitting his ass again in the same leg.

"Arggggh!"

"I don't want to witness this," Summer cried. "Please, can I just leave? I can't handle any more of this."

"Sure, you can leave," I said, turning the gun toward her. "In a body bag."

Pew

The bullet went straight through her head and out through her lace front. Summer's body fell with a thud, and I didn't blink twice. But I was going to miss that pussy I just killed, literally.

"Fuck! Summer, I'm so sorry, baby. I brought this shit to your doorstep. Believe it or not, I loved you the only way I knew how."

"Tell her that shit on the other side, nigga! Tell the devil I said hello," I smiled sinisterly as I emptied my clip into his face.

Pulling my phone out, I sent a text for Scony to send someone to clean this shit up. I couldn't leave them here, especially with my DNA on Summer's tongue.

Chapter 26

Phantom

"Daddy!" Layla smiled as I entered the hospital room. I'd only been away from my baby girl for a few hours, but to her it was a lifetime.

"Hey, Daddy's baby. These are for you," I said, handing her the dozen pink roses I picked up from the florist on the way back to the hospital. "Are you ready to dominate this therapy session?"

"I am, but I'm so ready to go home," she pouted.

"Guess what? You are going home today, munchkin. You can finally heal back at my house. How does that sound?" I asked as I sat on the edge of the bed.

"Thank God! The food here is terrible and plus, my bed feels way better than this bed."

"Lawd, Lay, you are truly a princess. We will be getting you out of here soon as possible."

Layla flared her arms in the air as me and my mama laughed at her.

My mind was strictly on my baby because after getting the call about Stone killing Heat and Summer, I was preparing myself mentally to ride down on the Black Kings. Even though I was lowkey pissed I didn't participate in Heat's demise, I was anxious to kill some muthafuckin' body before everything was said and done. It then dawned on me that Tiff was still in the rotation and my heart started thumping in my chest. The hardest thing I would ever have to do is kill the mother of my child.

A knock on the door brought me back to reality and the transportation employee entered the room. "Miss Layla, you ready for your session today? I heard you've been handling your business while I was off."

"Todd! I've missed you. Yeah, I've been killin' the game. I can't be stopped!" Layla was so excited and that alone warmed my heart. My baby was growing up right before my eyes and being cooped up in the hospital can bring anyone's spirit down, but not her. The staff was superb when it came to Layla and my family was the truth.

"That's what I like to hear. Okay, I'm ready when you are. Let's do this," Todd said with a smile.

At that precise moment, Kenzie entered looking like the sexiest woman on earth, at least in my eyes. She had on simple get-up. A black pair of distressed jeggings, a green "Married to Tha Pen" shirt she copped from her favorite author Meesha, and a fresh pair of green Chucks. Her hair was pulled into a messy bun, and her plump lips had my mans doing a happy dance.

I'd been trying to drill a hole in her pussy ever since she agreed to be my woman. Kenzie had a nigga happy as fuck, but she was still hesitant about being in a relationship. Chanel had a lot to do with that, because her professional ass wanted to continue being petty.

"Kenzie, you're here! I've missed you so much," Layla squealed.

"Now you should've known I wouldn't let you down, pretty girl. Today is the day you will show up and show out more than ever. We gotta get ice cream wasted when you get home."

Layla smiled and looked at Todd. "I'm ready."

I lifted my baby into the wheelchair and stepped back as Todd pushed her out of the room. My mother was right behind her, while I stole a few kisses from Kenzie. Squeezing her ass, I pushed my wood against her stomach and nibbled on her ear.

"Move your nasty ass out the way and get out of this room," she blushed.

"Soon as we get Layla situated, I have something for you," I grinned. "I can't get enough of you, baby. Who told you to have that good shit between yo' legs? You mine now, and if I wanted to take you right here, I have that right." Biting her neck one last time, I finally let her escape out the room.

An hour later, Layla was exhausted from her session, and we were waiting for the doctor to release her. I watched as Kenzie dressed her as if she was a newborn baby. The love she showed my daughter brought tears to my eyes, because it should've been

Tiff taking care of our daughter. Instead, her monkey ass did what she did and ran. Tiff had no intentions of coming back and I was going to make sure she never returned, without remorse. The dread of killing her evaporated into thin air as the day she hit my baby replayed in my mind.

Layla was still sleeping in my arms when we entered my home. I took her straight to bed while my mama went to the kitchen to whip up a feast. Kenzie was lying across my bed with her eyes closed and I eased in right beside her. Slipping my arm under her head, I pulled her into my chest and kissed the top of her head. She didn't budge and I knew she was tired. My phone vibrated on my hip, and I maneuvered to grab it before it stopped ringing.

"What is it, Chanel?" I asked, closing my eyes.

"I want to apologize for bringing drama to your life. Xavier, you are the only man that has ever cared about me in a way only you could. I fucked up what we had and when you left me alone, I was broken. Telling you I was pregnant was my way of having you in my life forever, but that would never happen. I am pregnant, but it's not yours. I'm having a baby by a man that will never love me the way I want."

"We could've had an everlasting friendship, Chanel. Your attitude changed that, ma. You may not want to hear this, but I'm with the woman I love. There will never be a woman after her. This is it for me. I wish you nothing but the best. Allow that man to love you and give that shit your all."

"But I want you, Xavier!" Chanel screamed.

"And he just told your pinhead ass make that shit work with the nigga that knocked you up! Bitch, I gave him the opportunity to close this chapter of his life, without opening my mouth. You pushing it, hoe. I can make your gullible ass disappear, if you don't move the fuck around. I'm being nice right now, but I still owe yo' stupid ass a round. If you knew what was good for you, calling this number wouldn't be in your future plans."

Storm ended the call and that shit turned me the fuck on. My bitch was gutta with it and I loved that shit. Tossing the phone to the side, I hoovered over her and kissed her deeply. The fire in her eyes dissipated and Kenzie came back into the world of the living. When she was mad, Storm came out instantaneously. I was about to fuck the shit out of Kenzie though. I didn't think I stood a chance sticking my dick in Storm. She would give me a run for my muthafuckin' money and I wasn't having that shit.

Making my way down her body, I pulled her pants along with me as I licked my lips. Seeing she didn't on any panties bricked a nigga up quick. It felt like that muthafucka was trying to bust a hole through my jeans fighting his way out. He had to wait because I needed some of her sweet nectar to soothe the dryness in my throat.

I parted her lower lips and blew on her pearl. It peeked out at me the moment my breath hit the tip. Running my tongue along her folds, I wrapped my lips around it and sucked like my life depended on it. Kenzie's hands grasped the back of my head and forced me deeper into her honey pot.

"Yes, just like that," she moaned, grinding into my mouth.

My eyes closed as I savored her taste and fell in love all over again. The sweet taste of pineapple landed on my tongue, making me swallow every drop. As I hummed, Kenzie wrapped her legs around my neck, cutting off my air supply for a minute. I reached up and grabbed both her legs without missing a beat and folded them muthafuckas over her head. She was open for me to do any and everything to that pretty pussy. I went to work on her ass, making her scream out in pleasure.

"Oh, shit! Phantom, your mama is downstairs," she moaned as she fucked my mouth with everything in her.

"She knows what time it is. I'm a nasty muthafucka and this my shit, what she gon' do, whoop me?" I smirked as I went back to the platter before me.

Kenzie took over with holding her legs, so I took that opportunity to stick my thumb in her ass before clasping down on her treasure box. "That feels so good, baby. Don't stop!" She rocked her ass on my thumb, and I wished that shit was my dick. I hadn't tried anal with her and didn't think she was going to go for it.

Savage Storms 3

Playing in her sacred hole for a few, I decided to try my luck since I'd got that ass ready for me. It was well lubricated, and I had to see what it would do for me.

Easing up, I stood from the bed and got out of my clothes quickly. Standing with my dick at attention, I turned her onto her stomach and pulled her toward the edge of the bed. Kenzie arched her back to perfection and the roundness of her ass reminded me I'd missed a spot. I ran my tongue between her cheeks and put in work eating her ass. The way she clutched the sheets and cried out in pleasure, made a nigga proud. Kenzie was getting the ultimate sex package from me that day and I had no plans of stopping anytime soon.

"Fuck! What are you trying to do to me?" she asked, out of breath.

"I'm lovin' you in every way imaginable. There are no boundaries to this shit, Kenzie. Ain't no other nigga gon' catch yo' eye after the way I plan to nail you to the cross," I said, coming up for air.

My nose was glazed with her secretions and that shit smelled like heaven. I rubbed my member along her crack, and she tensed up. "Relax, beautiful. I got this." Moving slowly, I lined my tip up with her hole and pushed in slowly. The way Kenzie was breathing almost caused me to abort the mission. Then she pushed back, and that asshole popped, causing me to grip her hips as my fingers dug in deeply. My toes threw up every gang sign known to the streets.

"Oh yeah, that's what the fuck I'm talkin' 'bout," I growled, letting her take over. Kenzie was working my dick like she owned it, which she did at that point. I let lil mama do her thang, and I felt like a virgin getting fucked for the very first time. Her asshole was tight, and it had my tool in a death grip. My nut was building fast, and I didn't want to bust just yet.

I went back to pleasuring her pussy and caused her to collapse onto the bed. "Bring that ass back over here, Kenzie. Ain't no running allowed in our house. You know better," I said, tapping her leg.

Meesha

"I can't take that shit, Phantom! Keep your mouth off me and give me that dick, nigga!" She turned my way and crawled over to me seductively like an exotic cat. "As a matter of fact, let me even the fuckin' score 'round this bitch."

Before I could do anything, my wood disappeared down her throat and I literally saw stars. Fuck a Gawk-Gawk 3000, I got MaKenzie "Storm" muthafuckin' Jones in this bitch! There's not one bitch on God's green earth that has ever had me singing harmony from a blow job.

"Kenzie! Suck that shit, baby. I love you so much." She looked up at me with her lips wrapped around my meat and I let loose down her throat. I had tears in my eyes, and I couldn't do shit but fall to the side on the bed. When I say I was paralyzed from the waist down, I couldn't feel shit but the shivers that went up and down my spine.

***

Kenzie drained a nigga and we both fell asleep after I broke her ass down worse than she did me. She was snoring like a grizzly bear when I opened my eyes and looked at the time. Hours had passed and I went to the bathroom to freshen up before facing my mother. No matter what she had to say about the noise, what I'd experienced was well worth it.

As I descended the stairs, the aroma of fried catfish, spaghetti, and cornbread was in the air. Heading to the kitchen, my mama's voice stopped me in my tracks. She was sitting in the living room on the sofa as Layla slept on the loveseat. The TV was on some *True Crime* shit and the look in my mother's eyes said all I needed to know. She was pissed.

"Xavier, I don't give a damn if this is your house. You are a father and have a daughter that now lives here with you. I'm going to need you to practice silence, because the shit I heard earlier was uncalled for. You were killing that poor girl up there. Not to mention, she brought out your falsetto as well." My mama laughed lowly after saying that and I felt my face get hot as volcano magma.

"I'm sorry you had to witness my madness, Ma. Kenzie brings the beast out of me. Layla is sleeping so I'm quite sure she didn't hear anything."

"Nah, Daddy. I heard you up there cussing and fussing at Kenzie. It's not nice for you to talk to her like that. It was mean and I think you hurt her feelings. You have to go out and buy her something to make her happy again."

Layla said all of that while her eyes were closed. Me and my mama laughed, and I was even more embarrassed since I knew my daughter heard me beating up the pussy too. It was a good thing she didn't understand the dynamics of sex, or I would've been fucked. My mama gave me the side eye and I just shrugged my shoulders. What else could I have done? Not shit.

"Oh, and Daddy. Don't ever tell Mama Kenzie you will nail her to the cross. Those men did that to Jesus and he died. I don't want her to die. Go nail my real mama to the cross for hitting me with that car."

Layla mumbled the last part, but I heard her clear as day. Little did she know, she had just put the final call on Tiff's life and that shit was a wrap. My mama had a look of pity on her face for Layla, but I was gonna make her thoughts true and there wasn't going to be a trace of Tiffany left for anybody to find. Kenzie came bouncing down the steps, looking like Calgon had taken her away. I knew it was me that put that extra pep in her step, and it made me smile.

"Hey, Kimille. You got it smelling good down here," she said, hugging my mom as she stood to her feet.

"I bet it smell better than that room you just left out of. Y'all two nasty muthafuckas. Keep that shit behind closed doors next time," she whispered into Kenzie's ear. Her face turned beet red at the words my mama spoke. "Come on so we can eat. Layla, you hungry, baby?"

"My legs hurt. I need something for the pain, Granny."

"Okay, you have to eat a little bit first, then I will give you some medicine."

While they prepared the plates, I went upstairs and grabbed my phone. I hit up the crew to meet me at the spot Tiffany was being held in. She had to go and there was no better time than tonight. We arranged to meet in an hour to get that shit over with.

Chapter 27

Tiffany

I'd been sitting in a house for days after Tim scooped me up from the hotel. I rode in the trunk for hours and didn't know where the hell he'd taken me. There was no way for me to get out, because the door was deadbolted from the outside and the windows had bars on them. It wasn't the best place to live, but at least I had a rundown couch and a decent bed to sleep in. With the noodles in the kitchen, I was able to eat and wouldn't starve, so I couldn't really complain.

Being alone gave me the opportunity to think about what I'd done to my child out of spite. It was wrong and I wished I could go back in time, but the shit was over and done. Phantom arranged to have me here and I knew it was a matter of time before he would show his face to address what happened on that dreadful day. Had he not been all in that bitch's face, we wouldn't be where we were. His ass was partially to blame too.

The sun had gone down long ago, and I was preparing myself for another restless night of listening to the squeaks of the rats that shared the space with me. Keeping the lights on gave me some type of hope of them not getting too close to me. Hell, I left some noodles on the floor for their asses so they wouldn't think twice about fucking with me at any point in time. I was sitting on the edge of the sunken mattress when I heard the front door open. My body tensed up, because my soul told me tonight was going to be the last one I'd endure.

A handsome man with long locs appeared in the doorway, with a grim expression on his face. Under different circumstances, I would've taken a shot at getting to know him better. That shit wouldn't happen because if he knew where I was, that meant he was on Phantom's team and he was sent to teach me a lesson. My baby daddy didn't have the guts to kill me on his own, so he sent someone else to do the job.

"Get yo' ass up and come in the other room. I heard you like to hit little girls with cars and shit," he barked. Opening my mouth to speak, I was cut off abruptly. "Don't say shit, just move!"

Jumping to my feet, I rushed to the door and was pushed forward. I stumbled until I gathered my bearings by grabbing the knob on a closet door. When I looked up, I was looking into the deathly eyes of none other than Xavier Bennett. He stood at his full capacity with his arms folded over his chest as that bitch stood by his side. Why she was there was beyond me. Kenzie didn't have shit to do with none of this shit and the problem was between me and Phantom alone.

Everyone in the room was looking at me as if I was contaminated with a deadly virus or something. To be honest, I wasn't afraid. Whatever was going to happen, I was ready for it. Before I left this earth, I was going to get my one-on-one with Kenzie though. That was a fact.

"Why the fuck you bring this bitch here? If you're going to beat my ass for what I did, you didn't need an audience, Phantom." Yup, I was pushing buttons from jump. I was never leaving the dump I was in alive anyway. Why not? "The bitch wanted to be me from the beginning, and she finally took you and my damn daughter from me."

"First of all, nobody took me from shit. Secondly—" Kenzie placed her hand on Phantom's forearm as she shook her head vigorously as she stepped toward me.

"Nah, you don't have to explain shit to this bird ass bitch. See, you never had him," she said, pointing her thumb behind her back at Phantom. "As far as your daughter is concerned, you didn't love that little girl from day one. The gig is up, bitch. We read your fuckin' journal and you were plottin' long before you hit your daughter with your car. You are one poor excuse for a mother and deserve everything that's coming to yo' whack ass."

This bitch kept creeping closer to me, so I drew back and rocked her ass. I was stunned because her head swiveled to the side, but when she looked at me, she had turned into a completely different person. The punch didn't faze her at all, and she reached out and clutched my throat in a firm grip. Clawing at her hands, I couldn't get her to release the hold she had on me for nothing. Kenzie was strong as fuck to be so tiny.

"You know you're dying tonight, right? Beating your ass will defeat the purpose, because you ain't even worth me breaking a nail. See, your baby daddy wants to know why you did what you did to our daughter. Me on the other hand, really don't give a fuck about why, because jealousy sealed your fate."

I mustered up enough strength and gawked a glob of spit in her face. Kenzie hit me with a left hook and my face went numb from the blow. She never let my neck go and I was on the verge of passing out. Blood seeped down my throat as I tried my best to stay alert. Finally letting me go, I staggered backwards and charged at her. No one moved to stop what was happening and I knew I'd fucked up. Kenzie lifted her foot and kicked me square in my chest, knocking the wind out of me. Falling to the floor hitting my tailbone, I looked into Phantom's eyes, and he didn't come to my rescue. Reaching behind her back, Kenzie pointed a gun in my direction and all my bodily fluids left my body.

"Bitch, you are out of your mind. You had a chance to tell your side of the story, but at this point the shit doesn't even matter. Layla has a woman that will love her unconditionally and will have no problem sharing her father's love. Have fun in hell, you slimy muthafucka."

There was a loud bang and I felt life leaving my body slowly, as I laid back with my blood oozing out of my chest. Layla's face appeared before my eyes, and I regretted ever doing her wrong. Nothing Kenzie said was a lie. Deep down, I knew she was going to take care of my daughter way better than I'd ever done. Blinking rapidly, Kenzie stood over me and fired another shot, and my soul floated away from my motionless body.

Meesha

Chapter 28

MaKayla

Last week, I missed out on Kenzie sending Tiff to her maker and Heat meeting his demise. But I refused to let this lil bug I had, prevent me from getting in on the action of the last mission we were going on. The day had arrived for us to end the war against the Black Kings. Kenzie and I had gone to Lox's funeral, and it was a circus show. There were so many females crying over his casket and a fight even broke out between a couple of them. Not understanding how women could argue about who had the deceased while they were living, when he was no longer able to pleasure them because he was gone.

The sight was sad, and I couldn't stomach the shit for another minute. When we were leaving out, the dude we copped weed from was standing outside the church. Spotting us, he lusted over Kenzie and reminded us about the celebration they were throwing for Lox. After assuring him we would be in attendance, we left and went to rest up and wait for the sun to set.

I sat quietly in the car with Khaos as we watched these niggas party like it was 1999, mourning for their fallen comrade. It was well after ten and the crowd was thinning, because they'd been out and about all day with the funeral. There were no kids on the street and that was the main concern we had. What we had planned, it was for them niggas alone.

"Kayla, are you sure you're okay? Don't think I haven't noticed you haven't been feeling good."

"I'm straight, baby. I had a slight cold, that's all. There's nothing to worry about," I said, staring in his eyes. "If I didn't feel better, I wouldn't be here."

"That's a lie. You missed out on other shit and just needed to have a hand in this shit. When we get home, you going right to bed."

"With your dick deep in my guts?" I smirked. "That would be the best remedy to make sure whatever invaded my body stays away."

"We are moments away from murkin' niggas and you thinking about fuckin'. Only you with yo' freaky ass. I got you though. If that's all it takes, you will never get sick again."

His cellphone pinged with a text, and it was go-time. The plan was for me and Kenzie to get out first, then the guys would follow on our command. Khaos kissed my lips, before I got out and strutted up the street. Kenzie met me in the middle of the block, and we continued on together. I spotted the dude that had his eye on my sister, and he fell right into our trap.

"What's up, shawty? I didn't think you was going to make it," he said, smiling from ear to ear. "We out here doing it big for my boi. But what's up with yo' sexy ass?" He pulled Kenzie into his body as if he had her on lock or something. She pushed him back slightly and he swayed from whatever he had running through his system.

"You don't have to touch me. I don't know you like that," Kenzie said as she looked around, taking in all the niggas that were present.

"You can get to know me. Shid, you were checkin' for Lox hard. That nigga gone and I can step in where he left off." Licking his lips lustfully, the shit made my skin crawl, and he wasn't even talking to me.

I counted about eight niggas chillin' with cups and bottles in their hands. I took that time to text the information to the group text. Dude on the other hand, continued to come on to Kenzie and she allowed that shit this time. I knew exactly what was about to happen, so I texted *"move in"* to the group. He grabbed her ass firmly and ran his tongue down the side of Kenzie's neck. His homeboys were looking on, raising their cups in the air.

"Yard, who the fuck is that? You finally gon' get some pussy, nigga?" Everybody laughed as Yard continued to slob all on my sister's neck. The shit was disgusting because that shit rolled down the side of her neck like sweat.

Wrapping her arms around Yard's neck, Kenzie buried her head under his chin and moved her mouth across his throat. "That's for Dreux, muthafucka."

Yard clutched his throat as blood oozed through his fingers and Kenzie stepped back and grabbed her piece from the small of her back as his body fell at her feet. I followed suit and sent a single bullet through the back of a bitch head, hitting one of the niggas in the forehead. I was always looking for a way to kill two birds with one muthafuckin' stone.

Taking cover as the bullets started flying in our direction, the crew came from every direction, popping anything moving as we turned Drummond Street into a real-life game of Call of Duty. Screams could be heard over the blast of gunfire, but that didn't stop us from completing what we started. Out of my peripheral, I spotted a nigga sneak out the cut with his gun trained on Khaos. Stepping away from the vehicle I was behind, I sent a lone bullet into his chest and Khaos emptied his clip in his body.

Khaos blew me a kiss and winked at me as I felt something hot in my upper shoulder area. Falling to the ground, Kenzie screamed and let her nine ride, hitting two niggas that was running in my direction. I pushed back on my legs until I was able to lean against the car I'd fell into. Tears threatened to run down my face as I felt around for my gun.

"Somebody check on my sister!" I heard Kenzie yell in the distance.

I was losing blood quickly. Taking my shirt off, I tied it around my arm to stop the blood, but I started feeling faint and passed out.

***

"She's going to be alright. Her body just went into shock, that's all. They were able to stop the bleeding and removed the bullet. With the help of Kenzie, she was able to get a few pints of clean blood."

I could hear my brother's voice, but I was unable to open my eyes. The feeling of being watched was strong and the shit was scary, because I felt like they were standing around looking down at me like a bitch was dying. One thing I could say, I didn't feel an ounce of pain, so I must've been heavily medicated because I felt as if I could float out of that damn bed and go my ass home.

"Yeah, Kenzie over there sleeping her ass off too. She needed that rest, because she was too hyped about getting down on them niggas. To see her so worried about Kayla getting hit without stopping busting her gun was a sight to see. Scony, you got some crazy ass sisters, man."

"You two muthafuckas stuck with their asses now," Scony laughed. "Maybe now they will stay out the streets and become the wives my granny wanted them to be."

"Good luck with that shit," G chimed in. "Kayla and Kenzie too deep into this shit just to stop now. Both of them know the consequences of the job they chose. It's going to take more than these two to get them out of the game."

There was a knock on the door and all conversation seized. I was trying to open my eyes, but I was losing with every turn. Relaxing my mind, I just laid there listening to what was going around me. Someone cleared their throat, and I heard the shuffling of papers.

"Um, MaKayla as you know sustained a gunshot wound to her clavicle bone. We were able to remove the bullet, but she sustained a break that will take time to heal. She will have to wear a sling for a few months, so the bone can heal. The wound will be something that will need close attention. It can be worse than what it is if infection sets up," the person I assumed was the doctor said, while rustling the papers in his hands. Clearing his throat, he continued. "We took blood work and Miss Jones is expecting."

"Expecting what?" Scony and Khaos asked together.

"Well, we had to take blood while prepping her for surgery and conducting a pregnancy test is mandatory, so we will know how to medicate the patient. The results came back positive, so I guess congratulations are in order here."

At that point I was glad I couldn't open my eyes, because they would've been resuscitating my ass from dying right there of natural causes. What the fuck was I going to do with a baby? Snow's lil ass was a handful to care for, let alone a damn human. Kenzie woke up for that shit because she was cackling like a fuckin' hyena.

"Damn, I'm about to be an auntie. Better Kayla than me. I'm not for shitting out nobody's kid. Thank God Layla was already in the world when I met yo' ass, Phantom. My sister is going to be mad as fuck, because her days in the streets are over," she continued to laugh. That shit was short lived when the doctor got to her.

"I'm glad you are awake, twin sister. We had to take blood from you as well, and it seems the two of you will bring babies into this world together. I have experienced twins being pregnant together on numerous occasions. Congratulations!"

I was finally able to open my eyes and I turned my head and grinned devilishly at my sister. I've always told her ass about laughing at other people's pain, because that shit always came back to bite a muthafucka in the ass. Khaos came over to the bed and kissed me on the lips, with tears in his eyes. I wanted to be mad at him for planting his seed in my womb, but I didn't have the strength to do so. He didn't say anything. Khaos just stood there watching me with nothing but love in his eyes.

Kenzie, on the other hand, was pissed. "Phantom, you set my ass up! I'm not keeping this baby!" she said, sitting up on the side of the bed. Phantom glared at her before turning to the doctor.

"Is there anything else you would like for us to know?" he asked calmly.

"Both of you ladies should set up appointments with your doctors. Getting prenatal medication and finding out how far along you are, is very important. Other than that, you two will be on your way home, soon as I get the discharge papers together. Congratulations once again."

The doctor wasn't out of the room twenty seconds when Phantom stormed across the room and yoked Kenzie up by her shirt. "If

231

you even think about terminating this pregnancy, I will have to die behind killing yo' ass. We gon' die together with yo' selfish ass!"

"You trapped me, nigga! I agreed to be your woman, and a mother to your daughter that's old enough to wipe her own ass. I didn't sign up to fuck up my body carrying a big waterhead ass baby for your ass. How the fuck am I supposed to make money all big and shit?"

"That shit is cancelled. I told you that mission was going to be your last and God agreed. Go to your damn Kindle app and download some books on motherhood, because that shit is about to be your next mission."

Epilogue

Nicassy

The past six months have been nothing but blissful beginnings for Savon and me. I moved back to Houston with my man, and he was lovin' on me as if we were never apart. When I was back in Atlanta, I stayed out of the way to get my head together. Being out in the streets and getting revenge never crossed my mind. When I stated I wanted out of the life, I meant it. Savon came back to me whenever his night ended.

Knowing I didn't have to worry about Heat coming after me helped me a lot, so I could get my life back on track. I found a job at a hospital as the head nurse in the maternity ward and it felt good being back in the workforce. Celeste was so happy to see me, and we were inseparable from the moment she laid eyes on me. I was fortunate enough to be there to help deliver her daughter, Savonia.

Savon ended up killing her baby daddy because he walked in while he was smacking his sister around. So, he stepped up and the baby didn't want for anything, because her uncle spoiled the hell out of her. He wouldn't have it any other way. Savon swore to anyone who would listen that Savonia was his junior. I went along with it until we had a little one of our own.

Standing in the mirror admiring my long tresses, Savon walked up behind me and encircled his arms around my waist. Today was my birthday and he was taking me out for a very intimate dinner, just the two of us. With both Kenzie and Kayla being pregnant, they didn't want to come celebrate with me. Kenzie said if she couldn't turn up and drink her troubles away, she'd rather stay home. It was so cute to see both of my sisters bringing life into the world together.

"You ready to go, baby? We have twenty minutes to get to the restaurant."

"We will get there on time. I'm ready."

Meesha

We drove to the restaurant as K-Ci and JoJo serenaded us on the way. The lyrics always did something to me, but they had a new meaning at that time. Savon was the man I prayed for all my life. The way I came into his life almost ruined my happily ever after, and I'm glad we got past that part of our lives. Starting over fresh with the man I'd fallen deeply in love with, actually gave me a new outlook on our relationship and our future. When we pulled up to the restaurant it seemed as if it was closed. All the lights were out, and I looked at Savon curiously.

"Babe, the restaurant is closed for business. I thought we had reservations."

"We do. You thought I was going to sit around with a bunch of strangers on your day? Plus, this our shit and I can close the muthafucka down if I want to. Happy birthday, baby. This is one of the first gifts I have in store for you."

I smiled hard because Savon listened when I told him one of my dreams was to open a steak and seafood restaurant. I had more than enough money to do it myself, but I guess he wanted to surprise me and that he did. "Thank you so much! I love you."

"I love you too. Now come on, so I can show you around. If there's any changes you would like to make, just let me know and I'll have it done," Savon said, kissing me tenderly on the lips. He got out of the car and threw his keys at the valet attendant and came around to open my door.

"First thing we have to do is name this place. How will folks know where they want to come eat?"

"We'll handle that tomorrow. Come on, we're late now." Savon hooked my hand into his arm and led me into our brand-new establishment. I had butterflies in my stomach as we entered, and the lights came on.

"Surprise!"

Tears stung my eyes as I looked around at all of our friends and family. Everyone was in Houston to celebrate my birthday with me, and it was the best surprise I'd ever had in my life. No longer able to keep the tears at bay, they cascaded down my face, and I was glad I used waterproof make-up. Kenzie and Kayla stood before me looking like twin blimps. Pregnancy looked good on both of them. Scony and his wife was amongst the crowd, along with G and his wife, who was also expecting. Celeste and Sammie were in attendance along with their parents. The biggest surprise was seeing Dreux standing between Phantom and Khaos.

I turned to love on my man and my hand flew to my mouth. Savon was down on one knee, and I couldn't believe what was happening in front of me. He held the biggest diamond ring in a velvet box in the palm of his hand.

"Angel, we've had our ups and downs, but I don't fault you for any of that shit. When I fell in love with you, that's exactly what I did, fell in love with a woman that loved me enough not to go through with ending my life. Many would've looked at me crazy if they heard our story from a third person," he laughed. "God knew I needed you just as much as you needed me. I'm here to stay and I want my forever to be with you. Will you marry me, Nicassy?"

"Yes! I will marry you, baby. There's no way I fought tooth and nail to ever turn you down. I look forward to being Mrs. Savon Cole."

"She said yes, y'all! With that being said, welcome to Cole's Paradise," he screamed as everyone clapped and whistled as we made out like teenagers.

Storm, Kane, and myself have been through hell and back to get to this point of our lives. We all deserve the happy ending that we have received. There wouldn't have been a story without all the trials and tribulations we endure. We had to go through all we had in order to make it through the Savage Storms that tried to tear us apart.

I hope you all enjoyed us, because we enjoyed every moment of telling our story in a way only we could. Thank y'all for walking this journey with us. I hate for it to end, but unfortunately, Kenzie and Kayla fucked it up for everybody.

The End

Meesha

Follow Me…

Facebook: https://www.facebook.com/mesha.king1
Instagram: https://www.instagram.com/author_meesha/
Twitter: https://twitter.com/AuthorMeesha
Tiktok: https://vm.tiktok.com/TTPdkx6LEW/
Website: www.authormeesha.com

Lock Down Publications and Ca$h Presents assisted publishing packages.

BASIC PACKAGE $499
Editing
Cover Design
Formatting

UPGRADED PACKAGE $800
Typing
Editing
Cover Design
Formatting

ADVANCE PACKAGE $1,200
Typing
Editing
Cover Design
Formatting
Copyright registration
Proofreading
Upload book to Amazon

LDP SUPREME PACKAGE $1,500
Typing
Editing
Cover Design
Formatting
Copyright registration
Proofreading
Set up Amazon account
Upload book to Amazon
Advertise on LDP Amazon and Facebook page

Meesha

***Other services available upon request. Additional charges may apply
Lock Down Publications
P.O. Box 944
Stockbridge, GA 30281-9998
Phone # 470 303-9761

Submission Guideline

Submit the first three chapters of your completed manuscript to ldpsubmissions@gmail.com, subject line: Your book's title. The manuscript must be in a .doc file and sent as an attachment. Document should be in Times New Roman, double spaced and in size 12 font. Also, provide your synopsis and full contact information. If sending multiple submissions, they must each be in a separate email.

Have a story but no way to send it electronically? You can still submit to LDP/Ca$h Presents. Send in the first three chapters, written or typed, of your completed manuscript to:

LDP: Submissions Dept
Po Box 944
Stockbridge, Ga 30281

DO NOT send original manuscript. Must be a duplicate.

Provide your synopsis and a cover letter containing your full contact information.

Thanks for considering LDP and Ca$h Presents.

NEW RELEASES

TOE TAGZ 4 by AH'MILLION
A GANGSTA'S QUR'AN 4 by ROMELL TUKES
THE COCAINE PRINCESS 2 by KING RIO
SAVAGE STORMS 3 by MEESHA

Savage Storms 3

Coming Soon from Lock Down Publications/Ca$h Presents
BLOOD OF A BOSS **VI**
SHADOWS OF THE GAME II
TRAP BASTARD II
By **Askari**
LOYAL TO THE GAME **IV**
By **T.J. & Jelissa**
IF TRUE SAVAGE **VIII**
MIDNIGHT CARTEL IV
DOPE BOY MAGIC IV
CITY OF KINGZ III
NIGHTMARE ON SILENT AVE II
THE PLUG OF LIL MEXICO II
By **Chris Green**
BLAST FOR ME **III**
A SAVAGE DOPEBOY III
CUTTHROAT MAFIA III
DUFFLE BAG CARTEL VII
HEARTLESS GOON VI
By **Ghost**
A HUSTLER'S DECEIT III
KILL ZONE II
BAE BELONGS TO ME III
By **Aryanna**
KING OF THE TRAP III
By **T.J. Edwards**
GORILLAZ IN THE BAY V
3X KRAZY III
STRAIGHT BEAST MODE II
De'Kari

Meesha

KINGPIN KILLAZ IV

STREET KINGS III

PAID IN BLOOD III

CARTEL KILLAZ IV

DOPE GODS III

Hood Rich

SINS OF A HUSTLA II

ASAD

RICH $AVAGE II

MONEY IN THE GRAVE II

By Martell Troublesome Bolden

YAYO V

Bred In The Game 2

S. Allen

CREAM III

By Yolanda Moore

SON OF A DOPE FIEND III

HEAVEN GOT A GHETTO II

By Renta

LOYALTY AIN'T PROMISED III

By Keith Williams

I'M NOTHING WITHOUT HIS LOVE II

SINS OF A THUG II

TO THE THUG I LOVED BEFORE II

IN A HUSTLER I TRUST II

By Monet Dragun

QUIET MONEY IV

EXTENDED CLIP III

THUG LIFE IV

By **Trai'Quan**

Savage Storms 3

THE STREETS MADE ME IV
By **Larry D. Wright**
IF YOU CROSS ME ONCE II
By **Anthony Fields**
THE STREETS WILL NEVER CLOSE II
By K'ajji
HARD AND RUTHLESS III
THE BILLIONAIRE BENTLEYS III
Von Diesel
KILLA KOUNTY III
By Khufu
MONEY GAME III
By Smoove Dolla
JACK BOYS VS DOPE BOYS II
A GANGSTA'S QUR'AN V
By Romell Tukes
MURDA WAS THE CASE II
Elijah R. Freeman
THE STREETS NEVER LET GO II
By Robert Baptiste
AN UNFORESEEN LOVE III
By **Meesha**
KING OF THE TRENCHES III
by **GHOST & TRANAY ADAMS**

MONEY MAFIA II
LOYAL TO THE SOIL II
By **Jibril Williams**
QUEEN OF THE ZOO II
By **Black Migo**
THE BRICK MAN IV

Meesha

THE COCAINE PRINCESS III
By King Rio
VICIOUS LOYALTY II
By Kingpen
A GANGSTA'S PAIN II
By J-Blunt
CONFESSIONS OF A JACKBOY III
By Nicholas Lock
GRIMEY WAYS II
By Ray Vinci
KING KILLA II
By Vincent "Vitto" Holloway

Available Now

RESTRAINING ORDER **I & II**
By **CA$H & Coffee**
LOVE KNOWS NO BOUNDARIES **I II & III**
By **Coffee**
RAISED AS A GOON I, II, III & IV
BRED BY THE SLUMS I, II, III
BLAST FOR ME I & II
ROTTEN TO THE CORE I II III
A BRONX TALE I, II, III

Savage Storms 3

DUFFLE BAG CARTEL I II III IV V VI
HEARTLESS GOON I II III IV V
A SAVAGE DOPEBOY I II
DRUG LORDS I II III
CUTTHROAT MAFIA I II
KING OF THE TRENCHES
By **Ghost**
LAY IT DOWN **I & II**
LAST OF A DYING BREED I II
BLOOD STAINS OF A SHOTTA I & II III
By **Jamaica**
LOYAL TO THE GAME I II III
LIFE OF SIN I, II III
By **TJ & Jelissa**
BLOODY COMMAS I & II
SKI MASK CARTEL I II & III
KING OF NEW YORK I II,III IV V
RISE TO POWER I II III
COKE KINGS I II III IV V
BORN HEARTLESS I II III IV
KING OF THE TRAP I II
By **T.J. Edwards**
IF LOVING HIM IS WRONG…I & II
LOVE ME EVEN WHEN IT HURTS I II III
By **Jelissa**
WHEN THE STREETS CLAP BACK I & II III
THE HEART OF A SAVAGE I II III
MONEY MAFIA
LOYAL TO THE SOIL
By **Jibril Williams**

Meesha

A DISTINGUISHED THUG STOLE MY HEART I II & III
LOVE SHOULDN'T HURT I II III IV
RENEGADE BOYS I II III IV
PAID IN KARMA I II III
SAVAGE STORMS I II III
AN UNFORESEEN LOVE I II

By **Meesha**

A GANGSTER'S CODE I &, II III
A GANGSTER'S SYN I II III
THE SAVAGE LIFE I II III
CHAINED TO THE STREETS I II III
BLOOD ON THE MONEY I II III
A GANGSTA'S PAIN

By **J-Blunt**

PUSH IT TO THE LIMIT

By **Bre' Hayes**

BLOOD OF A BOSS **I, II, III, IV, V**
SHADOWS OF THE GAME
TRAP BASTARD

By **Askari**

THE STREETS BLEED MURDER **I, II & III**
THE HEART OF A GANGSTA I II& III

By **Jerry Jackson**

CUM FOR ME I II III IV V VI VII VIII
An **LDP Erotica Collaboration**
BRIDE OF A HUSTLA **I II & II**
THE FETTI GIRLS **I, II& III**
CORRUPTED BY A GANGSTA I, II III, IV
BLINDED BY HIS LOVE
THE PRICE YOU PAY FOR LOVE I, II ,III

DOPE GIRL MAGIC I II III
By **Destiny Skai**
WHEN A GOOD GIRL GOES BAD
By **Adrienne**
THE COST OF LOYALTY I II III
By Kweli
A GANGSTER'S REVENGE **I II III & IV**
THE BOSS MAN'S DAUGHTERS I II III IV V
A SAVAGE LOVE **I & II**
BAE BELONGS TO ME I II
A HUSTLER'S DECEIT I, II, III
WHAT BAD BITCHES DO I, II, III
SOUL OF A MONSTER I II III
KILL ZONE
A DOPE BOY'S QUEEN I II III
By **Aryanna**
A KINGPIN'S AMBITON
A KINGPIN'S AMBITION **II**
I MURDER FOR THE DOUGH
By **Ambitious**
TRUE SAVAGE I II III IV V VI VII
DOPE BOY MAGIC I, II, III
MIDNIGHT CARTEL I II III
CITY OF KINGZ I II
NIGHTMARE ON SILENT AVE
THE PLUG OF LIL MEXICO II

By **Chris Green**
A DOPEBOY'S PRAYER
By **Eddie "Wolf" Lee**

Meesha

THE KING CARTEL **I, II & III**
By **Frank Gresham**
THESE NIGGAS AIN'T LOYAL **I, II & III**
By **Nikki Tee**
GANGSTA SHYT **I II &III**
By **CATO**
THE ULTIMATE BETRAYAL
By **Phoenix**
BOSS'N UP **I , II & III**
By **Royal Nicole**
I LOVE YOU TO DEATH
By **Destiny J**
I RIDE FOR MY HITTA
I STILL RIDE FOR MY HITTA
By **Misty Holt**
LOVE & CHASIN' PAPER
By **Qay Crockett**
TO DIE IN VAIN
SINS OF A HUSTLA
By **ASAD**
BROOKLYN HUSTLAZ
By **Boogsy Morina**
BROOKLYN ON LOCK I & II
By **Sonovia**
GANGSTA CITY
By **Teddy Duke**
A DRUG KING AND HIS DIAMOND I & II III
A DOPEMAN'S RICHES
HER MAN, MINE'S TOO I, II
CASH MONEY HO'S

Savage Storms 3

THE WIFEY I USED TO BE I II
By Nicole Goosby
TRAPHOUSE KING **I II & III**
KINGPIN KILLAZ I II III
STREET KINGS I II
PAID IN BLOOD **I II**
CARTEL KILLAZ I II III
DOPE GODS I II
By **Hood Rich**
LIPSTICK KILLAH **I, II, III**
CRIME OF PASSION I II & III
FRIEND OR FOE I II III
By **Mimi**
STEADY MOBBN' **I, II, III**
THE STREETS STAINED MY SOUL I II III
By **Marcellus Allen**
WHO SHOT YA **I, II, III**
SON OF A DOPE FIEND I II
HEAVEN GOT A GHETTO
Renta
GORILLAZ IN THE BAY **I II III IV**
TEARS OF A GANGSTA I II
3X KRAZY I II
STRAIGHT BEAST MODE
DE'KARI
TRIGGADALE I II III
MURDAROBER WAS THE CASE
Elijah R. Freeman
GOD BLESS THE TRAPPERS I, II, III
THESE SCANDALOUS STREETS I, II, III

249

Meesha

FEAR MY GANGSTA I, II, III IV, V
THESE STREETS DON'T LOVE NOBODY I, II
BURY ME A G I, II, III, IV, V
A GANGSTA'S EMPIRE I, II, III, IV
THE DOPEMAN'S BODYGAURD I II
THE REALEST KILLAZ I II III
THE LAST OF THE OGS I II III

Tranay Adams
THE STREETS ARE CALLING

Duquie Wilson
MARRIED TO A BOSS I II III

By Destiny Skai & Chris Green
KINGZ OF THE GAME I II III IV V VI

Playa Ray
SLAUGHTER GANG I II III
RUTHLESS HEART I II III

By Willie Slaughter
FUK SHYT

By Blakk Diamond
DON'T F#CK WITH MY HEART I II

By Linnea
ADDICTED TO THE DRAMA I II III
IN THE ARM OF HIS BOSS II

By Jamila
YAYO I II III IV
A SHOOTER'S AMBITION I II
BRED IN THE GAME

By S. Allen
TRAP GOD I II III
RICH $AVAGE

Savage Storms 3

MONEY IN THE GRAVE I II
By Martell Troublesome Bolden
FOREVER GANGSTA
GLOCKS ON SATIN SHEETS I II
By Adrian Dulan
TOE TAGZ I II III IV
LEVELS TO THIS SHYT I II
By Ah'Million
KINGPIN DREAMS I II III
By Paper Boi Rari
CONFESSIONS OF A GANGSTA I II III IV
CONFESSIONS OF A JACKBOY I II
By Nicholas Lock
I'M NOTHING WITHOUT HIS LOVE
SINS OF A THUG
TO THE THUG I LOVED BEFORE
A GANGSTA SAVED XMAS
IN A HUSTLER I TRUST
By Monet Dragun
CAUGHT UP IN THE LIFE I II III
THE STREETS NEVER LET GO
By Robert Baptiste
NEW TO THE GAME I II III
MONEY, MURDER & MEMORIES I II III
By **Malik D. Rice**
LIFE OF A SAVAGE I II III
A GANGSTA'S QUR'AN I II III IV
MURDA SEASON I II III
GANGLAND CARTEL I II III
CHI'RAQ GANGSTAS I II III

Meesha

KILLERS ON ELM STREET I II III
JACK BOYZ N DA BRONX I II III
A DOPEBOY'S DREAM I II III
JACK BOYS VS DOPE BOYS
By **Romell Tukes**
LOYALTY AIN'T PROMISED I II
By **Keith Williams**
QUIET MONEY I II III
THUG LIFE I II III
EXTENDED CLIP I II
By **Trai'Quan**
THE STREETS MADE ME I II III
By **Larry D. Wright**
THE ULTIMATE SACRIFICE I, II, III, IV, V, VI
KHADIFI
IF YOU CROSS ME ONCE
ANGEL I II
IN THE BLINK OF AN EYE
By **Anthony Fields**
THE LIFE OF A HOOD STAR
By **Ca$h & Rashia Wilson**
THE STREETS WILL NEVER CLOSE
By **K'ajji**
CREAM I II
By **Yolanda Moore**
NIGHTMARES OF A HUSTLA I II III
By **King Dream**
CONCRETE KILLA I II
VICIOUS LOYALTY
By **Kingpen**

Savage Storms 3

HARD AND RUTHLESS I II
MOB TOWN 251
THE BILLIONAIRE BENTLEYS I II
By Von Diesel
GHOST MOB
Stilloan Robinson
MOB TIES I II III IV V
By SayNoMore
BODYMORE MURDERLAND I II III
By Delmont Player
FOR THE LOVE OF A BOSS
By C. D. Blue
MOBBED UP I II III IV
THE BRICK MAN I II III
THE COCAINE PRINCESS I II
By King Rio
KILLA KOUNTY I II
By Khufu
MONEY GAME I II
By Smoove Dolla
A GANGSTA'S KARMA I II
By FLAME
KING OF THE TRENCHES I II
by **GHOST & TRANAY ADAMS**
QUEEN OF THE ZOO
By **Black Migo**
GRIMEY WAYS
By Ray Vinci
XMAS WITH AN ATL SHOOTER
By **Ca$h & Destiny Skai**

Meesha

KING KILLA
By Vincent "Vitto" Holloway

BOOKS BY LDP'S CEO, CA$H

TRUST IN NO MAN
TRUST IN NO MAN 2
TRUST IN NO MAN 3
BONDED BY BLOOD
SHORTY GOT A THUG
THUGS CRY
THUGS CRY 2
THUGS CRY 3
TRUST NO BITCH
TRUST NO BITCH 2
TRUST NO BITCH 3
TIL MY CASKET DROPS
RESTRAINING ORDER
RESTRAINING ORDER 2
IN LOVE WITH A CONVICT
LIFE OF A HOOD STAR
XMAS WITH AN ATL SHOOTER

Meesha